DEFENDING THE NEST

Several armed AAnn standing beneath the nearest wing glanced up in surprise as the thranx crawler rumbled into view. Ryo shot one of them before the others could move, and the group broke and ran frantically for the ramp which led to the belly of the shuttle.

Ryo caught an AAnn halfway up the ramp with a second bolt and watched while the creature jerked and twisted downward. Several energy beams reached toward the crawler from the retreating soldiers but, fired wildly and in haste, they missed the agile machine as Bor zigzagged.

By now the thranx were crossing under the stern of the first shuttle and careening toward the second. Ryo sent several shots crackling toward the twin exhaust jets, hoping to disable some vital component, but he had no way of knowing if the bursts were effective.

By this time panic was giving way to reaction among those on board the two craft. Suddenly a powerful wash of energy radiated from the bow of the second shuttle, carbonizing the ground ahead and to the left of the charging crawler.

"Turn, turn" shouted Aen . . .

Also by Alan Dean Foster
Published by Ballantine Books

THE ADVENTURES OF FLINX OF THE COMMONWEALTH

The Tar-Aiym Krang

Orphan Star

The End of the Matter

Bloodhype

THE BLACK HOLE

CACHALOT

ICERIGGER

MISSION TO MOULOKIN

WITH FRIENDS LIKE THESE . . .

Nor
Crystal Tears

Alan Dean Foster

A Del Rey Book

BALLANTINE BOOKS • NEW YORK

A Del Rey Book
Published by Ballantine Books
Copyright © 1982 by Alan Dean Foster

Library of Congress Catalog Card Number: 82-8836

ISBN 0-345-29141-7

Manufactured in the United States of America

First Edition: September 1982

Cover art by Michael Whelan

For the tiger with the little-girl voice
    and the velvet claws,
My agent, Virginia Kidd, with thanks for
Ten years of encouraging purrs
    and constructive scratches.

It's hard to be a larva. At first there's nothing. Very gradually a dim, uncertain consciousness coalesces from nothingness. Awareness of the world arrives not as a shock, but as a gray inevitability. The larva cannot move, cannot speak. But it can think.

His first memories, naturally, were of the Nursery: a cool, dimly lit tubular chamber of controlled commotion and considerable noise. Beneath the gently arched ceiling, adults conversed with his fellow larvae. With awareness of his surroundings came recognition of self and of body: a lumpish, meter-and-a-half-long cylindrical mass of mottled white flesh.

Through simple, incomplete larval eyes he hungrily absorbed the limited world. Adults, equipment, walls and ceiling and floor, his companions, the cradle he lay in, all were white and black and in-between shades of gray. They were all he could perceive. Color was a mysterious, unimaginable realm to which only adults had access. Of all the unknowns of existence, he most pondered what was blue, what was yellow—the taste of the withheld spectrum.

The adults who managed the Nursery and attended the young were experienced in that service. They'd heard generations of youngsters ask the same questions in the same order over and over, yet they were ever patient and polite. So they tried their best to explain color to him. The words had no meaning because there were no possible reference points, no mental landmarks to which a larva could relate. It was like trying to describe the sun that warmed the surface high, high above the subterranean Nursery. He came to think of the sun as a brightly blazing something that produced an intense absence of dark.

As he grew the attendants let him move about in his crude humping, wormlike fashion. Nurses bustled through the Nursery, busy adults gifted with real mobility. Teaching machines murmured their endless litany to the studious. Other adults occasionally came to visit, including a pair who identified themselves as his own parents.

He compared them with his companions, like himself squirming white masses ending in dull black eyes and thin mouth-slits. How he envied the adults their clean lines and mature bodies, the four strong legs, the footarms above serving either as hands or as a third pair of legs, the delicate truhands above them.

They had real eyes, adults did. Great multifaceted compound orbs that shone like a cluster of bright jewels (light gray to him, though he knew they were orange and red and gold, whatever those were). These were set to the sides of the shining valentine-shaped heads, from which a pair of feathery antennae sprouted, honestly white. He was fascinated by the antennae, as all his companions were. The adults would explain that two senses were held there, the sense of smell and the sense of faz.

He understood fazzing, the ability to detect the presence of moving objects by sensing the disruption of air. But the concept of smell utterly eluded him, much as color did. Along with arms and legs, then, he desperately wished for antennae. He desperately wished to be complete.

The Nurses were patient, fully understanding such yearnings. Antennae and limbs would come with time. Meanwhile there was much to learn.

They taught speech, though larvae were capable of no more than a crude wheezing and gasping through their flexible mouth-parts. It took hard mandibles and adult lungs and throats to produce the elegant clicks and whistles of mature communication.

So he could see after a fashion, and hear, and speak a little. But sight was incomplete without color and he could not faz or smell at all. By way of compensation the teachers explained that no adult could faz or smell nearly as well as the primitive ancestors of the Thranx, back when the race dwelt in unintelligence even deeper in the bowels of the earth than they did now, when artificial light did not exist, and the senses of faz and smell necessarily exceeded that of sight in importance.

He listened and understood, but that did not lessen the frustration. He would worm his way around the exercise course because they insisted he needed exercise, but he was ever conscious of what a pale shadow of true mobility it was. Oh, so frustrating!

Larval years were the Learning Time. Hardly able to move, unable to smell or faz, barely able to converse, but with decent sight and hearing a larva was adequately equipped for learning.

He was a particularly voracious student, absorbing everything and asking greedily for more. His teachers and Nurses were pleased, as was the teaching machine attached to his cradle. He mastered High and Low Thranx, although he could properly speak neither. He learned physics and chemistry and basic biology, including the danger posed by any body of water deeper than the thorax, where the adult's breathing spicules were located. An adult Thranx could float, but not forever, and when the water entered the body, it sank. Swimming was a talent reserved for primitive creatures with internal skeletons.

He was taught astronomy and geology although he'd never seen the sky or the earth, for all that he lived beneath the surface. The Nursery was exquisitely tiled and paneled. Other sections of Paszex, his home town, were lined with plastics, ceramics, metals, or stonework. In the ancient burrows on the planet Hivehom, where the Thranx had evolved, were tunnels and chambers lined with regurgitated cellulose and body plaster.

Industry and agriculture were studied. History told how the social arthropods known as the Thranx first mastered Hivehom, adapting to existence above as well as below the surface, and then spread to other worlds. Eventually theology was discussed and the larvae made their choices.

Then on to more complex subjects as the mind matured, to biochemistry, nucleonics, sociology and psychology and the arts, including jurisprudence. He particularly enjoyed the history of space travel, the stories of the first hesitant flights to the three moons of Hivehom in clumsy rockets, the development of the posigravity drive that pushed ships through the gulf between the stars, and the establishment of colonies on worlds like Dixx and Everon and Calm Nursery. He learned of the burgeoning commerce between Willo-wane, his own colony world, and Hivehom and the other colonies.

How he wanted to go to Hivehom when he learned of it! The mother world of the people, Hivehom. Magical, enchanting name. His Nurses smiled at his excitement. It was only natural he should want to travel there. Everyone did.

Yet something more showed on his profile charts, an undefined yearning that puzzled the larval psychologists. Possibly it was related to his unusual hatching. The normal four eggs had bequeathed not male and female pairs but three females and this one male.

He was aware of the psychologists' concerns but didn't worry about them. He concentrated on learning as much as possible, stuffing his mind full to bursting with the wonders of existence. While these strange adults mumbled about "indecisiveness" and "unwillingness to tend toward a course of action," he plowed through the learning programs, mitigating their worries with his extraordinary appetite for knowledge.

Couldn't they understand that he wasn't interested in any one particular subject? He was interested in *everything*. But the psychologists didn't understand, and they fretted. So did his family, because a Thranx on the Verge always knows what he or she intends to do . . . after. Generalizations do not a life make.

For a while they thought he might want to be a philosopher, but his general interests were of specifics and not of abstruse speculations. Only his unusually high scores prevented their moving him from the general Nursery to one reserved for the mentally deficient.

On and on he studied, learning that Willow-wane was a wonderful world of comfortable swamps and lowlands, of heat and humidity much like that of the Nursery. A true garden world whose poles were free of ice and whose large continents were heavily jungled. Willow-wane was even more accommodating than Hivehom itself. He was fortunate to have been born there.

His name he knew from early on. He was Ryo, of the Family Zen, of the Clan Zu, of the Hive Zex. The last was a holdover from primitive times, for only towns and cities existed now, no more true hives.

More history, the information that the development of real intelligence was concurrent with the development of egg-laying ability in all Thranx females. Gone was the need for a specialized Queen. Their newly evolved biological flexibility gave the Thranx a natural advantage over other arthropods. But Thranx still paid respects to an honorary clanmother and hivemother, echoes of the biological matriarchy that once dominated the race. That was tradition. The people had a great love of tradition.

He remembered his shock when he'd first learned of the

AAnn, a space-going race of intelligence, calculation, cunning, and aggressiveness. The shock arose not from their abilities but from the fact that the creatures possessed internal skeletons, leathery skins, and flexible bodies. They moved like the primitive animals of the jungles but their intelligence was undeniable. The discovery had caused consternation in the Thranx scientific community, which had postulated that no creature lacking a protective exoskeleton could survive long enough to evolve true intelligence. The hard scales of the AAnn gave protection, and some felt that their closed circulatory systems compensated for the lack of an exoskeleton.

All these things he studied and mastered, yet he was unsettled in mind because he also knew that of all the inhabitants of the Nursery who were on the Verge, he alone was unable to settle on a career, to choose a life work.

Around him, his childhood companions made their choices and were content as the time grew near. This one to be a chemist, that one a janitorial engineer, the one on the cradle across from Ryo to become a public Servitor, another opting for food-processing management.

Only he could not decide, would not decide, did not want to decide. He wanted only to learn more, to study more.

Then there was no more time for study. There was only time for a sudden upwelling of fear. His body had been changing for months, subtle tremors and quivers jostling him internally. He'd felt his insides shift, felt skin and self tingling with a peculiar tension. An urge was upon him, a powerful desire to turn inward and explode outward.

The Nurses tried to prepare him for it as best they could, soothing, explaining, showing him again the chips he'd studied over and over. Yet the sight of it recorded on screen was clinical and distant, hard to relate to what was occurring inside his own body. All the chips, all the information in the world could not prepare one for the reality.

Worse were the rumors that passed from Nurserymate to Nurserymate in the dark, during sleeping time, when the adults were not listening. Horrible stories of gross deformities, of monstrosities put out of their misery before they had a chance to see themselves in a mirror, which others said were allowed to survive for a life of miserable study as scientific subjects, never to be permitted out in society.

The rumors grew and multiplied as fast as the changes in his own body. The Nurses and special doctors came and went and monitored him intensively. Around it all, encapsulating all the mystery and terror and wonder and hope, was a single word.

Metamorphosis.

The process was something you could not avoid, like death. The genes insisted and the body obeyed. The larva could not delay it.

He had studied it repeatedly with a fervor he had never applied to anything else. He watched the recordings, marveled at the transformation. What if the cocoon was wrongly spun? What if he matured too soon and burst from the cocoon only half formed or, worse yet, waited too long and smothered?

The Nurses were reassuring. Yes, all those terrible things had happened once upon a time, but now trained doctors and metamorphic engineers stood by at all times. Modern medicine would compensate for any mistake the body might make.

The day came and he hadn't slept for four days before it. His body felt nervous and ready to burst. Incomprehensible feelings possessed him. He and the others who were ready were taken from the Nursery. Befuddled younger larvae watched them go, some filling their wake with cries of farewell.

"Good-bye, Ryo . . . Don't come out with eight legs!" "See you as an adult," shouted another. "Come back and show us your hands," cried a third. "Tell us what color is!"

Ryo knew he wouldn't be returning to the Nursery. Once gone, there was no reason to return. It would belong to another life, unless he opted for Nursery work as an adult. He watched the Nursery recede as his palette traveled in train with the others down the long central aisle. The Nursery, its friendly-familiar whites and grays, its cradles and compassion the only companions he'd ever had, all vanished behind a tripartite door.

He heard someone cry out, then realized he was the noisemaker. The medical personnel hushed him, calmed him.

Then he was in a great, high-ceilinged chamber, a dome

of glowing darkness, of perfectly balanced humidity and temperature. He could see the other palettes being placed nearby, forming a circle. His friends wiggled and twisted under the gentle glow of special lamps.

On the next palette rested a female named Urilavsezex. She made the sound indicative of good wishes and friendship. "It's finally here," she said. "After so long, after all these years. I'm—I'm not sure I know what to do or how to do it."

"Me either," Ryo replied. "I know the recordings, but how do you tell when the precise moment is, how do you know when the time is right? I don't want to make any mistakes."

"I feel . . . I feel so strange. Like I—like I have to. . . ." She was no longer talking, for silk had begun to emerge magically from her mouth. Fascinated, he stared as she began single-mindedly to work, her body contorting with a flexibility soon to be lost forever. Bending sharply, she had begun at the base of her body and was working rapidly toward the head.

Layer upon layer the damp silk rose around her body, hardening on contact with the air. Now he could see only her head. The eyes began to disappear. Around him others had begun to work.

Something heaved inside him and he thought he was going to vomit. He did not. It was not his stomach that was suddenly, eruptively working, but other glands and organs. There was a taste in his mouth, not bad at all, fresh and clean. He twisted, doubled over, working the silk that extruded in a steady, effortless flow as if he'd spun a hundred times before.

He felt no claustrophobia, a fear unknown to a people who mature underground. Up, high, higher, around his mouth and eyes now, the cocoon rose. The upper cap narrowed over his head. It was almost closed when a pair of truhands reached in and down through the remaining gap. Moving quickly, in time to his mouth movements so as not to become entangled in the hardening silk, they held a tube that was pressed against his forehead.

The hands withdrew. Nothing else remained to concentrate on except finishing, finishing, finishing the work. Then the cocoon was complete and the sedative that had been injected into him combined with his physical exhaustion to speed him into the Sleep. A dim, fading part of him knew he would sleep for three whole seasons . . .

But it wasn't long at all. Only a few seconds, and suddenly he was kicking with a desperate intensity. *Out*, he thought hysterically, I have to get *out*. He was imprisoned, confined in something hard and unyielding. He shoved and kicked with all his strength. So weak, he was so terribly weak. Yet—a small crack, there.

The sight renewed his determination and he kicked harder, punched with his hands and began to pull at the pieces that cracked in front of him. The prison was disintegrating around him. He whistled in triumph, kicked with all four legs—then sprawled free and exhausted onto a soft floor.

On his thorax the eight spicules pulsed weakly, sucking air. He turned his head and looked up, using his truhands to brush at the dampness still clinging to his eyes.

Then other hands were on him, turning him, helping him untangle. Antiseptic cloths brushed at his eyes and there was a sharp smell of peppermint. A voice spoke soothingly. "It's all over. Relax, just relax. Let your body gather its strength."

Instinctively he turned toward the sound of the voice as the last film masking his eyes was sponged away. A male Thranx looked down at him. His chiton was deep purple, so he would be quite elderly.

Realization came in a rush. Purple. The adult's chiton was purple, and purple was a color that had been described to him and now he knew what it *was* and the ceramic inlay in the doctor's forehead was a single bar of silver crossed by two bars of gold and his ommatidia were red with gold and yellow central bands and they gleamed in the light of the room and . . . and . . . It was wonderful.

He looked down at himself, saw the slim body, the segmented abdomen, the four glistening wing cases, vestigial wings beneath, the four strong, jointed legs spraddled to his left. He raised a truhand, touched it with a foothand, then repeated the motion with the other pair, then touched all four sets of four fingers together.

All around him he heard uncertain clicks and whistles as strange voices struggled to master new bodies. Someone brought a mirror. Ryo looked into it. Staring back at him was a beautiful blue-green adult, still damp but drying rapidly following Emergence. The valentine-shaped head was cocked to one side. Cream-white feathery antennae fluttered and smothered him in the most peculiar sensations. Smells, they were; rich, dark, pungent, musky, glowing, vanilla. The smells of the postcocoon recovery room, of his metamorphosed friends. He knew he'd been asleep not a few minutes or seconds but for more than half a year, that his body had changed and matured from a pulpy, barely conscious white thing into a gloriously streamlined adult.

He tried to gather his legs beneath him and found ready hands on either side, helping him up. "Easy there . . . don't try to rush yourself," a voice told him.

Erect, he turned and discovered a wide window. On the other side stood a host of excited, mature Thranx. Ryo recognized the markings of two, his sire and dame.

They were no longer kindly gray shapes. They had color now. Evidentally they recognized him, for they made greeting signs at him. He returned them, realizing that he now possessed the means for doing so.

The hands left him. He stood by himself on all fours, abdomen stretched out behind him, thorax and then b-thorax inclined upward with his head topping all. He looked back over his shoulder, down at his body, then down at the floor. He stepped carefully off the soft padding onto the harder outside ring. Experimentally, he walked in a slow circle.

"Very good, Ryozenzuzex." It was the elderly doctor who'd supervised his Emergence. "Don't rush yourself. Your body knows what to do."

Around Ryo his companions were taking experimental deep breaths, cleaning their eyes, testing legs and fingers, females wiggling their shining ovipositors, extending and recoiling them.

I can walk, he thought delightedly. I can see colors. He sensed the pressure of air around him and his brain sorted the implications. I can faz, and I can smell, and I can still hear. He thanked those who'd assisted him and marveled at the clarity of his speech; sharp clicks, beautifully modulated whistles—all the intricate convolutions of Low Thranx. Years of study paid off now.

He marveled at that, too, his four mandibles moving

smoothly against each other as he made sounds of pure pleasure. Only one thing hung in his thoughts to mar his happiness: his body was complete but his future was not, for he still had not the vaguest idea what he wanted to do with himself.

Eventually he drifted into agricultural services, for he felt a positive joy at finally being able to go Above and, unlike his highly gregarious fellow citizens, took pleasure in working outside the town.

He drowned his personal uncertainties and confusion in work. Pushed by his clan, he took as premate a bright and energetic female named Falmiensazex. Life settled into a comfortable, familiar routine. His clan and family ceased to worry about him, and the old, nagging indecision faded steadily until it was nearly forgotten.

▌▐ It was the midday of Malmrep, the third of Willow-wane's five seasons and the time of High Summer. The weather was rich with moisture and the air rippled with heat.

Ryo checked the readout on the console. Two assistants accompanied him on the scouting expedition into the jungle. They were to survey the feasibility of planting two thousand bexamin vines.

He'd argued long and patiently with the Inmot local council who had intended to plant the newly drained and cleared land in ji bushes. Ryo insisted that it was time to diversify local operations further and that bexamin vine, which produced small hard berries of deep ocher hue, was the most suitable candidate for planting.

The berry fruit was useless, but the single seed that lay at the center of each, when crushed and mixed with water and a protein additive, produced a wonderfully sweet syrup that was nearly as nutritious as it was tasty. But the fifteen-meter-long vines required more attention that the most delicate ji bush. Nevertheless, the council voted three to two in favor of his suggestion.

Ryo was quite conscious of how much was riding on the success of this planting. While failure would not shatter his solid reputation within the Company, a good bexamin crop would considerably enhance it. Whether a grand triumph was a good idea he wasn't sure, but he didn't seem to be progressing in any other directions. So he thought he might as well rise within the Company structure.

"Bor, Aen," he said to his two assistants, both of whom were older than he, "break out the transit sighters. We're going to lay a line down that way." With right foothand and truhand he gestured to his left, to the northeast.

They acknowledged the order by unpacking the instruments and fixing them to the proper mounts on the side of the crawler. Ryo made sure the stingers were unstrapped and ready for use in case they should meet with an errilis.

But nothing sprang from the tangled vegetation to challenge them as they powered up the instruments. Minutes passed and Bor was removing a reflective marker from its case when an explosion threw him violently to the crawler deck. The concussion bent the thinner trees eastward. Vines and creepers were torn free of their branches. Only his

11

grip on the steering pylon enabled Ryo to maintain his footing.

During the silence that followed, the three of them lay stunned, not knowing what to make of the violence. Then a frantic cacophony of screeks and wails, moans and weeping rose from the startled inhabitants of the jungle as they recovered from their own shock.

A trio of splay-footed inwicep birds ran past the crawler, their meter-wide webbed feet barely tickling the swamp water, their necks held parallel to the surface and their thin blue tails stretched out behind them for balance.

"Ovipositors acute!" muttered Bor. "What was that?" As if to punctuate the query there was another roar, less cataclysmic but still strong enough to rattle the treetops.

Both assistants looked to Ryo for an explanation, but he could only stare south, the way they'd come, and perform instinctive gestures of befuddlement. "I've no idea. It almost sounds as if the generator nexus went up."

"A collision at the transport terminal perhaps," suggested Aen.

"Not possible." Bor made a gesture of assurance. He was the eldest of the trio. "Only a monitor breakdown for the northern sector of the continent would allow such a disaster. Even if that came to pass I can't visualize any collision of modules producing such an explosion."

"That would depend on what they were carrying," said Ryo, "but I agree with you. A more likely source of such energy would be the Reducer complex south of town where they distill fuel alcohols."

Aen concurred. "We'd best hurry back and see what we can do to help. There may be fire in the burrows."

"I have clanmates who work at the Reducer." Bor was no less concerned than his friends.

"And I," added Aen.

Ryo gunned the engine of the crawler. Broad exterior treads spun in opposite directions. The vehicle turned on its axis and Ryo sent it rumbling back down the path they'd crunched through the raw jungle. Ooze and water sprayed from the speeding machine's flanks as Bor and Aen hurriedly restowed the survey equipment.

A fresh shock awaited them as they reached the edge of the jungle and were about to touch the farthest of the plan-

tation access roads. Two large shuttlecraft of peculiar mul-
tiwinged design were resting there. In landing they'd made
a ruin of several neatly tended fields of weoneon and asfi.

The local airport was south of Paszex, a fact that Ryo
could not reconcile with the presence in his familiar fields
of the two strange ships. It was the older Bor who roughly
took the controls from him and hurriedly backed the crawler into the cover of the jungle.

The action ended Ryo's immobility, if not his confusion.
"I don't understand. Is it some kind of emergency? Is that
why they didn't set down at the port and . . . ?"

Bor interrupted him, pragmatism assuming sway over
politeness.

"Those are not Thranx, or anything else friendly. They
are AAnn shuttlecraft. Don't you recall them from Learning Time? There has to be an AAnn warship somewhere in
orbit around Willow-wane."

Bor's words brought the segment of study back to Ryo in
a rush.

Powerful, antagonistic, and crafty were the words that
best described the endoskeletal space-going AAnn. Their
star systems lay farther out along the galactic plane than
the Thranx worlds. Though war had never been declared
between the two races, occasional "mistakes" were made
by individual AAnn commanders who "overstepped their
orders." Or so the AAnn apologies always insisted.

Since the Central government on Hivehom was always
practical about such matters, the errors never led to full-
scale combat. Such isolated incidents were irritating but
rarely outrageous. The Grand Council therefore chose to
protest such incidents through diplomatic channels.

This policy was not much comfort to the three outraged
individuals driving the crawler, an unusual state of affairs
among a people normally respectful of authority.

The trio could not sympathize with diplomats, since all
they could see were two invading craft that had destroyed
laboriously groomed fields, and the plumes of dark black
smoke that rose like mutilated ghosts above Paszex.

"We must do *something*." Ryo stared helplessly through
the trees. Across the fields drifted the hiss of discharging
energy weapons mixed with the lighter crackle of Thranx

stingers and an occasional nasty *cur-rrrupmph!* from explosive shells.

"What can we do?" Bor's tone was one of calm acceptance. "We do not have—" His voice rose at the thought and his eyes gleamed like diamonds. "We do have weapons."

Ryo's hands pulled the largest stinger rifle from its holster. He needed all four to handle it. "Bor, you drive the crawler. Aen, you navigate and keep watch for the AAnn."

"Pardon," Aen objected, "but in accordance with our respective positions it would be my place to drive, Bor's to shoot, and yours to navigate."

"Rank is hereby superseded by circumstance." Ryo was checking the charge on the rifle. It was full. "I order you to disregard position."

"If you wish me to ignore position then you cannot give me an order to do so," she argued smoothly. Bor settled the argument by plunging the crawler through the trees onto the field of cab-high asfi. They were soon submerged in ripe yellow pods just starting to droop from their green-and-black-striped stalks.

Noise and gunfire continued to issue from the direction of the town. That was natural. Also promising, Ryo thought. Having touched down unopposed in an unprotected colonial region, the invaders quite likely would anticipate little in the way of armed resistance. Certainly nothing as absurd as a counterattack.

Ryo ordered Bor to aim the crawler for the parked shuttles. Ryo wished simultaneously for an energy rifle. That would be much more effective against machinery, the stingers having been designed for use against living beings.

They approached quite near to the shuttles and still no one appeared to challenge them. The shuttlecraft were the first true space-going vehicles Ryo had ever seen. Paszex and Jupiq and even Zirenba did not rate a spaceport. Only facilities for less powerful suborbital craft.

At Aen's suggestion, Bor swung the crawler sharply left and off the main cultivation path. Now they were smashing crudely through the dense rows of asfi stalks. Fruit and stalks flew in all directions.

Such casual destruction was normally worthy of severe condemnation, but under the circumstances Ryo didn't worry about possible social consequences. And then, suddenly and unexpectedly, a single creature was standing just ahead and to the right of the rapidly advancing crawler.

The AAnn was relieving himself and the abrupt appearance of the crawler was a shock. He stumbled over his short pants and growled unintelligibly.

The blunt, heavy jaws were filled with sharp teeth. A pair of black, single-lensed eyes peered from high on the two sides of the head. A single tail curved from behind. The large, clawed feet wore devices that resembled steel spats. Its short pants were matched by a shirt of dull color and a helmet forested with electronic sensors.

A thick cord connected a bulky hand weapon to a power pack slung around the AAnn's waist. The muzzle swung around to point at the onrushing crawler.

Civilized thoughts were subsumed by fury and Ryo never hesitated. Had he been the average worker, he would have died, but in the swamps Ryo had acquired reflexes that most hive dwellers lacked.

There was a sharp *crack* from the stinger and a tiny bolt of electricity jumped from its tip to strike the AAnn squarely in the chest. The AAnn convulsed, jumped a meter clear of the ground, and fell back twitching. He was motionless by the time the crawler rumbled past. Now the enormity of what Ryo had just done finally struck. He'd deliberately slain another sentient creature. For an instant Ryo was a little shaky.

They could hear anguished, high-pitched whistles from the direction of Paszex. Primitive instincts overwhelmed the last of thousands of years of civilization. The hive was being attacked. Ryo was a soldier defending the burrow entrances. All that mattered now was defense.

By now they were quite close to the nearer of the two shuttlecraft and Ryo was hunting for a section of the ship that might prove vulnerable to his weapon. If he'd had an energy rifle he would have begun by shooting at the multiple landing gear or at the transparent crescent that marked the command cabin above the nose. But these were warcraft. There were no exposed antennae or exterior engines.

Several armed AAnn stood beneath the nearest wing. They glanced up in surprise as the crawler rumbled into view. Ryo shot one of them before the others could move.

The group suddenly broke and ran frantically for the ramp that led from the ground to the belly of the shuttle.

Ryo caught another AAnn with a second bolt halfway up the ramp, watching coldly as the creature jerked and twisted downward. Several energy beams reached from the other retreating soldiers toward the crawler but, fired wildly and in haste, they missed the agile machine as Bor sent it winding in unpredictable directions.

Now they were crossing under the stern of the first shuttle and careening toward the second. Ryo sent several shots crackling toward the twin exhaust jets and then the rocket openings between, hoping to disable some vital component. He had no way of knowing if the bursts were effective.

By this time panic was giving way to reaction among those on board the craft. Suddenly a powerful wash of energy radiated from the bow of the second ship. It carbonized the ground ahead and to the left of the charging crawler.

"Turn, turn!" shouted Aen. Bor responded with soft clicking noises indicating acknowledgment and mild annoyance.

The crawler raced for the concealment of some tettoq trees. A second energy blast seared the earth where the crawler had been heading moments earlier.

Other rushing, mechanical sounds reached them. Looking back over the stern of the crawler as they disappeared into the shelter of the tettoq boles, Ryo could make out moving figures hurrying toward the shuttles. Some were on single-tracked machines that carried soldiers in pairs. Others ran on foot. All were pouring out of the town.

The fire from the second shuttle was joined by a flare from the first. Beams from both swept the tettoq orchard in search of fleeing enemy. One struck near enough to explode the crawler's rear tread. But by that time the overworked vehicle was limping into the far thicker cover offered by the jungle.

Almost reluctantly, a final, fiery burst cut down two massive lugulic trees, which fell with a ripping crash just to the left of the damaged crawler, carrying down vines and lesser trees with them. Then a rich, rising whine filled the air.

"Can you see what they're doing?" Bor asked, maintaining as complex an evasive course as he could manage with the damaged tread. Ryo and Aen tried to stare through the trees.

"The ramps have been taken in," Ryo said excitedly. "Judging from the noise, I'd say they're preparing to leave."

"Surely not because of our little diversion?"

"Who knows?" Pride filled Aen's voice. "They were certainly surprised. Perhaps they think several dozen of us, mounting deadlier weaponry, are preparing to attack them."

"Such speculation is unbecoming," Ryo murmured.

"The circumstances support it," she replied.

"Then again," Bor put in, "it may be that their flight has several possible causes."

"Meaning what?" wondered Ryo.

Bor brought the crawler to a halt and joined them in gazing through the wall of trees. "Either they have accomplished whatever evil they planned for our poor hive or else," and he pointed skyward with a truhand, "one of the warships that occasionally but regularly visits our system had received word of this attack and has drawn near."

The whine of the lifting jets achieved a respectable thunder and the three Thranx watched as the warcraft taxied through more of the fresh asfi, picked up speed, and gradually rose into the eastern sky. Of defensive aircraft from distant Ciccikalk there was still no sign.

As to whether a Thranx warship had actually arrived on the orbital scene and prompted the retreat, they would have to wait to find out. The echo of the jets faded. There was nothing to hint that anything out of the ordinary had happened, nothing save the columns of black smoke, the crushed vegetation in the fields, and the faint, awful smell of something burning.

Paszex had not been completely destroyed. One of the natural advantages of living underground is that all but the uppermost levels of a community are relatively impregnable to all but the heaviest weapons. From their primitive beginnings the Thranx had always lived beneath the surface of the earth.

Still, substantial and heartrending damage had been

done. Besides the casual destruction of carefully tended orchards and fields, the hive's module transport station was twisted, running metal. Many of the air intakes and ventilation stacks had been burned away like so much dry straw. No real military purpose could have been served by such destruction; it seemed to have been done more for amusement than tactical advantage.

The hive's communication center and satellite terminal had also been destroyed, but not before the operators had succeeded in transmitting a message to Zirenba. From there it was instantly relayed to Ciccikalk, whence help had been summoned.

Many were dead and every clan had new ancestors to honor. But there were no recriminations, no days of wailing and weeping. Because the water lines were untouched the Servitor staff could efficiently extinguish all but the most persistent fires. Because the Servitors were also responsible for such diverse functions as keeping the peace and cleaning up the garbage, restoration and repair were well coordinated from the beginning.

Families tallied their losses, clanmothers compiled rosters of the dead, while the job of putting Paszex back together again proceeded smoothly. Since the AAnn had been too busy or too contemptuous to destroy the synchronous-orbit communications satellites above Willow-wane, reestablishing contact with the rest of the planet was simply a matter of placing portable communication discs above the town.

Ryo cared little for such details as he'd raced through the smoke-filled corridors in search of Fal.

She'd been working in the Nursery. If he'd known that, he wouldn't have worried so much about her. But he couldn't be sure she was at work when the AAnn attacked. She could have been anywhere in the hive. It was a considerable relief to learn that she was safe and unhurt.

When the first explosions had sounded, followed immediately by the alarms, she'd assisted in the transfer of the larvae to the special Nursery chambers below the hive's fifth and bottom level. There she and the other attendants waited out the battle in comparative safety.

The emergency lower Nursery had its own sealed air supply as well as weapons, and could have held out for three seasons without revealing itself to long-term invaders. Such security for the young was a holdover from the Thranx's primitive past. Even after attaining intelligence and civilization, the Thranx had never forgotten that the most basic ingredient for the survival of a people is the protection of the young.

Eventually the town learned that the timely arrival of a Thranx warship had, indeed, forced the hasty AAnn retreat. That did not prevent Ryo, Bor, and Aen from being accorded the status due local heroes.

They had been responsible for the deaths of at least three of the bandits—the local council would not dignify the AAnn by calling them invaders—and one of the two AAnn shuttles had been destroyed by the Thranx warship before rendezvous with its mother ship. The Thranx captain had ascribed the fatal shot to an improperly supervised gunnery officer, subsequently "reprimanded." So there was something of a trade-off, incidentwise. Nevertheless, a few were convinced that the success was due to Ryo's stinging rifle. But there was now no way to prove this, so Ryo and his companions naturally refused to accept credit for it.

That did not keep the hive council from voting them commendations and thanks. There was even talk of some kind of presentation at the capital. That never materialized, but weeks later Ryo learned that he had been nominated for a single crimson star by the grateful colonial government, and that the award had been approved by the appropriate bureau on Hivehom, in Daret. The star was to be set in his chiton just behind his left shoulder.

Some military and civilian heroes of great accomplishment could boast twenty and thirty such stars, acquired through long and meritorious service. A few even carried the coveted yellow sunburst. But thousands of respected achievers had never received a single such honor. The award was quite a coup for Ryo's clan, though he cared little for it. Anyone would have done as he had, presented with the same options. Nonetheless, it was argued, it was he who had done it.

As the weeks passed, supplies were air-ferried from Zirenba, and Jupiq and Paszex's other sister towns contributed what they could. Medical and food supplies were the first to arrive in quantity, followed by technicians, building materials, and sophisticated replacement components from Ciccikalk.

The damaged fields were soon readied for replanting. New ventilation and exhaust stacks were quickly set and sealed in place.

The greatest damage was to the module transport terminal. Ryo went there one day to see how repairs were progressing. It was important to the Company because most of Inmot's local unprocessed produce was shipped via module to Zirenba.

The guide tracks on which the magnetic repulsion modules cruised were still being poured and cast. The thick gray-white plastic would solidify quickly into a nearly unbreakable, flexible line. New coils were being sealed into position. Under the critical gaze of a large crew of local and imported technicians the station was being rebuilt in the most modern style and much expensive sunglass crystal was used as shielding.

The new station would be larger and more efficient as well as more attractive than its predecessor, though the citizens of Paszex would gladly have traded it for the old one and a retraction of the cause of its destruction. Ryo wondered if the lavish new terminal was the government's subtle apology to the scarred inhabitants.

A big celebration was held when the first modules arrived over the new track from Jupiq, but Ryo missed the event, being deep in the jungle at the time. He watched it via screen later that night, saw the dozen oblong passenger modules link up outside Jupiq to form a single silvery segmented train, then split up outside Paszex to arrive in stately individual procession.

At least the system was operational again. Goods and individuals could once more travel freely between Paszex and the rest of Willow-wane. Only decorative detail remained to be added to the terminal. More government money. More apologies.

A formal clan evening meal was served that night. The clan hall was utilized and the meal set two timeparts later than normal to allow everyone time to dress properly. Fine jewelry and inlays were brought out for the occasion. There were neck pouches and body vests of orange and silver mesh, pink threadwork so fine that it seemed no hand or machine could manage the weave. Females and males alike sported inlays of cerulean and carnelian, obsidian and chalcedony, faceted gems, fine ceramic and enamel in curlicues, triangles, and bars. Most gleamed from excavations made between mandibles and eyes, though more official inserts shone on a few shoulders and necks.

After the meal Ryo's crimson star was awarded in a formal ceremony. The four-pointed insignia was presented by a minor government functionary who'd traveled from Zirenha for the occasion.

The official presented the small transparent case to the venerable Ilvenzuteck, Ryo's clanmother, who handed it proudly to the inlayer. The craftswoman set to work with blades and chisels, painlessly excavating a gap from the chiton of Ryo's left shoulder while the rest of the clan looked on approvingly.

Permaglue was brushed on the base of the star, which was then carefully set in place, the metal fitting flush with Ryo's exoskeleton. The inlayer, an old Thranx, took satisfaction from a perfect fit on the first attempt. No glue oozed from the edges of the incision. She'd done this many times before, though mostly with cheap ceramics and rarely before an audience. She applied a little saliva to shine the star, inlayer tradition.

The decoration would remain a permanent part now of Ryo's body, for all to see and admire. If he ever did any traveling, it would be amusing when strangers asked him in what campaign, during what exploration he'd achieved the award. He would have to confess that he'd earned it for acceding to the impulse to prevent belligerent aliens' from knocking down tettoq trees and asfi bushes.

A loud whistling arose from the assembled clanate, from elders, adults, and adolescents alike. The whistle of approval rose shrilly and then snapped off, neatly concluded. Ryo acknowledged it while Fal beamed proudly at him from her seat nearby.

She looks particularly beautiful tonight, he thought, with the simple yellow stripes in her forehead and the three pink dots topping each. She wore matching neck and body attire of violet iridescent material. Violet and silver thread had been applied with temporary glue around her b-thorax and spicules. Silver wires formed double helixes around both arching ovipositors, an agonizingly long task at which her brother and friends had helped.

For a moment Ryo thought to boldly announce their intention to mate, but of course he could not do that without consulting her first, though he knew she would agree instantly. It was just as well, he thought. Lovely as she was, he still wasn't certain he was ready for that.

So he stood, accepting the accolades of his clan, the four-pointed crimson star shining on his shoulder. As he thought of the lady who loved him and the certain promotion to the Inmot local council, he was quiet, contemplative.

No one in the assembled crowd of friends and relatives could have guessed that the thought uppermost in Ryozenzuzex's mind was this: he did not hate but, instead, greatly envied the AAnn of the shuttles . . .

The ship was nearly as young as her captain. Six great oval projection fans formed a circle in front of it, attached to the octahedral bulk of the craft proper by long metal corridors and a webwork of struts and braces.

Each fan generated a portion of the posigravity field, a crude precursor of the KK drive that was to come following the Amalgamation. This field pulled the ship through Space Plus, for all that it was ungainly, unstreamlined, and resembled an angular metallic squid. Generation of the posigrav field used a great deal of energy and Space Plus was no place for timid physics. It was a region inhabited by ghost stars, where visible light turned diffuse and X-ray stars became visible. Other peculiarities were normal to Space Plus, the region of theory wherein the ships of Deep Space uncertainly made their way. A captain had to be ready to deal with all sorts of manipulative physical phenomena, some that were not matter, others that were not energy.

Below Space Plus lay normal space ("below" here signifying a place more colloquial than relativistic), where could be found predictable stars and habitable planets. Below *that* were the unnatural atomic and subatomic vagaries of Space Minus, or Nullspace, a region of eternity best not touched, where tachyons and other nonexistent particles became real and where ships and messages sometimes vanished more utterly than if they'd dropped into a collapsar. Nullspace was, according to a most respected Thranx theosophical physicist, "the inside-out of real."

Captain Brohwelporvot strolled the control room of the *Zinramm*. Though he was on his third expedition for Deep Space Research he was still nervous about his first command. Relaxed in their saddles, his crew formed a circle around him.

Through the forward observation port the distant purple glow of the posigravity drive field marked the burrow the *Zinramm* was tunneling through Space Plus. They were a quarter of a season out from Hivehom system. In addition to verifying and extending the charts for this considerable section of space, they'd entered and studied two new planetary systems, one holding a world that was marginally inhabitable—a discovery by itself sufficient to make this the most productive of the three expeditions Broh had so far directed.

Still, as they had time left, he drove ship and crew deeper through the Arm. Nothing ever quite satisfied Broh, no discovery sated his curiosity or sense of duty. His internal drive was one of the reasons he'd been selected to command the *Zinramm* when his years did not seem to merit it.

The scanner made a sign toward his captain with a foot-hand, the other foothand poised delicately above lower contacts and his truhands remaining on the controls.

"What is it, Uvov?"

"Object, sir. Extrasystemic, twenty squares right of our present course. Moving at moderate speed and inclined slightly up from the plane of the ecliptic."

"Intercept course?" Broh stared over the scanner's shoulder at quadruple colored screens.

"Three timeparts," replied the scanner, after a moment's calculating.

"Identification?"

"Impossible to say at this distance and velocity, sir. It's quite small. Wandering asteroid perhaps. Cometary nucleus. Or? . . ." He left the always hopeful question unanswered.

Broh said nothing. Such gaps were what the journey of the *Zinramm* were supposed to fill. He considered. They were in no hurry to get anywhere and any object traveling this far out from a system was worth a casual inspection. Turning, he called across the disk of the room.

"Emmt."

"Sir," the pilot replied, swiveling slightly to look back at him.

"Maintain course for two timeparts, then drop to normal space."

"Yes, sir." She turned to her instrumentation and commenced programming.

"Defense?"

"Ready, sir."

"Place ship on third-degree alert, one degree of uncertainty. Personnel, sound stations for drop to normal space."

The bridge was a quiet maze of moving multidigited arms and legs as the command crew scrambled smoothly to comply with the sudden rush of orders. There was no confusion, no uncertainty to the preparations. Not like the first time, Broh thought ruefully. Now everyone knew precisely what was expected. They worked without hint of excitment, the thrill of such encounters having been dulled by numerous similar incidents that invariably proved to be of minor scientific utility.

Soon the computer called up the count from engineering. "Bite . . . one, two, three . . . ," and on toward eight and the drop from Space Plus. Broh braced himself in the captain's saddle.

There was a violent wrench, the ship shuddered like a leaf in a whirlwind, and Broh was certain his insides would spill out through his mouth. The nausea passed with merciful speed and no unseemly regurgitation. The forward observation port showed relaxed, normal stars of recognizable color and shape instead of the ghostly auras that had earlier marked their location. Nothing else was visible via the port, but the search screens were alive with information. "Scanner," he called briskly, "do you have the object?"

"Coming up on screen one, sir."

The large screen set on the wall to the left of the port flickered momentarily. Then the subject of their temporary drop from Space Plus became visible and the attitudes of those who could spare a moment from their assignments changed drastically. Startled clicks echoed through the bridge. The object was not an asteroid, or a comet head.

Analysis confirmed what the eye supposed: the object was largely metallic. Further information merely confirmed the obvious. The artifact was a ship. Three cones formed the front section of the vessel, attached by struts and beams to a sphere. The arrangement hinted at a different, but not radically so, propulsive system.

The senior science council had arrived on the bridge, drawn from their studies by the announcement of the forthcoming sublight encounter. Now they crowded next to the captain's position and stared at the screen. There were three of them, in age all quite senior to Broh. They waited, however, for him to make the proper command inquiries.

Now more than ever in his brief and comparatively uneventful career, Broh was aware of his lack of experience. Not that he would permit that to show. In some ways the science council outranked him. He was grateful for that. It would allow him to ask obvious questions without seeming stupid.

"AAnn or related design?" he asked sharply.

"No," replied the first observer. She studied the screen intently. "At least, not of any AAnn designs I've ever seen. The projection fans—for such we must assume they are—are quite different from ours or the AAnn's, though somewhat more similar to the AAnn's."

"Also the number of projection units—three—is the same as the AAnn employ." The second observer pointed toward the image and described silhouettes in the air. "But see, they are far more flat than ours or the AAnn's. I wonder how that affects the field that wraps around the ship in Space Plus." He muttered about the displacement of reality and other arcane matters that were as much solipsistic and metaphysical as hard science.

Of course, there was no firm boundary between reality and unreality when one was dealing with such concepts as Space Plus and Space Minus. When brilliant generalists like the three observers got together, even theology sometimes took on the aspect of a hard science.

The alien vessel grew steadily larger and magnification was correspondingly reduced until finally they found themselves looking at a real-size image.

"Try signaling," the third observer suggested.

"What frequency?" Communications asked.

"All," Broh said. "Try standard hive channels first, then AAnn frequencies."

"But the first observer already has said it's not a recognizable AAnn type, sir."

Broh ignored the insubordination. "It may be a new type," he responded. "Or an ally of the AAnn we know nothing of."

"If it's an ally," the scanner commented, "it's been badly treated." Screen two, to the right of the viewport, suddenly came to life with a close-up of the alien's fore section. Two of the three cone-shaped units had been badly damaged. Broh requested an analysis and opinion of the damage.

"It could have been meteoric material, but I think not," said the analyzer. "See the way the metal folds and twists back on itself there at the leading edges? And there, along the support beams, surely that's the mark of heavy-energy weaponry."

"Possibly," murmured the first observer. She was more interested now in the after section of the ship.

"No response to inquiries, sir," Communications announced. Broh mulled that over. Coupled with the signs of severe damage, everything indicated that they were looking at a dead ship, a wandering derelict. He put the thought to the council.

"It could be a clever trap," suggested the second observer. "The damage could have been falsified to lure us close enough to be taken before we had a chance to signal. Such a ploy would be typical of the AAnn."

"If that's the case," said Broh, "we'll know in less than a timepart."

If the alien was a thangner hiding in its silken burrow, it was a most patient one. It continued to coast as they approached, its engines apparently quite dead. Not a hint of energy issued from the three cone projectors.

"If that's a decoy, it's fooled me," Communications muttered.

Broh frowned inwardly. It was not the communicator's place to offer such a comment. He would have to speak with the officer later.

"Still nothing on all bands," the communicator said coolly. "Trying unassigned frequencies now. I'll run the whole spectrum."

The images on screen two shifted. "There appears," the analyzer pointed out judiciously, "to be damage to the main body of the vessel as well as to the projection units."

Broh made a clicking sound, gestured. "Bring us around toward the main body, then."

Slowly the *Zinramm* changed direction toward the stern of the strange craft. Now they could see a few weak lights glowing from behind intact ports. These were located mostly near the upper rearmost section of the ship. The ports were circular instead of triangular, but no one on the *Zinramm*'s bridge made the obvious lewd comments. The main body was larger than that of the *Zinramm*—larger than that of most Thranx vessels—but, save for the few dimly illuminated ports, the alien craft was dark as night.

Broh whistled into the communicator that hung from his

headset to activate the proper section of the *Zinramm*'s internal communications system. "Outside? Anzeljermeit, I want a burrowing party of five."

"*Five*, Captain?" came the querulous acknowledgment.

"Five should be sufficient. I do not believe the damage to this alien is camouflage. And if it is, it will make no difference how many are in the group."

"Arms, sir?"

Broh hesitated. For this he had prescribed procedure to draw upon.

"Small arms only. In one-tenth of a timepart. Lock six."

"We'll be ready, sir."

Broh rose from his saddle, turned to the science council. "I have no power to compel you but I would like it very much if you—"

The second observer cut him off with a concomitant gesture of apology. "This is what we live for, Captain. Such a moment is the joy of a life. You could not keep us from boarding that marvelous mystery if you wished to. There is hardly a need to ask us to accompany you."

"I thought as much." Broh's gesture indicated mild amusement mixed with high gratification. "The law requires that I ask."

"Of course," said the third observer. "Let us not waste any more time in discussion of the accepted."

The five Outside specialists were suited and waiting in lock six when Broh and the science council arrived. The *Zinramm* would not dock with the alien vessel. Broh was not that confident of the derelict's harmlessness, so the party moved from the lock into a small shuttlecraft, one normally used for conveying explorers to the surface of a solid body.

The lock sealed behind them. Anzeljermeit, leader of the Outsiders, fired the shuttle's engines very briefly. The shuttle slipped free of its compartment and out into space, angling toward the intimidating bulk of the alien ship. Anzeljermeit's four subordinates struggled to maintain the pose of professional indifference, but there was no mistaking their tense posture.

The alien was perhaps half again the size of the *Zinramm*. The perfect spherical body was unsettling to those on the shuttle. They were used to ships, those of the AAnn as well, that boasted a comforting alignment of planes and sharp angles. A vessel shaped as a smooth globe was something most disturbing.

At least the skin of the alien was marred by the expected projections. Antennae and samplers were more or less recognizable. Several blunt nozzles were not, though if they were anything but the business ends of weapons Broh would have been much surprised. They remained comfortingly angled away from the approaching shuttle and the motionless mass of the now distant *Zinramm*.

Anzeljermeit carefully adjusted the attitude of the shuttle, directing it around the flank of the alien and toward the stern. It did not take long to locate what had to be an exterior lock. The officer barely touched the maneuvering rockets. Tiny puffs of gas flared from the shuttle's sides, moving it closer to the alien before firming its position in space.

The lock opening was no less aberrant than the shape of the alien ship. It was a squared ellipsoid, nothing like the familiar triangular hatches on the *Zinramm*. It looked a lot more like an AAnn airlock. The several similarities were beginning to trouble Broh. The shape of the lock was the first unarguable sign they had that the aliens might physically be related to the AAnn.

Boarding would be no problem. The tube that would extend from the shuttle was flexible and would conform itself to the alien opening while sealing tightly. Broh gave the necessary orders.

The Outside officer adjusted the shuttle slightly, so that it presented its left side to the stern of the alien. The boarding tube extended and secured itself to the alien craft. There was a pause while checks were performed.

"Mating completed," Anzeljermeit announced tersely.

There was no reaction from the alien ship. Now Broh had to make a more difficult decision. To enter the alien they might have to blow the lock cover, an action that could be interpreted as offensive. Since no hint of life had manifested itself from the ship, he'd come to believe she was truly a derelict, floating free, engines as dead as her crew following an armed encounter.

But the few feeble lights showed that some power remained on board. Even a dead ship might boast automatic defenses. Therefore he dearly wanted to avoid having to blow the lock.

Anzeljermeit left two of his people in charge of the shuttle to relay information from the burrowing party to the *Zinramm*'s secondary scientific complement. Broh knew that in the event of trouble they were to return immediately to the *Zinramm*. While interrank relationships were reasonably casual on board Thranx ships, discipline was absolute when invoked.

The suited burrowing party entered the shuttle's lock, which closed behind them. The three sections of the outside door slid apart and they floated into the connection tube.

Ahead lay the exterior of the alien ship. The skin was painted black or composed of some black metal. It did not shine the comfortable silver of the *Zinramm*. It was with some relief that Broh had noticed earlier it was also not the garish orange of an AAnn craft. Crowded together in the narrow confines of the boarding tube they pondered what to do next.

The Outsiders had brought solid charges for blowing the lock if that proved necessary. Broh let the science council take its time studying the lock configuration.

They quickly discovered several hinged covers, which when raised, revealed contact disks. These were perfunctorily inspected. The observers conferred, then the first spoke to Broh via suit communicator. "We believe these to be simple, if bulky, controls for operating the lock, as should be present on any such entryway in the event of internal power failure."

"They could also," the second observer noted grudgingly, "be a method for inducing anyone trying to enter to blow himself toward the nearest star."

"An assumption that presupposes both paranoia and belligerence," said the third observer. "Two qualities which I would prefer not to ascribe to the builders of this vessel."

"We're not debating preferences, but actualities," said the second observer. "However, I naturally defer to the majority opinion." He moved toward the rear of the tube. "You activate the controls. I will wait here."

The third observer made a gesture indicative of acceptance coupled with hopeful anticipation and just a smidgen of mild amusement. She turned and reached with a suited truhand for the lower of the two exposed disks. The Outside officer and his companions waited impassively, not having been allowed to retreat.

Broh's inclination was to agree with the majority of observers, but he wished their decision to try the lock controls had been unanimous.

As the third observer depressed the disk the lock hatch promptly slid up into the wall of the ship. A brightly lit chamber was exposed beyond. A second hatch showed ahead. They were indeed entering an airlock, then.

It was more than large enough to hold them all, including the recalcitrant second observer who floated behind, grumbling but willing to admit he'd been wrong.

Corresponding disks were sunk in the interior wall. Their function was simple to divine. When all seven burrowers were inside, the third observer depressed the counterpart to the outside disk. The exterior lock door slid shut.

There was faint motion in the lock. Sound sensors detected the whistle of escaping gas. Lock pressurization was automatic. Suit instrumentation immediately analyzed the gas. It was a pleasant surprise to discover that the atmosphere that had been injected into the lock was technically breathable.

"Oxygen breathers like us," murmured the first observer as she settled to the floor. "Artificial gravity perhaps a tiny bit stronger than ours."

"Also like the AAnn," Broh pointed out.

"Not exactly like us." The second observer was studying his suit instruments. "Check your climatology readings."

The atmosphere that now filled the lock was breathable, but desperately cold and almost unbelievably dry. Since the air had been provided promptly there was no reason to assume that either factor was the result of a malfunction in the ship's systems, though such a possibility could not be ruled out.

Broh stared disbelievingly at his humidity indicator, which registered close to zero. As the third observer pointed out, that was disconcertingly like the climate the AAnn were known to prefer.

"That much is true," the second observer admitted. "The lack of reasonable moisture in the air here is indeed similar to suspected AAnn home planetery conditions. However, the temperature in this lock is low enough to kill them even faster than it would doom us."

"Maybe," the first suggested, "this ship's automatic monitors are functioning properly save for a breakdown in the heating elements."

"That's possible," Broh agreed, breaking into the learned discussion lest it grow too esoteric, "but as near as I can tell everything else seems to be functioning properly. I fear we must assume that holds true for the temperature controls the same as everything else."

"A frozen race," the Outside officer muttered.

"Of course," the first observer continued after making a polite gesture in recognition of the officer's comment coupled with mild condescension toward one of inferior mental powers, "allies of the AAnn would not necessarily have to enjoy the same climate as the AAnn, any more than their ships would have to be based on similar designs."

"True enough." The third looked thoughtful. "I've been fortunate enough to have had the chance to study the interior of a captured AAnn vessel. I can say that insofar as airlocks are concerned, the differences between that ship and this one are considerable. I reserve final judgment until we have seen more of this one, of course."

There was a crackling in Broh's headset, an urgent flurry of inquisitive clicks and whistles.

"Captain, sir?" said a slightly distorted voice.

"Speaking." Broh's reply was sharper than he intended.

"It's nothing specific, sir." Broh recognized the voice of the Outsider manning the shuttle. "But we hadn't heard from you since instruments showed that you'd boarded the alien and closed the lock door behind you."

"My error," Broh replied. "We should have checked back with you sooner. The builders of this ship remain unknown and," he glanced for confirmation at the science council, "at least so far there is nothing to indicate they are AAnn or AAnn-allied. You may relay this very tentative and preliminary information back to the *Zinramm*."

"And happy they'll be to hear it, too—tentative though it may be," the other Outsider on the shuttle commented.

"We've spent enough time here." Broh moved to the hatch barring the far end of the lock and studied the controls. They were duplicates of those outside the ship. He touched what should have been the proper one for opening the door. Nothing happened. He tried the other, with the same disappointing result.

"Try them in opposite sequence," suggested the first observer. Broh did so and was rewarded when the hatch slid sideways into the wall. The outer hatch had retracted upward. Broh wondered idly if the disparity of direction was functional, aesthetic, or designed to satisfy some sense he could not imagine.

A corridor gleamed beyond, brightly lit and beckoning. They cautiously exited the lock, pausing repeatedly to marvel at various peculiar aspects of the walls and ceiling. The science council continually had to be urged onward, or they would have spent a timepart arguing over the function and purpose of each tiny control or extrusion.

As they moved deeper into the alien ship the party encountered smoke. Broh and the Outsiders kept their hands close to their holstered stingers, their attention on each new doorway and opening.

The lighting was harsh, though whether this was due to damage or intention they had no way of knowing. Broh wondered at the sources of the smoke. They paused at one complex instrument panel that was a flickering galaxy of exploding sparks and melted metal. Broh studied the ruined panel and the metal that had run beneath it, then moved on to examine a similar console that was still intact. It boasted a screen in its center and bulky controls below.

More interesting was the saddle set into the deck before it. It had to be a saddle, since it seemed an unlikely place to put an abstract sculpture. It was much higher off the floor than any Thranx could manage. Not that they could have rested on it even if it had been lower. It was impossibly small and flat, yet very different from the AAnn saddles the science council had studied.

"I don't see how that could belong to any large intelligent creature," the first observer said. "It seems too small to support anything but a krep-size animal, yet everything else aboard this ship hints that it was built and used by large creatures. The dichotomy is puzzling."

"It seems certain that whoever they are, they're completely alien," Broh said. The Outsiders' nervousness increased.

Every screen they encountered thereafter was placed well above normal eye level. Only standing on one's hind legs would enable one to see the topmost controls. Everything save the peculiar stunted saddles pointed to creatures larger than the Thranx or the AAnn.

They moved deeper into the ship, pausing at regular intervals to check in with the two Outsiders running the shuttle.

The one thing Broh had wished for and which they hadn't encountered were alien atmosphere suits. Used, perhaps, while abandoning ship? Stored elsewhere? He didn't know, but his mental reconstruction of this ship's crew was not very pleasant.

Still, his conceptions might be way out of line. The drindars of Hivehom, for example, though primitive dumb creatures, could conceivably fit the alien saddles.

They entered a new chamber, much larger than any they'd seen so far, and found long platforms and dozens of small saddles that were not fastened to the decking.

"A communal meeting hall," suggested the second observer. "For the carrying out of clan rituals, perhaps?"

"Maybe," the third murmured, "but something makes me think otherwise."

They walked through it into still another room of uncertain function. It was filled with a profusion of portable devices. Rummaging through cabinets that opened to the touch, one of the subordinate Outsiders discovered a collection of what appeared to be personal items.

"Utensils, possibly," suggested the first observer.

They crowded around the tiny collection of alien artifacts. There were open-ended containers and low-relief concave slabs of vitreous material. Nowhere did Broh see anything resembling a drinking vessel. Surely the crew of the ship consumed liquids, Broh thought.

They found other devices of obscure purpose, but a whole drawer was full of knives, something with an oval scoop attached to one end, and a multipronged tool that resembled a miniature fishing spear.

"I believe their intake would not prove entirely bizarre," said the second observer. "It's possible we might be able to eat some of the same food."

That brought forth a thoroughly disgusted noise from

one of the Outsiders, for which he promptly performed a gesture of third-degree apology, mixed with two degrees of embarrassment.

"An experiment that I would prefer to forgo for now," Broh said, fighting to conceal his own distaste at the thought.

Since there was no other way out of the room they returned the way they'd come, through the chamber of the long platforms and inflexible stunted saddles, and into the corridor beyond.

They continued on into the bowels of the ship and soon found a new chamber filled with fresh mysteries. There were multiple platforms, but they differed considerably from those in the meeting hall. There were also small videoscreens and a great many garish objects decorating the walls. To everyone's delight, these platforms resembled nothing so much as enormous sleeping lounges.

"The first real indication of any physical similarity," said the Outside officer. "Perhaps they are more like us than we thought."

"Then how do you explain those impossible little saddles?" asked one of the two subordinates.

"I don't," the officer replied. Without waiting for word from a member of the science council he elected to climb up onto one of the lounges, that being as good a name for them as anything.

"How is it?" the subordinate wondered.

"Almost normal. Comfortable, even." He glanced over at his captain. "Permission to remove suits, sir."

"I don't know . . ."

The first observer nudged him. "Let him. The experiment should be tried. The air tests acceptably well."

"If you concur," Broh said reluctantly. He signed to the officer.

Carefully Anzeljermeit unsealed the right-center portion of his suit, exposing his thorax to the alien air. After an anxious pause, he did the same to the seals covering his spicules on the left side. His thorax pulsed.

"Reaction?" inquired the third observer.

The reply came as a momentary gasp, grew slowly stronger and more normal. "Dry enough to rust your blood. It's a bit of a shock." He unsealed and flipped back the

upper section of the suit, including the transparent headpiece, and sat unsuited to the shoulders. His antennae fluttered, then spread unrestrained as he sampled the air.

"You can smell the dryness, and the cold chills your
guts, but those details aside, it is quite breathable, as the
instruments indicated. Add a lot of moisture to it and cook
it some and I'd say it would be comfortable enough. What
is your opinion, Quoz?"

The Outsider standing next to the lounge unsealed the
upper third of her own suit and flipped it back. Now two
pairs of antennae waggled freely in the chamber.

"I agree," she finally said, with somewhat more enthusiasm than her superior. "It's quite palatable."

The first observer began to unseal her own suit. "I, for
one, am tired of canned air. It's not every day one has the
opportunity to sample an alien atmosphere."

Soon they were all working at their suit seals, keeping
the lower section in place and well heated. Lounging on the
peculiar alien platform, Anzeljermeit watched them easily,
pleased in the knowledge that he'd been the one with the
courage to go first. Then he made a gesture of uncertainty
compounded by concern and sat up fast.

"Where's Iel?" He looked toward the far corners of the
chamber, his gaze coming to rest on the doorway leading
out into the corridor beyond.

The other Outsider turned a slow circle. "I don't know,
sir,"

The officer slid off the lounge. "I'll have his rank for
this. Wandering off without authorization."

"Gently go, sir. You know Iel. Impulsive and easily
bored. Well, maybe not impulsive, but incautious."

"That may not matter much on board the *Zinramm*, but
here we—"

Distant, frantic whistling sounded from somewhere far
away.

"Quickly!" the officer commanded.

Suits were hurriedly resealed and the burrowing party
rushed in the direction of the whistles. They hadn't gone
far from the chamber with the lounges when Outsider Iel
rounded a far corner, running on all sixes as if the Ruler of
the Distant Darkness itself were after him. On their suit

communicators they could hear his frantic breathing, his breaths coming in short, tight gasps.

"So something's given you a good scare, has it?" said Anzeljermeit sharply, not immediately noticing the attitude with which the Outsider held himself, antennae folded flat back inside his suit, mandibles clenched so tightly together Broh thought they must shatter. "Serves you damn well right, too, for going off on—" His voice faded like a fast-moving breeze.

A thing had materialized in the corridor behind the terrified Iel.

It raced in pursuit of him, moving with horridly fluid loping movements of its lower limbs. The massive shape towered over the diminutive Iel. It seemed to fill the corridor, though in reality it was not all that large. Its voice was a deep-throated thunder that reminded Broh of Hivehom's more dangerous carnivores.

Surely that's what it had to be, a beast escaped from some on-board holding pen or traveling zoo. But it wore clothing, and moved with more than feral purpose. Despite what his revolted insides shouted, Broh knew it had to be one of the alien crew.

It continued to utter incomprehensible noises as it chased Iel. Broh drew his stinger but determined not to fire until the last possible moment.

At that point the abomination noticed the burrowing party crowded together at the end of the corridor. It halted abruptly, generated a tremendously violent sound that rattled Broh's head, and vanished back the way it had come.

Outsider Iel finally reached them and skidded to a stop. He started to say something. Then a shadow darkened his ommatidia and he keeled over on his left side. His superior and Broh bent over him, dividing their attention between the unconscious Iel and the now deserted corridor.

Broh watched while Anzeljermeit inspected his subordinate. "He doesn't appear to be injured, sir," the officer finally concluded. "His suit is intact and the seals don't seem to have been breached—but it's difficult to tell, since they're self-repairing. In any case, his breathing is normal, if labored."

"You mean he does not appear to have been injured

physically." The third observer was gazing with a mixture of awe and revulsion down the corridor. He made a gesture of astonishment mixed with fourth-degree worry.

"I don't wonder that he went comatose," the first observer said. "Did you see the thing clearly? What an impossible organism!"

"Surely it was one of the crew." Broh rose to his feet.

"Much as I would like to think otherwise, I fear I must concur," said the second observer.

The captain's attention was on the still empty corridor. "No telling how many of them there are. However, we must keep in mind that this one carried no weapon."

"If that was an attempt at a friendly greeting," said Anzeljermeit, "I'll eat my left leg."

"Which one?" asked Quoz.

"Both of them. And without spices."

"I'm afraid there's no question but that violence was directed toward Iel," Broh murmured regretfully. Things had not gone as he'd hoped. He rechecked his stinger's charge. "Fall back to the shuttle. Have the *Zinramm* send over another. I want a full complement of our Outsiders here."

"Yes, sir." Anzeljermeit whistled into his suit pickup preparatory to contacting his unit.

"Rifles as well as small arms this time," Broh added reluctantly.

"Your pardon, Captain," the third observer said, "but is that wise at this point? Admittedly I would not have liked to exchange positions with that poor fellow a moment ago, but surely we have matured beyond mere shape-fear? We must try to contact them."

"So we will," Broh agreed, "but I must note, with all due respect, that you observers are my responsibility, as are all on board the *Zinramm*. I am instructed according to procedure to use the most extreme caution should any new alien intelligence be encountered. I have seen nothing thus far that would induce me to relax such procedure." He continued to stare down the corridor, trying to visualize once again the horror that had charged at them. "Least of all would I relax it now."

"As you command," said the third observer. "While it is not complementary to what is supposed to be my scientific attitude, I must admit that your position is perfectly understandable."

"Me also." The second observer was visibly shaken. "Did you see the thing? I can barely allow that it may be intelligent."

"We have no absolute measure of that yet," Broh said thoughtfully. "It is surely a member of the crew, but it may be a subordinate type. The real masters of this vessel may be another, higher species that employs the kind we saw for menial functions. Our ancestors had specialized functions. Primitive Thranx workers were of superior intelligence compared to ancient soldiers. We may simply have encountered an alien soldier, functional but comparatively mindless."

"A plausible theory," the first observer admitted. "Or it may be a member of a different, less advanced race. The relationship may hold between two dissimilar species."

"Exactly. The one we've seen may have acted belligerently, but as yet no one has been hurt." Broh turned to Anzeljermeit. "No one is to shoot until I give the orders."

"Very well, sir." The officer was speaking rapidly into his suit communicator, relaying via the shuttle the request for reinforcements. He spent a moment listening, then spoke to the rest of the group. "Pilot says that she has requests from Science for a more detailed description of the alien being."

"In due time," Broh told him. "We'll provide visuals as well. And if we can persuade or capture one, the department will have it to study in person."

Again the officer relayed the message. "They say they're not sure they're ready for personal inspection and study, sir."

"They'd best prepare themselves." Broh used his most authoritative tone. "That is our task. As an exploration team we must deal with the ugly as well as the beautiful. As to the request for a more detailed description of the alien, you may relay our initial impressions."

"I don't know if the computer will settle for the simple declaration that the alien ship is crewed by monsters," murmured the second observer.

"It will have to, for now," said the third. "Unscientific

and emotional the description may be, but it has the virtue of concision. It should prepare the crew for actual contact."

They waited in the corridor, unconsciously edging toward the airlock, their eyes working constantly lest the nightmare spring upon them again before reinforcements could arrive from the *Zinramm*.

IV Fal turned up the volume on the teaching unit and nudged her current charge. The bulky, mottled-white mass stirred listlessly in the cradle. She spoke to it in a gently admonishing tone.

It was Learning Time, yet Vii was dozing off. That was not permissible. Worse, it was not the first time. Tests revealed that Vii suffered from a minor chemical imbalance that could be overcome through intensive conditioning and without the use of drugs. Conditioning was safer, but harder on the Nurses.

So Fal devoted more time to Vii than to the others. She held her patience as she prodded the would-be sleeper back to wakefulness. While she waited for any questions she thought again about the message she'd received from her clan cousin Brohwelporvot.

It had been many years since she'd actually seen him, that day long ago when he'd arrived in Paszex for her Emerging. He'd been introduced to her newly adult form by the clanmother of the Sa. Though only related to the Sa, the clan was still inordinately proud of him because of their connection to the Por. Willow-wane was a colonial world and Paszex in its most primitive region, so there was little for the town's clans to boast about. Through connection with the Por clan of Hivehom they could claim Brohwelporvot as a relative, and he was no less than a starship captain.

For some reason Broh had taken a special liking to the new adult, and they corresponded intermittently over the years. Which made the most recent communication all the more unusual. Normally Brohwelporvot was the most prosaic and rational of correspondents. Yet his latest communication was not only rambling but infused with emotional overtones.

The larva Vii broke into her thoughts with a question regarding the information being displayed on the teaching screen. Fal strained to understand the awkward larval words. Only a trained Nurse could easily comprehend the soft-mouthed babble of the young.

She answered the question and then responded to the larva's request by once again turning down the volume of the machine. She watched Vii carefully, but her insistence

41

seemed to have finally produced the desired result and the larva gave no sign of drifting back to sleep.

Yes, a very strange communication, Fal mused. If she hadn't personally known its source she would almost have thought it hysterical. She considered reporting it to her clanmother. That would be a good idea, she decided. Perhaps a wiser head could make better sense of it. It could do no harm to seek another's opinion, even if Broh had instructed her not to mention the content of the communication to anyone else. She would tell Ryo also, of course. It was his right, and his own intelligence might see to the heart of the garbled communication.

Idly she checked the monitors set into the upper duty strap of her vest. Soon it would be bathing time. That was a chore she looked forward to; washing the grubs down, knowing that their pasty white flesh would soon give way to a jewel-like cocoon from which a new adult would eventually emerge fresh and glistening into the world. It gave Fal never-ending delight that she and her associates in the Nursery helped to bring about that miraculous transformation.

After evening meal, when she and Ryo had settled down for a presleep of learning, entertainment, and conversation, she moved to the apartment console and ran the personal messages of the day. She slowed the one from Broh.

"Isn't it the most peculiar thing you've ever seen?" she asked him as the communication crawled slowly up the screen. "So emotional and so disjointed. It's not like him at all, Ryo"

But her mate hardly heard her. At first he'd concealed his boredom by listening politely to her concerns as they'd watched the message unravel. Lines and angles formed words before him.

As the tone and content of the communication emerged, however, something pierced him like a surgical probe. He raised his head off the saddle cushion and stared fixedly at the screen. Fal he barely heard.

When it was over there was a buzz and a light flashed to the left of the screen. Ryo immediately left his saddle and walked up to adjust the controls. The communication replayed, still slower this time.

"You see what I mean, then," she said, when the repeat

had concluded and the screen displayed daily news. She leaned to the right and let her legs touch the floor.

"Yes." Ryo's reply sounded thinly, as if he were trying to whistle through his spicules instead of his mandibles. That was a trick some Thranx could manage, but he didn't seem to be doing it intentionally.

"Well, what do you think of it?"

"Think of it." He turned to face her. His fingers were twisting in instinctive patterns indicative of great excitement. "It's simply the most marvelous thing that's ever happened!"

That was not at all the reaction she'd expected from Ryo, though if she'd thought more deeply about it she might not have been so surprised. In fact, she might not have mentioned Brohwelporvot's message at all.

"It means we've found a completely new, completely alien space-going intelligence!"

"A race of monsters, according to Broh." Fal was put off by the strength and direction of his response.

"Initial impressions count for nothing. I have to see them for myself, of course."

"That's an amusing thought."

"I am very serious," Ryo replied, adding an unmistakable gesture of fifth-degree assertiveness.

"I don't believe you. Why fill with dirt the burrow so laboriously excavated? You make less sense than that communication."

Because something inside me says that I have to do this, he thought. It all tied in somehow with what he thought he'd been missing all these years. The message of a frantic, distant relative had fanned the hidden ember into a forest blaze. Now it was too late to put it out.

Fal was rambling, her voice and gestures full of bewilderment. "No sense, no sense. It's not your place to do something like this. You cannot. What of your assignment, your work?"

"It can be done by others."

"That's not what I mean. You're about to be promoted to Company council. The hive thinks well of you— And what of us? You have other responsibilities." She slid off the lounge and firmly entwined antennae with him. "You have other responsibilities." She caressed him warmly.

He tried to think of a better way to put it, could not. "It's a thing I have to do, Fal."

"But you don't say why. Can't you explain?"

"No better than I already have."

She let loose his antennae, backed away. "I can't accept decision without reason. You must not do this. I will not permit it."

But Ryo was already moving through the apartment, slipping on day vest and pouch, stocking items in his clothing. "I'll contact you as soon as I'm able. I am sorry, Fal. There's nothing else I can do."

"There is. Nothing is forcing you to do this." She spaced each click and whistle deliberately.

"I'll contact you as soon as I can," he said again. Then he was out the exitway and into the cool night corridor beyond.

Fal stood in the center of the front room, stunned. It had happened so fast: he'd read the message, there'd been some excitement, a little talk, and then he was gone. On the way to far Hivehom and perhaps also to insanity. She was too fond of him to allow it. There was too much to throw away. She walked rapidly to the console.

The Servitors met him halfway to the transport terminal, holding themselves a little more stiffly than was normal. They were not dispensing aid to the aged or collecting garbage now.

"Good evening," Ryo said, executing a hasty gesture of greeting.

"Good eve to you, citizen," said the leader of the group. There were four of them, all bigger than Ryo. Soldier throwbacks, he thought. He tried to step around them. They shifted to block his way.

"Is something the matter?" he inquired of the leader.

"Perhaps. Perhaps not. We act on a request from your clanmother and family."

"I don't understand," he said as they turned him bodily about, a foothand on each of his own. "I've committed no crime. What does this mean?"

"We are not certain ourselves," the leader told him. "Only that our action has been sanctioned by the hivemother as well. I am sorry," he added apologetically, and seemed to mean it. "You are aware of the customs. Such a request must be carried out."

Request. Ryo turned the word over bitterly in his thoughts as he stood in the clan meeting hall. It was very late. The four Servitors had departed, still apologizing.

Seated before him were at least a dozen Ryo recognized. Fal was there . . . that surprised him, though it shouldn't have. His sire and dame. Two of his three sisters . . . the other had moved away to Zirenba. Several clan elders.

"My free movement as a citizen has been interfered with," he said. His gaze settled on Fal. She looked away from him, nervously cleaning one eye with a damp truhand.

"I am sorry, Ryo. I thought this necessary, best for you as well as me. You have your responsibilities."

"We're not mated," he said, more bluntly than he intended. She ceased her cleaning.

"I am aware of that. What I have done was done out of my feelings for you, whatever you may feel for me. You must believe that." Her whistle was painfully plaintive.

"Come here, Ryozenzuzex." It was a command, but a gentle one. He stepped forward until he was standing before a Thranx he'd met only twice before.

Twenty-five hundred members of the Zu clan lived in Paszex, and Ilvenzuteck was their spiritual if not legal head. The clanmother was very old. Her chiton had faded to deep purple, was nearly black in places. Her antennae drooped and her eyes were dull as death, but there was nothing corpselike about her speech. Her gestures were minimal but lucid, her whistles properly pitched, the clicks sharp and devoid of any suggestion of uncertainty.

"Falmiensazex has told me of your desire to leave us. Indeed, to leave Paszex and Willow-wane to fly off to Hivehom on some bizarre quest."

Ryo glanced toward Fal, who was not looking at him. "Did she tell you that my reasons involve more than merely a crazed desire?"

"She did not elaborate. She merely said that it had to do with a desire that you felt required satisfaction but could not describe in detail."

"That much is true enough," he admitted.

"Such feelings can be treated."

"Physically I'm fine, Clanmother. Mentally I've always been slightly different." He noticed his sire making small, half-unconscious gestures of sad affirmation. "But never aberrant enough to warrant treatment. My personal achievements and successes speak to that." He did not need to point out the shining star set in his shoulder. Ilvenzuteck had witnessed its setting.

"They do indeed," she said. "If they did not, we might be holding this conversation under more difficult circumstances. But this has nothing to do with eccentricity or any desire of yours. You have responsibilities here: to the Inmot Company, to your hive, to your family, and," she added with a gesture, "to Falmiensazex. To your family-to-be. Many ancestors are sitting in this chamber with us. They fill the empty saddles and sit in judgment. You cannot abandon them, too. We all have our secret desires, our secret wishes. Unfortunately, the universe is not so constructed that we may be permitted to fulfill them."

"I'm sorry, but—"

She interrupted him, as was her privilege. "You must not pursue this thing. It drives you toward destruction. I will not let you throw away so promising a life, Ryozenzuzex. As your clanmother, I forbid it. That holds no legal power, as you are aware. But if you hold to your heritage at all, such abstracts will not tempt you."

"And if I try to go anyway, 'heritage' notwithstanding?"

"I have registered my decision with the hive council. Hivemother Tal-i-zex concurs. So do your parents and your premate. So will your employers. Many witnesses to this conversation will testify to your oddness of habit. They will do so to protect you from yourself, out of love for you."

Ryo calmly studied the assembled faces and bodies and saw this to be so. He would have expected nothing else.

"It is your future happiness they hold dear. As I do," Ilvenzuteck said gently.

"I do not doubt that," he replied, truthfully enough.

"If you try to leave," she continued softly, "your clanmates will stop you. If you get past them, the hive council will have you recalled, citing your importance to the welfare of the hive.

"You have done well on the scale of this hive, slightly in terms of Willow-wane itself, and not at all in terms of interplanetary society. Speaking practically, you could not reach Hivehom. You have not the resources. Your credit is locked in mutual file with your premate Falmiensazex, and a limit node has been placed upon it."

He threw Fal a sharp look.

"For the same reasons, Ryo," Fal told him. "If our positions were reversed, you would do the same for me. I've worked for that credit as hard and as long as you. You've not the right to do whimsy with it."

"Let me have my share then." His tone was coaxing, affectionate.

"No. When this attack fades from your mind and you are your rational self once more, you will be grateful for what all your friends have done for you. You have many friends, Ryo."

"It does not matter," Ilvenzuteck said. "Even if you had access to all the credit it would not be nearly enough to carry you to Hivehom. You have no concept of the costs of the greater society. Your Learning Time did not include that."

"I'd get there. One way or the other, I'd get there."

"Is that truly your wish, or only what you think you wish?" she continued shrewdly. "You've listened to me. You've seen the reaction of all who love you most. Is it not possible they are right and you are wrong? Against experience, tradition, and love you can marshal only a vague 'desire.' Who then musters the better argument, Ryozenzuzex? You are intelligent. Use that intelligence now and speak truthfully with your inner self."

He seemed to slump, his body to droop between his legs. "I cannot fight your arguments, Clanmother. I suppose you are right. You are all right." He did not sound pleased, but the intensity had left him. "It was the excitement of the moment, the possibilities I saw. But I see now that they are not for me. Foolishness. I am ashamed."

He executed a gesture of embarrassment mixed with mild humor. "When inspected dispassionately from outside, it does indeed appear irrational and immature."

"There's no need to feel embarrassed," his sire said.

"You are admired for your confession to reality. If your curiosity is so great, perhaps you should have chosen information processing for a career."

"Not a bad thought. Maybe someday I still could, as a second profession."

"Perhaps," Ilvenzuteck said soothingly. She was watching him closely. "How do you feel?"

"Not too well," he said. "Tired."

"Understandable. Enough of this silliness, now. Go back to your admirable apartment with your premate."

"If you want to, that is, Ryo." Fal was worried.

"Of course I want to." He looked around gratefully. "I thank you, thank you all, for what you've done. For your concern and your affection. I've been an idiot, and not for the first time. But for the last."

Fal approached him and they entwined antennae lovingly.

"That's much better." Ilvenzuteck sighed in relief. "A night best forgotten. We've all been roused from a sound sleep and all must work tomorrow. So, everyone to home, and let it be the last said of this matter."

Days passed. Unexpectedly a second message arrived from Brohwelporvot. Fal didn't hesitate to show it to Ryo. The wording and phrasing were calm, controlled, wholly typical of Broh as opposed to the previous hysterical and life-disrupting communication.

Broh's message explained that everything in the previous communication was the result of overwork and overworry and the pressures of a difficult command in which he did not yet feel comfortable. No monsters existed, no contact had been made with a spherical black alien craft, and he, Broh, had been dispatched to a rest facility for a vacation. He was feeling quite chipper, and she should not worry. Someday he would explain in more detail about the nightmares that could afflict one in Deep Space, and they would both have a fine long-range laugh over it.

Fal replayed the message a second time for Ryo. He absorbed it and immediately agreed that it explained sensibly everything that had gone before. It was not even necessary to repeat it at a slower speed because he'd arrived at a similiar conclusion about the first message on his own. It was good to have his theory confirmed.

Clearly Broh had dictated the message himself, for his own face was imprinted on the bottom of the communication. And to allay any possible lingering suspicion on Ryo's part, Fal had confirmed the message's authenticity via a brief, terribly expensive personal voice-picture conversation with Broh himself, on Hivehom, a copy of which conversation she played for Ryo.

The whole incident had been a fantasy that had been precipitated by a bad dream. No longer would it cloud their lives. Ryo was quite in agreement, even chiding her for having to show the recording to him. The first communication had not so much as tickled his thoughts since the meeting in the clan hall.

Now he had to rest, for tomorrow would be a difficult day in the jungle. There was tiresome clearing to supervise, and would she please stop troubling him with such trivialities?

But during sleeptime he lay conscious and awake, his thoughts churning like a tropical storm. Something had forced Brohwelporvot to compose and transmit the second communication. Something or someone had decided to cover matters with the one person, however indifferent, who'd been informed of things she ought not to know.

Half a season passed. The incident seemed completely forgotten. Life was easy and smooth with him and Fal. The discreet surveillance the hive council had set on Ryo was gradually withdrawn.

He received the expected promotion to the local Inmot council and in-field supervison of clearing and planting passed to another. The bexamin vines throve, increasing still further his stature within the Company and the hive.

So when word came through Company channels that Ryo was required in Company council in Ciccikalk he showed no surprise and certainly no excitement over what was just a boring business trip to the capital. He made no unusual preparations for the trip and was normal in voicing his dismay at having to travel so far from home and hive. Only he knew as he sped southward that he would not be returning to Paszex very soon.

His otherwise empty eight-person module traveled fast and silent. The first night an unexpected bump jolted him awake, but it was only the sound of another module linking to his own. A few passengers boarded at the next stop. They took no notice of him. His anonymity would be preserved until he failed to appear at the Company council meeting. Then communications would pass querulously between Ciccikalk and Paszex. With luck it would be some time before his disappearance was linked to a possible recurrence of his youthful mental aberrations.

The module train curved southwestward, gradually turning and accelerating due south. In time it crossed into more heavily populated country, and after four days the train began to slow.

For half a day Ryo watched as roads, ventilators, and surface facilities began to appear like growths on the land. His module was in hill country and still slowing when the train finally pulled into the transport center of Zirenba, where he changed for Ciccikalk. Seven additional days of steady southerly travel revealed vast panoramas of cultivated fields that put those of Paszex to shame. Huge black ventilator stacks hinted at great subterranean manufacturing complexes.

And finally it was night again and the long train of crowded modules was pulling into the central passenger terminal at Ciccikalk. As each module halted the doors automatically sprang open. The simple portion of his journey was at an end. From now on he would have to move as a fugitive.

Ciccikalk was a metropolis of nearly three million, home to 20 percent of the planet's population. The central terminal was only one of a dozen of similar size that ringed the city's boundaries, and was as large as Paszex.

Ryo had expected great size, but not confusion. No statistic can convey the feel and scope of a large city to someone from a small town.

Overhead, myriad signs flashed showing modules and their destinations or those arriving from outlying communities and towns. The terminal was filled with Thranx pressing tight upon one another as they made their way to tracks and exits.

Ryo found himself fighting for control. To one side, he saw a line of rest saddles, forced his way through the crowd to them, and settled gratefully into one. Now he could watch and study the teeming terminal without having to fight for a place to stand.

He tried to remember what he'd learned about Ciccikalk. Three million was the metropolitan population. There were several million more living and working in the peripheral cities and towns. As opposed to Paszex's five levels, there were forty-three beneath him here, wrenched from the rock of the planet. In addition to this prodigious feat of excavation, a dozen upper levels had been cut into the hills that ringed the Cicci Valley, and that was the hardest fact to grasp; that there were more than twice as many levels here *above* the surface as there were in all of Paszex.

Though still dazed he tried to review his somewhat sketchy plan of action. The fare to the capital had cost him all but his last unmonitored chit. He had exactly eight credits left. That would not buy him the right to look at a shuttlecraft, much less passage on a posigravity transport. It might keep him alive for a month. That did not take into account the problem of lodgings. He could not touch his joint account with Fal.

He would have to ration himself very closely. Perhaps he might find sleeping quarters in the poorer sections of the city. When to eat was not a concern. Nothing ever closed completely in a city the size of the capital. This was not sleepy Paszex.

The lack of credit to buy time did not worry him, since he doubted he would have a month. Eventually his image would be circulated and connect with the observation of some Ciccikalk Servitor and he would be picked up. He would *have* to use his credit stick to purchase passage on a ship. With luck, by the time the transaction was registered and the authorities were alerted, he would be on a ship making the break into Space Plus.

If he took a vessel's last shuttle prior to departure, and if that shuttle docked just before its ship departed Willow-wane orbit, he might get away before the Servitors could freeze the ship. Once away from Willow-wane, he was confident he could find some way to reach the surface of Hive-hom undetected, even if the Willow-wane authorities messaged ahead via Nullspace communications.

First Ryo had to find a place to stay while he studied the transport manifests for the most suitable departing ship.

He also wanted a meal. The internal city transport module he entered was designed to assist travelers and was full of helpful information, though its attitude became slightly reproachful when Ryo indicated he wished to stay at the cheapest hotel possible.

Noise and some of the confusion faded as the vehicle slipped out of the frenetic transport terminal. Ryo relaxed a little. The burrow corridors narrowed as the module descended. It eventually went horizontal at the Thirty-third Level, turned eastward, then north, and finally deposited him at Level 33, Subannex 1,345.

At that point the corridor was just wide enough for two transports to pass each other and the ceiling hung barely a meter above Ryo's antennae, but he felt right at home in the comfortable claustrophobic surroundings.

Nearby was the entrance to Dulinsul, the establishment that the module had reluctantly recommended. A number of simply dressed Thranx were at the saddles inside, conversing, drinking, or eating the evening meal. Ryo selected a booth near the back, placing his order through the tiny speaker set into the table surface, and stretched out on the hard, unpadded saddle. A dour elderly Thranx with one antenna eventually delivered the food by hand.

A single curved spout emerged from the prosaic drinking tankard. No intricate scrollwork here, Ryo mused. The tray that came with it held steamed vegetables, two different tuber pastes, a long section of Higrig fruit, and the requisite bowl of soup. The meat in the soup was tough but flavorful and the rest adequate. Ryo consumed all the food as if he were sitting in the finest gourmet restaurant in the city. He'd made it safely to Ciccikalk. Success was all the spice he needed.

"The way you're inhaling that food, I'd say you're pretty hungry."

He looked up. Standing next to him was a diminutive adult. Female. Her face and wing cases were adorned with garish ornamentation; paste jewels and bright sequins that were simply glued on instead of being properly inlaid. From her body vest and neck pouch metal tinsel hung nearly to the floor. Strands of imitation gold filigree hung loosely from her ovipositors.

"Travel always makes me hungry," he replied, turning to

his food. He took a long suck from the spout of the tan-kard.

She eyed it curiously. "What are you having?"

"Quianqua fruit juice," he said apologetically, and then wondered why he'd used the apologetic inflection.

"Piss juice, you mean." The female turned, gestured toward the front counter. Without being asked, she settled into the saddle opposite Ryo. Light flashed from her ommatidia. The thin gold bands that crossed the center of the eye were wider than most. "You don't look like the assembly-line type."

"I'm not," he admitted. "I'm a raw land surveyor and have been working to the north."

"Out of the hive, then?"

"Yes, I'm here on exploration-related business and trying to husband my credits." She seemed to be enjoying the conversation. As was he. It was relaxing to have someone to talk to he could feel safe with. She did not strike him as a Servitor operative.

His descriptions of the jungle and wild lands to the north fascinated her. By her own admission she'd never been outside Ciccikalk. A common condition of large-hive citizens, Ryo mused. It limits their horizons.

The kitchen worker arrived with two tankards of something that smelled wonderful. The drinking spouts were slightly more elaborate than that of the tankard he'd started with, each having a single neat spiral worked into it. They were what passed for fancy utensils in the Dulinsul.

"I think you'll like this," she said, taking a deep suck from her own spout.

The drink lightened his thoughts and lifted his worries. The sensation was not unlike being tossed by the Southern Jhe, though the fear of drowning was absent.

"You're right, it's marvelous. What is it?"

"Masengail wine. I'm glad you like it, since you're paying for it."

"I am?"

"I introduced you to it. Isn't that enough?" Again the trilling laugh.

"Fair enough." He sipped more deeply. It made him feel lovely.

V He'd been wrong about many things in his life, but never so wrong as he'd been about the wine. It had lightened his thoughts and lifted his worries, and while it couldn't drown him like the Southern Jhe, it did help him bash his head against something. Or bash something against it.

He leaned against the wall and gingerly felt of his head with a foothand. The chiton was not cracked, for which he was grateful. However, his head did feel as if someone had unscrewed it from his b-thorax and then replaced it backward and upside down. Improper orientation seemed to afflict the street too, though the longer he stared at it the more it seemed to right itself. But the pain intensified as the view solidified.

He took a couple of steps and nearly toppled over. Eventually he succeeded in reaching a corridor corner where the standard direction plate was imbedded in the wall. He read it several times before he could understand it.

It informed him that he was on Level 40, Subannex 892. Vaguely it occurred to him that he was not where he ought to be. Squatting down on the street, he tried to order his thoughts.

Slow inspection revealed that in addition to the lightness between his eyes, his body had been lightened in several other places. His single remaining credit chit was gone, along with his pouch tools and anything else of value. Gone were identification, personal effects, and the credit stick that he now would not have to worry about alerting Servitors with. He'd been left his vest and pouch, and that was all.

Patiently he reconstructed the far-away-and-long-ago events that had left him on an unknown burrow corridor with an aching skull. There had been the Masengail wine and the lovely stranger. Teah, her name had been. She never had given him her full name. Conversation and more wine. A lot more wine, and then the suggestion that since he had no place to stay that night he spend it with her. There were implications of nonprocreative sex.

A walk through some unusually dark and ill-maintained streets, then darkness descended. The dim feeling of being moved. Waking up dazed, in pain, and on his side on the left-hand corner of burrow street marker Level 40, Subannex 892.

I've been robbed, he thought hysterically, and started to laugh, his whistling filling the narrow corridor, bouncing off nearby walls. Our carefully planned, wonderful society, every Thranx knowing his or her place and obligations, laws firmly laid down and adhered to, led to this.

He wondered what old Ilvenzuteck, so steeped in tradition and custom, would have thought of the situation. Such a thing could never have occurred in the isolated, neat little hive of Paszex. The old wreck would probably faint from shock. Inside him a small sane fragment of self was aghast at the insult he'd just composed. His own sisters and family would have shunned him had he said it in their presence.

Amazing how reaching part of your goal only to be relieved of the rest of your dream as well as your possessions and nearly your life can enlighten you as to the true nature of the world, he thought wildly. He continued to laugh.

A couple of Thranx coming home from late-night work passed him on the other side of the corridor, keeping their eyes averted. He yelled and screamed at them and they scuttled a little faster.

The laughter faded, the ill-modulated whistling died out. He was alone on the dimly lit corridor between two silent shopfronts.

For two days he wandered aimlessly through the hive. Without planning it, he eventually found himself back in the central transport terminal.

If nothing else, he thought dully, he could charge a communication back to Paszex. He suspected his family would reaccept him and hoped that possibly Fal might as well. The dream that had driven him to Ciccikalk, that had pushed him so far, had faded to a persistent ache centered somewhere along the back of his neck, where the robbers had struck him.

He no longer bothered with his appearance. The reaction of other citizens to his presence was evidence that he'd become something less than presentable. He'd had nothing to eat for two days, but water was available from public fountains. His stomach contorted inside his abdomen, and he was growing faint from hunger.

I won't make that communication, he thought weakly. I

won't admit defeat and return home. I'll die in Ciccikalk first. Better a fool dead trying than a living failure. Yet he retained enough sense to realize how foolish that declaration sounded. If something did not happen very soon he knew he would send that communication. He would abandon the absurdity that had bothered him since Learning Time, and return placidly to his proper home and work.

The Thranx in front of him was exceedingly well dressed. His body vest and neck pouch were woven of rich but unostentatious imported fabrics. His chiton was just turning from blue-green to violet. The inlays on his upper and lower abdomen were alternating insets of blue and silver metal arranged in simple patterns. Everything about his posture and attire bespoke intelligence, breeding, and wealth.

There was a slight bulge in the elder's neck pouch. Probably carries a fat packet of credit chits in there, Ryo thought coldly. A nice, heavy roll of eighty-credit pieces that he can boast about to the less fortunate. The elder's credit stick would be useless to Ryo, of course, but the loose chits might be enough to buy him a one-way passage to Hivehom.

But how? He couldn't beg an eighth fraction of a chit here in a public facility and certainly not eight hundred. Talk to him, quick, before he goes on his way, came the sudden crazy thought! Ask him for directions, for sympathy, ask anything so long as it will get him over here. No, over there, behind that great pillar, out of sight.

A quick blow to the neck just beneath the skull, enough to knock him out and if you break his b-thorax, so what? Parading about the terminal as if he owned it! Does he have any dreams? Doubtful, that. Probably inherited his wealth from the maximum bequest allowed by law. Doesn't deserve it anyway, has no real use for it. Unlike those of us who still have the courage to dream, even if such dreams are unhealthy and involuntary because they drive us, compel us, force us—

"Excuse me, sir," he found himself saying politely, "I wonder if I might talk with you a moment?"

"Most certainly, friend." The voice was perfectly modulated, an imperceptible blend of whistles, clicks, and syllables. A voice accustomed to conversing in High, not Low, Thranx. Not like us simple country folk, thought Ryo.

"I'm new in the hive."

"I can tell that," the elder said sympathetically.

I'll bet you can, Ryo thought grimly. In a few moments you'll be spared the necessity of thinking.

"Just over here, sir, if you would be that kind. I have my map there." He pointed to the huge pillar. Around them modules whined and people talked loudly, intent on their own business. It would only take a second, just a second, and no one would notice. "It's with my luggage."

"I'd be happy to assist you, youth." The elder dipped antennae politely. "Let's have a look at your map."

They were very close to the pillar now. "That's odd," observed the elder, peering in apparent confusion at the floor. "Where did you say your luggage was?"

"Just there," Ryo told him encouragingly, "just back in the shadows."

Desperately he tried to swing the ready foothand at the elder's neck, but his quarry was far away now, far away on the other side of the jungle, across the raging Southern Jhe, looking back at him curiously and making sad sounds as he faded into the distance.

Then someone threw the terminal floor at him. Very unfair, he thought, damnably unfair to throw an entire floor at a drowning soul. The floor pressed him down, down into the depths of the thundering, roiling river . . .

The one thing he would not have expected to feel on a return to consciousness was sunshine. It warmed his eyes and forced him to turn away from its brilliance. He was suddenly sick, but there was nothing in his gut for him to throw up.

A gentling voice said, "You slept an entire day and night. About time you woke up."

Ryo sat up very slowly, rolling onto his side and raising his upper torso. At once he became aware of several things that in combination nearly overwhelmed him: an impression of subdued wealth, morning sunshine, and the wonderful, throat-rending aroma of freshly cooked food.

"I would ask if you're hungry, but the answer is clear from the moisture at your mandibles."

Ryo searched for the source of the voice. Standing close on his right was the old Thranx he'd encountered in the transport station. For an instant Ryo froze. But the elder didn't seem at all concerned. Slightly amused, if anything.

"Well, are you hungry or aren't you?" He turned away, his back presented fearlessly to the figure on the lounge. "Of course if you're not I can have it thrown—"

"No, no." Ryo scrambled off the sleep lounge. "I *am* hungry."

"Of course you are," the elder said pleasantly as he led Ryo into the eating area.

It was beautifully appointed, with that same clear eye for good taste that had been evident in the sleeping chamber. The central table was of laminated hardwoods that were a rainbow of natural colors. The walls were compacted natural earth, glue-bonded and inlaid with crosswise metal strips to form an ocher and silver dome overhead. No natural light penetrated here.

Ryo attacked the waiting banquet with utter lack of shame. His belly screamed its needs at him and they would be satisfied at the expense of etiquette. The elder looked on interestedly.

When his insides finally signaled *enough* and he leaned back in the comfortable saddle, Ryo thought to study his host. Yes, he was the same Thranx who'd nearly met an early end in the terminal. The inlays on his abdomen were the same, as was that peculiar forward inclination of the skull. At first Ryo had thought the cranial tilt an affectation. Now he saw that it was a permanent part of the elder's physiognomy.

His stare was noted. "I broke my neck—oh, six or seven years ago," the elder said pleasantly.

Embarrassed at having been caught, Ryo looked away.

"I was climbing a tree, if you must know," the elder finished.

Ryo was startled. Yaryinfs climbed trees. Muelnots, shrins, and ibzilons climbed trees. Thranx did not. They were not built for it. Not their legs or their truhands. Only the foothands were properly constructed for such an effort, and you could not haul yourself up a woody trunk with only two limbs.

"Why were you trying to climb a tree?"

The elder whistled softly. "Wanted to see what it was like from the top, of course."

"But you could have been lowered into the treetop by a hoverer or raised on a picker arm."

"You don't understand—but neither did anyone else. You see, I am a poet." He stepped forward, touched antennae to Ryo's across the table. "My name is Wuuzelansem."

"Ryozenzuzex," he replied automatically. He thought back to a bit of recreational reading, or perhaps it was part of a conversation on current aesthetics. "The *Eint* Wuuzelansem?"

The elder executed a third-degree declamatory gesture. "I am the same."

"I have heard of you. More than that, I recall some of your poetry."

"Well, that's not necessarily a good thing." Wuuzelansem let out a deprecatory chuckle. "Nevertheless, I suppose I am gratified. What is your profession?"

Ryo immediately went on guard.

The poet noticed the reaction. "Oh, never mind. You needn't tell me if you don't wish to. I know one thing. You're not a professional mugger."

Ryo was startled a second time.

"That was your intention in central station, was it not?"

After an instant's hesitation Ryo performed a gesture of embarrassed agreement.

"Well, I suppose hunger can make one do anything."

"How did you know I wasn't a mugger?"

"Because of the way you went about it." Wuu spoke matter-of-factly, as if discussing the plumbing. "You see, I know many muggers and robbers. They live in a state of perpetual danger and constant conflict. That can provide the basis for some interesting poetry. I document in rhyme. I am also fair with them, so many are my friends.

"The hive authorities frown on that relationship, of course. Such individuals are not supposed to exist in the wondrous capital of Ciccikalk." Whistling laughter rose from the experienced throat. "My boy, the universe is full of things which are not supposed to exist but continually confound us by doing so. Places in space where reality disappears, suns that rotate not around one another but among dozens, Nullspace where things that are too small to exist suddenly become real, muggers and robbers—all difficult to believe in, all subjects for poetical discourse.

"Now then," he settled himself into the saddle opposite Ryo, "since I've hauled you back here and cared for you, you can at least be honest with me. If I'd wanted to turn you over to the Servitors I could have done so earlier, more safely, and at considerably less personal expense."

So Ryo told him, the whole story pouring out through his broken confidence. When he'd finished, Wuu pondered silently for several minutes. Then he led Ryo wordlessly from the eating area back into the sleeping chamber. A wide pane of acrylic looked out of the side of the hill. The sun was just below the horizon and rain clouds rose slightly above it, their pink underbellies glowing as brightly as faceted kunzite.

"Alien monsters, hmm?" Wuu turned from the view to face Ryo. "It sounds like a lot of garbage to me." Ryo said nothing. "Garbage strong enough to drive you to leave your premate, your family, your clan, and your hive, to make your way to a city like Ciccikalk. To some, I suppose, garbage can become an obsession."

"It's not garbage," Ryo declared angrily. "It's part of a dream."

"Ah yes." Wuu sounded amused. "Very overrated, dreams. Nonetheless your persistence and natural intelligence mark you as something more than a mere fanatic. It strikes me you may have fallen into something worth pursuing. It should be fun, anyway. What say that you and I make our way to Hivehom and see if we can't find out?"

Ryo could not have been more startled had Fal suddenly rushed into the room to throw herself wholeheartedly into the journey. Fal—he found himself thinking of her frequently, but always the dream surged into his brain, overpowering thoughts of anything else, goading him, guiding him, inexorable in its demands, unrelenting in its mental pressure.

"Are you sure . . . do you know what we may be getting into if my suspicions turn out to have grounds, sir? There could be danger."

"I would hope so! Otherwise there would be no fun in this. If there were no fun and danger, there'd be no poetry to it. And if there was no poetry in it, there would be no reason for me to go. Now, would there?"

Ryo did not know how to answer that.

"Look, out there." The Eint turned and indicated the hillside window, from which the view extended across the valley of the Cicci.

On the far left towered silver tubes that belched the scrubbed emissions from immense manufacturing complexes. To the right were the intake stacks that supplied fresh air to the millions swarming below. In the distance, slightly to left of center, a tiny bright spot rose cloudward at a speed too extreme and angle too sharp for it to be an aircraft.

"Yes, it's a shuttle. The port is that way." Wuu stood alongside Ryo, contemplating the rising dot of light. "No telling where that one's going, with its queen ship. To Hivehom perhaps, or Amropolous or another world. We could be on such a ship very soon, if you're agreeable."

Ryo said nothing, simply stared at the distant reflection until it vanished into the cloud layer. When it was gone he turned to stare at his benefactor, hardly daring to believe.

"It's not possible. You could follow the tale to its end, could return and tell me about it. I cannot go with you. I have no access to credit."

Wuu executed a gesture not favored in polite society. "Credit is nothing. I am showered with it for doing that which I would do for nothing."

"Well then, there is the matter of identification," Ryo continued stubbornly. "Mine was taken. Even if it had not been, I'm not sure I could reach a ship before the Servitors contacted it and had me held in confinement. I must be listed in every computer terminal on the planet by now."

"Then we must fashion a safe identity for you, my boy." Wuu considered the problem, then explained, "I have been widowed twice. Both times through unfortunate accidents. There are no natural offspring, but it would surprise no one were I to announce that I had adopted several. You can pose as my adopted offspring, which I suspect you are already, in spirit if not legally.

"I told you that I know much of the underlife of Ciccikalk. In addition to those who prey upon the unwary I am also conversant with many engaged in other forms of extralegal activity. Some of them are writers. Such writing is never particularly inspiring, but their limited editions are masterpieces. You will retain your personal name, which is common enough not to arouse suspicion, I think. We will give you a new clan, family, and hive. You will become Ryozeljadrec. How does that strike you?"

"Heavily enough to make me a candidate for a long stay in an adjustment burrow, but if you really think it will be believed . . ."

"Knowledge and money combined can work miracles, my boy. Alien monsters, monstrous aliens—I feel a poem coming on already," and he rattled off a string of singsong High Thranx whistle words, harmonically arranged and lovely to hear.

"That's fine," Ryo said admiringly.

"Nothing, nothing. Garbage not worth setting to chip. Rough words, but we will find inspiration worthy of publication, my boy."

"I hope something good comes of all this. What if your—ah, forger proves not as efficient as you seem to think he will?"

"I have a title, this 'Eint.' It must be good for something. Surely it will enable us to brazen our way past any uncertainty. Since you don't have the experience for it, I shall do the brazening for us both. I do it all the time. Is not poetry a method of brazening one's way past a listener's defenses, in order to get directly at his emotions? Poetry's more than harmonics and math, you know. We'll manage our way, don't worry.

"There is one thing. Have you given thought to your family and premate?"

Suddenly Ryo did not feel very well.

"Constantly," he murmured.

"That is as it should be. You struck me as a responsible young fellow. We'll draft a communication to one of them. It will arrive in this Paszex of yours by a most circuitous route so that its origin cannot be traced. It will not go off at all until we are safely on our way and out of the Willowwane system.

"It will not tell them your whereabouts or intentions, but that you are well and thinking of them. If what you've told me so far is true, the last thing they will believe is that you've succeeded in making your way off-planet. It will be something of a shock to them when you return with the truth, but until then they will at least not consider setting a burial service for you."

Ryo watched the poet instead of the scene beyond the window. "You do realize what you're doing?"

"What's that?" asked Wuu. He'd settled himself before a beautifully inlaid computer console and was busily running his fingers across the square touchboard.

"You're breaking at least four laws on my behalf."

"Oh, *laws*." Wuu made a shockingly rude sound. "What do you think the task of poets is if not to break laws?" Information rippled across the console screen. "A transport departs from Hivehom in three days. I think we can be ready by then, my boy."

"So soon? But don't you have things to prepare, affairs that need to be tidied up before you can leave? We've no idea how long we'll be gone."

"My affairs always need tidying up," said Wuuzelansem, adding a third-degree twinkle. "Ryo, there are three great excuses one can use in life. To say that one is mad, drunk, or a poet. It makes amends for a great many delightful outrages one can safely perpetrate upon society.

"As to the preparation of your new identification, admittedly that will require something of a rush job on the part of the lady I have in mind, but I believe she can manage. She is a true artist. Wait until you see her work. She uses all four hands simultaneously with a flow nothing short of erotic. A thing of beauty—as your eventual identification will surely be. Beautiful and believable both.

"I will book passage for us on the transport. Not upper class, not lower, but middle. We don't want to be pushed around as we might be in lower and we don't want to attract the attention that upper would bring.

"We'll travel with the average this time 'round, in search of distinctly unaverage discoveries, and if no alien monsters should be skulking about on Hivehom—well, it's been a while since I've been off my home world. While the local and familiar are soothing to the soul, the mind requires somewhat more extensive stimulation. The journey itself will be worthwhile. I take it you have never been to Hivehom?"

"I've never been outside Paszex until my journey here."

"It will be something for you to see. A bucolic lad like yourself. Yes, three days should be enough."

"I don't know what to say or how to thank you for this," said Ryo, adding a little click and gesture of amusement, " 'Father.' "

"Good. You're beginning to get into the spirit of subterfuge. Treat me with respect, call me always as you would a real adoptive sire. We will surely gain acceptable verse from the drama."

Suitable attire was ordered for Ryo. In keeping with Wuu's intentions to stay as inconspicuous as possible, the clothing was new but not fancy. Those constraints aside, the vest and pouch were attractive and sturdy.

A day prior to their scheduled departure a secretive little Thranx appeared at Wuuzelansem's entryway to hand-deliver a tiny package. This produced a remarkable brace of identification documents, including even a credit charge stick. The latter was supposedly unforgeable, for the financial institutions of all Thranx worlds were extremely security-conscious. Ryo would use it only in an emergency.

"I will handle all fiscal transactions," said Wuu. "No sense in tempting fate. That stick will be the most difficult to pass, but it's important that you at least be able to show one. No one travels intersystem without a stick." He studied the younger Thranx. "How do you like your new clothing?"

Ryo dropped to all sixes, rose again and twisted his upper body, shook his abdomen. The vest stayed securely in place.

"I hardly know what to say."

"One wordless and one overflowing with words. We'll complement each other well." The poet made a gesture indicative of second-degree amusement mixed with disavowal of sarcasm. "Tomorrow then, we take ship."

"And if there are problems?"

"We'll deal with them as they present themselves. Spontaneity is one of the joys of existence, my boy, especially if you prepare for it in advance." He wagged a truhand at the younger male.

Ryo didn't sleep well that night as he dreamed unreassuring dreams that centered on a gigantic slobbering thing with a mouth full of crooked, snaggly teeth, crimson fur all over its body, and a half-dozen claw-fingered hands that groped anxiously after him. It wore its skeleton inside, like the yaryinf, and it wanted to suck out his head.

He woke uneasily to the soft chimes of Wuu's house alarm.

They packed little, carrying only hand luggage. "We're not going to an investiture ball," Wuu had pointed out, "and those who travel light travel fast."

Exiting the level complex in which Wuu lived, they took a shaft lift below surface and then a fourth-level transport to the nearest module terminus, where they boarded a direct module to the shuttleport.

"I regret only one thing that has happened thus far," said Ryo in the quiet of their private compartment.

"What's that?"

"That those who beat and robbed me should escape without punishment."

"Who says they suffer no punishment? I know what their lives are like. They are miserable most of the time and at best a little of the simplest pleasures may trickle down to them. They live in many ways worse than our primitive ancestors who grubbed a bare existence from the earth, for the advantages of modern society are denied them. Yet ignorant and unhappy though they are, they must somehow live too."

Wuu made an all-encompassing gesture with all four hands. "The universe is a jungle, my boy. You could spend all your life in Willow-wane's wildest reaches fighting poisonous flora and carnivorous fauna, be healthy and happy, and come to the Hive of Ciccikalk one day only to be run over by a transport module. If you regard every place as being dangerous and uncivilized you will find yourself much more relaxed in mind."

It was quiet in the module then. Ryo thought how very far from home he was and how farther still he was about to go. Very far from family and clan, and from Fal.

What would she make of the cryptic message he and Wuu had concocted and sent her? Would she forget him altogether? Assume he was lost mentally? He hoped she would simply sigh deeply and return to the Nursery in hope of his reappearance. Then again, she might seek another premate.

A mental shake shattered the thoughts like little crystals. He was pursuing a dream the way an addict pursues his next fix. All that mattered now was getting safely off-planet.

His nervousness increased exponentially as they walked up the ramp to the shuttle entrance.

"What if the identification fails?" he whispered to Wuuzelansem. "What if? . . ."

"Everything will be fine if you'll simply relax and look normal," was the poet's response. "Your antennae are so stiff they're going to crack. Straighten your posture, incline your thorax properly, and act like you're bored by the whole procedure, offspring."

"Yes . . . sire."

There was a pause while their names were checked against the passenger manifest. A line of Thranx waited to ascend the ramp. A single official stood there, looking indifferent as the machinery monitored both manifest and personal identification.

He didn't even look up as Ryo and Wuu passed through and announced themselves. Their ident slips were processed, checked, and efficiently spat back at them by the boarding console.

Wuu appeared slightly miffed as they continued up the boarding ramp into the shuttle. He hadn't been recognized.

"Not a reader or listener," he grumbled, referring to the official who'd passed them through. "Civilization is really run by unaesthetic illiterates."

"Is there then such a thing as an aesthetic illiterate?"

They launched into a discussion so animated and intense that Ryo almost didn't notice when the shuttle's jets hissed and the thick-bodied craft lifted into the air.

Airborne, Ryo thought in disbelief. Actually airborne. Like a hesornic. Like a dream.

They quickly rose above the clouds. Only a dim red line marked the horizon where the sun of Willow-wane was trying to hide. Airborne! What must it have been like, he wondered, for his distant ancestors whose wings had been, for the mating season at least, functional instead of vestigial? Was intelligence such a good trade-off for the momentary power of flight?

Before long rockets took over from the starving jets. The shuttle was now above the highest clouds, and the sky was fading from blue to purple, aging much like a Thranx. Many songs had employed the analogy. Then they were swimming through the long night and the stars were brighter than they'd ever been.

A scream rose from behind Ryo, down the central aisle. A female had tumbled from her saddle and lay on her back, kicking at the air with all four legs, pawing at it with her hands.

Two attendants rushed to her. One clamped a breathing pack over her thorax and administered air from a tank while the other injected a drug directly down her throat.

She quieted down immediately. Ryo glanced around and noticed that of the two dozen or so passengers on the shuttle, perhaps a fourth of them wore glazed looks and sat in their saddles as if in a trance. He'd been too absorbed by the view outside to notice it earlier. Now he looked questioningly at Wuu.

"The lady in distress experienced a severe attack of Outside. It particularly affects hive dwellers who spend most of their lives underground. An ancestral carryover that some of the race is still heir to, when we dwelt almost exclusively below ground and when to venture outside was to expose oneself to the prowling carnivores that then roamed the whole surface of Hivehom. This is probably her first flight and she suppressed the feeling as long as she could."

"What about those?" Ryo indicated the strangely subdued passengers.

"The same problem, but those are experienced travelers. Certain drugs safely counteract the Outside. The side effects are minimal but obvious. He turned to inspect Ryo.

"You feel no fear, no sense of panic?"

"Not a thing."

"Have you looked out the port?"

"I've been doing little else.

Wuu made a gesture of third-degree confidence mixed with mild curiosity. "Most Thranx on a first extraatmospheric journey experience a certain amount of mental discomfort. After repeated travel the discomfort passes. Some, of course, feel nothing. They are the exception rather than the rule. As I mentioned, I've done considerable traveling and therefore feel nothing at all. As for yourself, I should not be surprised that you are the exception in this way as well as in others."

"Open spaces have never bothered me," Ryo explained. "That was one of the things, I think, that helped me to advance so rapidly in my profession."

"Ah yes, the exploiter of new agricultural land. You put food on my table, so I won't start in on the morality of butchering Willow-wane's native jungle simply to plant asfi."

It developed that Ryo was not quite as immune to the vagaries of Deep Space travel as he first thought. When the ship passed beyond the last of the system's six planets and shifted into Space Plus he fell prey to the same nausea as everyone else, experienced or otherwise.

The stars became streaks and their colors changed as if they were being viewed through a shaded prism. Once the nausea passed there was ample time to enjoy the luxuries of middle-class shipboard life.

Days and nights fled apace, with the only indication of movement coming from the slowly changing starfield.

Eventually the passengers had to return to their cabins a last time. The ship dropped from Space Plus into normal space, stomachs were wrenched, and the stars resumed their normal colors and positions and shapes.

Ahead lay a bright and somehow familiar sun. There were twelve planets in the Hivehom system, the home world fully inhabited, of course, and three others less so. Several timeparts passed and then they were in orbit around Hivehom. The home world of the Thranx. The spawning place. The where-we-all-come-from.

VI As the shuttle descended Ryo stared avidly out the long port. Hivehom was a beautiful world. Not so beautiful as Willowwane perhaps, but then his own home was a paradise.

Hivehom had 20 percent more surface area than Willowwane, but only a little more habitable territory because it was a cooler world. As they dropped lower Ryo could make out white smears at the northern pole—solid water, he knew from his studies. It was hard to imagine a place where there was little vegetation, where the air was cold and yet so dry that your breath seemed to crackle in your lungs.

Then the shuttle fell too low to see that far north and there was only green, green and brown like on Willowwane. Air began to scrape the little craft and it skipped nimbly through the atmosphere as they dropped through the rain clouds above Daret, the capital city of the Thranx.

Fifty-five million citizens claimed the Hive Daret as their home. The capital city extended hundreds of kilometers in all directions, plunged two hundred and fifty levels toward the center of the planet. Low hills flanked the valley beneath which the city had been cut. A great river, the Moregeeon, meandered over the metropolis. Long barges plied its surface and for forty levels beneath its rocky bottom an intricate complex of artificial aquifers soaked up water to slake the city's enormous thirst.

Air intakes rose a half-kilometer into the damp sky. They vibrated slightly from the drag of immense suction pumps pulling air down to the lowest levels. The forests of intakes and ventilators resembled a city of windowless silver towers.

Six shuttleports ringed the valley of the Moregeeon, the smallest dwarfing the shuttleport serving Willow-wane's capital of Ciccikalk. The shuttle banked sharply to avoid a cluster of cloud-spearing ventilators.

Wuuzelansem pointed out the port as they leveled off slightly in preparation for landing. There, to the northwest, shone sunlight on the towers of Chitteranx, a satellite city of six million particularly wealthy Thranx. Still farther north lay the important metropolitan complex known collectively as Averick, famed for incredibly ancient temples

71

raised by some pre-Thranx intelligence. Both lay hard by the base of the vast frigid plateau that loomed like an island in Hivehom's sea of clouds and was rarely, even at this modern date, visited or explored.

Daret itself was close to Hivehom's equator. Its surface boasted a mean temperature of 33° C and average humidity ranging from 90 to 95 percent. With such ideal climatic conditions it was no wonder the valley of the Moregeeon had become the center of Thranx civilization.

The little craft leveled off and soon bumped slightly as its landing gear contacted pavement. They were down and taxiing toward a dock. Ryo tried to count the shuttles, lighter-than-air transports, and sleek aircraft as they eased toward disembarkation, but soon lost track of types and numbers.

The wonders of Hivehom from the air had fully occupied his attention during the descent. Now that he and Wuu were on the ground, his early worries returned. Slipping into Daret was likely to prove more difficult then leaving Ciccikalk had been.

As usual, he was buoyed by Wuu's bottomless supply of optimism. "Worlds may differ but bureaucrats are everywhere the same. Do you recall our departure from Ciccikalk? Did that Servitospector linger over your new identification?"

"I don't believe he ever looked at it," Ryo admitted. "He left everything to the computer. But shouldn't it be different here? Not only is this the mother world, but taking things out is not dangerous. Bringing things into another world can be."

"I don't think we'll have any difficulty." The debarking tube and ramp were rising from the ground toward the shuttle. No other structures marred the smooth surface of the shuttleport.

"We've come direct from Willow-wane, a known world. We're not carrying produce or sample material; in any case, there are few restrictions on what can be brought in."

Those few restrictions were enough to inspire a very thorough customs inspection, however. While Ryo and Wuu had indeed come direct from Willow-wane to Hivehom, other passengers had not. Ryo fought to conceal his nervousness as a bright-eyed Servitospector went through his identification. It seemed to Ryo that a lot of time was spent studying the identiplate.

Eventually they were passed through, accompanied by the kind of polite indifference the inhabitants of the capital reserved for those citizens unfortunate enough to have been born on other worlds. Ryo was too relieved at having successfully passed identification to feel any upset at such chauvinism. Wuu seemed to know where he was at all times and quickly located a hotel on Level 75, which was reasonably close to the city center.

Save for areas of historic importance, the center of Daret for twenty-five prime levels served only the growing Thranx government.

As their transport module carried them along wide corridors Ryo noticed burrows with stone facings. This was the heart of the eternal city of Daret, and Daret was the heart of the modern Thranx civilization. History pressed close all around him.

If he was slightly overwhelmed, Wuu was exactly the opposite. "Doesn't this mean anything to you?" Ryo asked him, gesturing out the module's single forward port. "Doesn't such grandeur inspire your poet's mind?"

"Yes, it does. Ten thousand years of bureaucrats."

They were to have begun their search the following morning, but Wuu insisted there was no need for hurry and offered to show Ryo more of the city. For example, there were the fabled Echo Falls. These fell from an opening in the underside of the River Moregeeon past a hundred and fifty levels to a great artificial cavern where the tremendous power of the vertical cascade was harnessed to supply energy for the city.

This and the poet's descriptions of other wonders caused Ryo to hesitate, but only briefly. It was unreasonable to expect the authorities to trace him quickly, but it worried him nonetheless and he was anxious to begin the hunt as soon as possible. Wuu grumbled at the thought of having to plunge so soon into the morass that was officialdom, and it had been Ryo's turn to supply the enthusiasm.

It was all basically so simple. "We just locate this Brohwelporvot," he'd explained blithely to the poet, "and he directs us from there."

Wuu had executed a gesture indicative of third-degree naïveté mixed with fourth-degree intimations of absurdity. "My boy, you are bright and persistent, but there is still much you have to learn. Consider the second communication that was received by your premate, the one that went to such pains to deny everything which had been communicated before. If we inquire after this perplexing fellow we would doubtless discover that he has been transferred to a 'rest' position somewhere many light-years from here. That is, if we can find anyone or any machine willing even to admit to his existence.

"In addition, such an inquiry would attract unwanted attention from whoever compelled him to send that second negative communication. You must know, my boy, that I am not at all convinced there is anything to all this blather about alien monsters and such. I simply find the prospect of pursuing so outrageous a rumor attractive.

"But if the opposite should be in some manner true, then we are likely—unless we are very careful—to find *ourselves* shipped off to some distant resting burrow until we agree to drop our private search. In any case, we will not find truth. If we would discover the latter, we must be circumspect as we delicately circumvent."

But even Wuu's most persuasive manner and persistent questions drew nothing in the way of useful information. As the days passed Ryo was beginning to believe that Fal's relative really *had* suffered a temporary mental breakdown.

Likewise discouraging to further inquiry was the condescension with which they were treated, because they came from a relatively undeveloped and unimportant colony world. This didn't trouble the philosophical Wuu, but it rankled Ryo's pride and went counter to everything he'd learned as a larva about the equality of all citizens. Clan- and hivemothers excepted, of course.

When a month had passed, even the normally indefatigable Wuu was beginning to show signs of losing interest. "We may have played the game to its conclusion, my boy," he murmured one evening in their hotel room. The hotel ran from Level 75 to Level 92. It was comfortable and boasted an exit on each level, but its novelty had long since worn off for both of them.

It is only natural for the interest of a poet to wane, Ryo thought. Desperately he tried to find some way to convince his sponsor to continue the quest, for without Wuu's knowledge and other resources Ryo knew he would never come any closer to the truth of the matter.

It came to them both as they boredly watched a fictionalized dramatization of the confrontation between Twentieth Emperor Thumostener and King Vilisvinqen of Maldrett over possession of the Valley of the Dead between the ancient cities of Yelwez and Porpiyultil. It was tense, stylized, and in keeping with proper anachronisms, militaristic.

"The military. Of course." Ryo put aside his drinking spout, letting it slide back into the wall as he raised up on his sleeping lounge. "We have to contact the military again."

Wuu sounded tired. "I've told you before, my boy, that any direct inquiry as to the whereabouts or even the existence of this Brohwelporvot fellow will draw either useless replies or unwholesome questions. Still," and he made a gesture of second-degree indifference, "since we have discovered nothing so far, perhaps it is worth a risk."

"No, no—I've no intention of going to the military authorities about Brohwel," Ryo replied.

Wuu set aside his portable drinking siphon and gazed curiously at his young companion. "Why else would we want to contact the military? Unless, of course, you plan a simple march up to the nearest office and intend once there to ask outright about the truth of their recent acquisition of a shipload of alien monstrosities?"

"Nothing of the sort. You see, I have another and wholly legitimate reason for making my way all the way from Willow-wane to Hivehom to contact military authorities."

"Don't be abstruse with me, boy," muttered Wuu. "I'm tired and feeling my age. One puzzle at a time is enough."

"It's just this . . ." Ryo began.

The military center was not located with the other government offices. It lay in a cube complex of its own near the outskirts of the metropolis. The two supplicants paid the transport module and entered through a triple-wide entrance off the busy corridor.

Swarms of workers scuttled through passageways and worked behind counters and at saddle-desks. Most of them displayed inlaid military insignia. Here and there Ryo noticed individuals in whose chiton gleamed crimson four-pointed stars to match his own. They were rather more common than he'd been led to believe, but his thoughts were too busy for the revelation to depress him.

He turned to face Wuu and found the poet staring at him expectantly, for now the burden of inquiry fell on Ryo's thorax. He led the way into the complex.

Eventually they found their way to a large information booth. The eight-sided interior was filled with chattering, whistling soldiers. No explanatory signs marred the various sides, nothing differentiated one from its neighbor. Ryo strode boldly to the nearest and looked across the counter at a busy Thranx. Sixteen fingers flew across an intimidating keyboard.

"Pleasant day to you," Ryo said to the soldier by way of introduction and greeting.

She looked over at him and he saw the light glance from the pair of emerald metal circles set into her left shoulder.

"This is Information West and what is it you need to know?" she inquired pleasantly.

"It's just that—that . . ."

"Yes?" His hesitation had not aroused any suspicions in her. Not yet, anyway.

He looked helplessly back toward Wuu. The poet ignored his stare, was gazing past him and admiring the soldier's ovipositors. Ryo inhaled, turned to the saddled soldier, and threw out the intricate half-lie.

"We are from Willow-wane. I am called," and he showed her the fake identiplate as he pronounced his adopted name. "I have many relatives in a small town called Paszex. It lies far to the north of the capital and is the northernmost hive on the planet save for Aramlemet.

"Four years ago Paszex was attacked and ravaged by a group of AAnn. Many died and property damage was substantial.

"At that time we were promised increased warship patrols for the isolated communities of the northern continent. No such developments have been forthcoming. I and my adoptive sire," and he indicated the expressionless Wuu, "have traveled all this way at our own expense, to get some satisfaction."

"I see," said the soldier thoughtfully, offering no comment. She swiveled her saddle to face the large console. The information displayed there was canceled by the touch of a key. Further touches produced different information.

"Here we are," she said, speaking without turning from the screen. "Record of the attack and related briefings. You say you have relatives still living in this Paszex?"

Ryo stiffened, which is not easy for a Thranx to do, but it was too late to back out or change his story. "I was there myself during the attack. I know what it's like firsthand. Not a pleasant experience."

He worried overmuch. The question had been put out of curiosity, not suspicion. The soldier did not follow it up. "I've never had the chance for combat patrol myself," she said, a mite less stiffly, "but I've studied many records of such incidents. I sympathize with you—informally, of course." She hesitated, considering. "You need to see someone in the office of the Supervising Officer in Charge of Ground-Side Protection, Colonial Burrow. That can be arranged, I think, and—"

Ryo hurriedly interrupted, making the complex gesture necessary to excuse his discourtesy. "If you don't mind," he said, "I've promised my relatives and clanmates back home that I'd try to find out exactly why the AAnn chose our poor little hive for attack. Paszex contains nothing of military interest. Their purpose in attacking it remains a mystery to all who live there."

"Death without purpose is ever a mystery," murmured Wuu.

"The dead are dead." The soldier eyed Ryo curiously. "What benefit could you and your friends derive from knowing the AAnn's motivations?"

"Such information would ease the pain that arises from uncertainty in the minds of the living," Wuu put in, "and perhaps also show us how to make ourselves less attractive to attack."

"I can understand that," the soldier said.

"So we'd prefer, at least at first," said Ryo, "to see

someone in charge of—oh," and he tried to make it sound casual, "general xenology. *Then* we could go to the Colonial Burrow Division of the Ground-Side Protection Office and find out why we're not getting the protection we were promised."

The soldier-clerk was uncertain. "The Xenology Ministry of Information is located among the general administrative offices at Daret Center. I fail to see why you'd put such a request to a military office."

"Because the motivation resulted in military action and a military psychology is involved," Ryo replied.

She stared back at him speculatively a moment longer. Then her curiosity vanished. Others waited impatiently behind Ryo and Wuu and it was not her business to analyze the requests of Outsiders, only to answer them.

"Of course. A perfectly reasonable request," she muttered. "The department you wish to visit is normally closed to nonmilitary inquiries. But since you've come such a long way, I will see what I can do for you."

"Thank you," said Wuu. "Up till now we've had very little help. We're very tired. Your assistance is most welcome."

"It's no bother," said the soldier, gratified.

The soldier studied her readouts as her fingers danced on the keyboard. "Xenology has its own divisions and subburrows, and a staff devoted to Motivational Analysis."

"That sounds promising," Ryo said.

"Here you are, then." She touched some keys and a pink plastic wand emerged from a hole. She picked it up, inserted it briefly into another hole. There was a pulse of light within the counter and a soft buzz. Then she handed it across the counter to Ryo.

"That's your directional pass." Rising in the saddle, she pointed to her left, toward a corridor. Stripes in a dozen different fluorescent colors ran along the framing walls, parallel to the floor.

"Follow the pink stripe," she instructed them. "Eventually you'll reach the Xenology Burrow. Motivational Analysis is located on the right. If you become disoriented or have any questions," she indicated the hole in the counter, "there are information-access points like this one set in the walls. Insert your pass for additional information." She settled back into her saddle.

"Thanks to you. Thanks greatly," said Ryo, taking the tiny wand. "Good day and night and a second metamorphosis to you."

"Good luck." The soldier was already talking politely to the next supplicant. Ryo was far more gratified than offended by the abrupt dismissal.

The tunnels and corridors of the military complex seemed endless, but no more so than those of Central Administration where they'd wandered hopelessly for days. They descended a dozen levels and crossed whole cubes before the use of the pass stick and judicious questioning of passersby finally brought them to an entranceway marked XENOLOGY—MOTIVATIONAL ANALYSIS. Ryo slipped the pass into the hole in the door, which parted obediently.

They stood in a circular, domed chamber. Three desks occupied the three triangular divisions of the chamber to left, right, and straight ahead. Peculiar creatures were mounted on the walls and tridimensional murals of alien landscapes camouflaged chip files and ceiling. Ryo shook as if he were preparing to mate.

An efficient-looking soldier in a green vest greeted them. Three metallic green stars and one brown one were set into his shoulder.

"What service may I perform for you, sirs?" He did not ask what they were doing in the chamber. Without the proper pass, they would not have been admitted. He naturally assumed they were on legitimate business.

Ryo repeated the story he'd told the information clerk.

"Yes, I recall many of those sporadic and nasty little attacks on Willow-wane," the soldier said sadly. "Your world is not the only colony to suffer such attention. There have been many such incidents. Too many. But we are scientists here, not combat burrow. There is no penalty for expressing opinion, however."

"It's refreshing to hear," Ryo admitted.

"Nothing of the sort ever touches us here, on Hivehom. The AAnn would never risk *that* extreme a provocation. Their elaborate explanations would not be strong enough to rationalize away an attack on the mother world itself—assuming they could get through the defenses, of course.

"So they content themselves with irritating us. Eventually such practices may bring about the war they strive so assiduously to avoid. Meanwhile they test our weapons and reactions and readiness far from areas of Thranx power."

"Precisely the problem we're here to address," Ryo said.

"And redress," Wuu added, for good measure.

"Naturally, I sympathize with your concern," the soldier said. "You wish explanations and answers. You've had no trouble from the AAnn since the incident you speak of?"

"No," Ryo admitted, "but we—"

"Come with me, please." The officer stepped back, made a sign to his busy pair of associates. There was some enigmatic professional discussion following which Ryo and Wuu were led into another room behind the outer chamber.

A large screen dominated the far end. Banks of chips set in proper file casings covered the entire right-hand wall. A dozen comfortably padded saddles filled the floor of the dimly lit room.

The officer moved along the wall, finally settled on a key, touched it. A sliver of rectangular plastic popped into view. He inserted it into the projector in the back wall, then handed Ryo a small cube dotted with indentations.

"This controls the speed, direction of movement, and other functions of the projector," he explained. "I've run it up to the section that deals with the attack on your home. Other such incidents are also documented on this chip. The chip reviews the history of such attacks and goes into detail on AAnn motivational psychology." He started toward the doorway to the outer chamber.

"If the material displayed does not answer your questions, I'll be happy to talk further with you if you finish before I go off shift. If I'm gone, the evening shift will be happy to assist you." The door closed behind him.

Wuu looked disappointed. "I haven't worked this hard and come all this way to look at sanitized military histories."

"Nor have I," said Ryo, "but it's a start, at least. Running the chip will give us time to decide what to try next."

They activated the projector and soon Ryo's thoughts

were not on what to do next but on the material playing across the screen. He was at once fascinated and appalled as the reconstruction resurrected those confused, frightened moments of so long ago . . .

VII After discussion of the attack and lengthy dissection of AAnn attitudes, the chip reported the stepped-up patrols around Willow-wane, the official protest lodged with the AAnn by ambassador Yeltrentrisrom, and a statistical summation integrating the attack on Paszex with all similar AAnn adventures.

Words, Ryo thought bitterly. Words and figures. Lives lost and burrows shattered—all interpreted statistically, for the benefit of study. He let the machine run. It began to describe other attacks on Willow-wane and on Colophon.

When the chip concluded Ryo was no nearer an idea on how they should proceed. Wuu was seated in one of the saddles, contemplating—or sleeping. Either way he was not to be disturbed, Ryo knew.

He peered through the doorway into the outer chamber. Three new soldiers occupied the three desks now.

The nearest looked toward the partly open door. "Having trouble with the projection unit? The depth perceiver has a tendency to go flat sometimes."

"No, nothing like that," Ryo replied. "I thought I had a question, but it can wait until the others return."

"That will be tomorrow morning," the soldier said pleasantly. "Are you sure I can't help?"

"Perhaps later." Ryo shut the door and retreated back into the study room. "Wuu, I wonder if perhaps we might—"

The poet was not in his saddle. He was standing opposite the chip bank, studying numbers and readouts.

"What are you doing?" The poet did not comment, however, simply continued to scan the wall.

"Ah," he muttered at last. "Here we are. Index." He touched controls and the little scanner set in the wall began to run through its enormous volume of information on alien contacts in which the military had been involved. In addition to the AAnn, there was material on the Astvet and Mu'atahl, two semi-intelligent nonspace-going races. The bulk of information dealt with nonsentient species with an emphasis on the carnivorous and belligerent types that the military was most likely to confront. But nothing touched on the mysterious rumor they'd come a—tracking.

A click sounded as the three sections of the door slid

apart. The soldier who'd offered to help Ryo walked into the room.

"You're not supposed to be doing that," he told Wuu reproachfully.

"Sorry." Wuu made a gesture of polite indifference as he shut down the index scanner. "You can understand our anxiety to learn all we can after coming all this way. Unfortunately, the information we're seeking doesn't seem to be in here." He gestured at the quiescent scanner.

The door sealed behind the soldier as he scuttled over. "See," he said to Ryo, "perhaps I can assist you after all. I'm very good with the files."

His eagerness to help, the friendliness that seemed genuine, led Ryo to exchange a gesture with Wuu that literally meant, "Why not?" They'd reached a dead end, their burrow search seemed blocked with granite.

When they put the query to him he responded with a reaction they'd already encountered: laughter. Not as loud or hysterical as some, but laughter still.

"I'm sorry. You must excuse my discourtesy," he told them, "but what you say is nonsense. Fascinating how rumors acquire a life of their own."

"Isn't it?" Wuu agreed resignedly. "And yet, rumor is the seed from which the flower of truth often blossoms, nurtured by hope and persistence."

"That's true." The soldier's attitude suddenly shifted. "I think I've heard that parable before."

"Really?" Wuu looked pleased.

"Yes. A colonial poet is the author. One of the better known outworld wordweavers. Quuzelansem."

"Wuuzelansem," Ryo said, gesturing toward his companion. "This is he."

For an instant the soldier was stunned. Wuu executed a gesture of modest affirmation.

"It is I, and my pleasure it is to meet a reader/listener."

"I am an avid follower of your work, sir, and that of Ciccikalk's Ulweilber and Trequececex as well—It's an honor to meet you, sir."

"Tut! Small honor, when our inquiries are met with laughter and scorn."

"Now, what then did you honestly expect, sir?" the soldier said unapologetically. "A question like that, a query so absurd as to—to—" He broke off abruptly. Neither of the two visitors was laughing with him. Without a word he turned, checked to make certain the door was sealed, then returned to confront them.

When he spoke again it was softly, his whistles barely audible. Then he chose a chip from the wall files, seemingly at random, inserted it into the projector and set it to playing. The actual material he ignored, pausing at the control cube only long enough to set the volume moderately high—just loud enough to mask their conversation, low enough not to attract attention.

"Wuuzelansem, I know your three books and hear that you're working on a fourth epic."

"As indeed I am, and a shadow play as well." It was then that Wuu had his small inspiration. "Would you like to hear something of the work in progress?"

"Would the eriat worm like to grow in a manure pile?" The overwhelmed soldier settled himself back into a saddle.

Wuu then gave a bravura solo performance from his new shadow play, executing all six parts and all six shadows as well, including that of a crippled larva. Ryo watched with as much delight as the soldier while the poet perfectly mimed the limbless larva with its blank, hungry stare and then shifted without a gesture break into the part of a hundred-year-old hivemother.

When all was done, it was everything the two spectators could do not to whistle their applause. Wuu stood before them, panting heavily.

"Something of an exertion." His sides were heaving. "It's difficult enough to write theater without having to be the theater as well. But one performs where one must, in the presence of demand, just as one takes inspiration when it is offered. I hope it was enjoyed."

The soldier left his saddle. His gestures, which until now had been acclamatory, turned suddenly furtive. He leaned close, the projector continuing to declaim nearby.

"Inspiration? I will give you some inspiration, Eint-Master. Inspiration of the darkest kind. Can you write blind poetry, as full of threats and nightmare and fear as the surface of a moon? Oh, I'll give you inspiration, yes!"

"Can it be that the stories are true, then?" blurted Ryo, unable after all this time to believe.

"No, the stories are not true, but the rumors are. As true as rumors can be. Understand, I am only a liaison, not even a subofficer. I'm far too low in the castes to know; merely one of second rank. To reach the truth you would have to meet with an officer of the fifteenth rank, and even then I am not so sure he would know."

"So high," Wuu murmured. Only one rank lay above the fifteenth in Thranx military hierarchy, and that was Burrow Marshal level.

"What of the substance of these rumors, then, if not of truth?" Ryo pressed their sympathetic friend.

"The substance is the stuff of nightmare. As the smoke says, one of our ships was prowling out the Arm along the galactic plane and higher." His whistles were short and sharp, the clicks brief and nervous. "It found *something*. Nobody seems to know precisely what. Many who know just the rumors are convinced it's part of a complicated exercise to prepare us in case such a find should someday actually take place.

"It's a hereditary fear, of course, this anticipation that some immensely powerful, malignant alien race is lying in wait for us Out There. It stems from our ancestral terror of the ancient surface world. Now all Hivehom is our burrow and other worlds as well, but the immensity of the night pit is a greater and more threatening surface than any we've ever faced.

"For all their boasting and tooth-gnashing, the AAnn have the same fear. Some horrible alien *something* awaits Out There—the terror that encircles a burrow dug by un-Thranx hands. The Throle that waited in hidden lair for our primitive ancestors.

"But if the rumors are true, that wandering ship found a horror that's grounded in reality, not our racial subconscious . . ."

Ryo decided not to mention his knowledge of Brohwel-porvot. Loquacious the fellow had so far been, and Ryo did not want to close down this wondrous source of information by letting the soldier know that the military secret, or rumor, or whatever, had been partially breached elsewhere.

". . . and whatever they found," he was concluding, "is rumored to be horrible beyond imagining."

"Intelligent?" Wuu asked.

"As I say, I don't even know that anything was actually found, only that *rumor* says it is some form of frightful life. Intelligent or not, I've no idea. There is intelligence, and then there is alien intelligence.

"The joint-shaking stuff comes not from those in a position to know about shape, which after all can only take so many forms, but from those whose specialties involve mental characteristics. Some rumors say the creatures are racially homicidal. That they have an inherent and inbred desire to kill anything and everything that comes their way, including even their own kind."

"Cannibalistic," Wuu muttered. "Like our ancestors."

"It's worse than that," the soldier said grimly. "Our ancestors at least slew out of purpose. Apparently these things kill because of abstracts."

"They don't sound properly sentient to me," the poet confessed. "Though I must say I know certain bureaucrats who might fit the same description."

"It is *not* a description—only rumors. And it's no joking matter." He was so deadly serious that even the normally irreverent Wuu was compelled to subside.

"You simply haven't heard the stories that have trickled down. Even among the bravest and most foolhardy of the highest ranks—those who are for mounting an attack on the AAnn home world—even they are absolutely terrified by the prospect the discovery of these creatures opens up. Which may, I remind you again, be nothing more than a clever training exercise conjured up to test the entire military caste."

"If that's the case they seem to be doing a lot of work to keep the test from affecting most of its intended subjects," Ryo said.

"But that's part of it, don't you see?" the soldier said earnestly. "The uncertainty adds to the effect. Besides, the rumors are only to test the military. If the information reached the public, the test would be ruined because its source would have to be disclosed to prevent panic among the general populace."

"Sounds like the 'test' might be a rumor planted to cover the real rumors." Wuu sounded intrigued. "The web is complicated."

"Whatever it is, truth or rumor, I want no part of it, as

you seem to. If they're trying to find out who's brave or curious enough to come forth and challenge the rumors in person, they'll have to find someone besides me."

As he listened to the soldier drone on, for some reason Ryo found himself thinking of Fal. So very far away now, she was. His thoughts turned to his clanmates, always so supportive and proud of him. He thought of his life assignment. It wasn't so dull compared to most. Sometimes it had been downright exciting, even when he had spent most of his time deliberating in an office chamber instead of working in the field.

Aren't there enough challenges in life, he found himself wondering, without trying to ferret out the darker secrets of the universe, without trying to probe regions best left to those appointed to search them?

What am I doing here? came the sudden thought. He looked around the study chamber, feeling the whole ancient weight of Hivehom, of endless Daret and its secretive and bustling military establishment. What was he doing in that chamber, a simple colonial agricultural specialist, a glorified fungus tender who followed in the path of those who'd tended growths in damp tunnels before the coming of reason? Perhaps . . .

Unexpectedly, the soldier emphasized a whistle, a proper name: Sed-Clee. It meant nothing to Ryo, but the force the soldier had put into the whistle and the terror embodied in his movements when he'd said it were enough to shock Ryo from his momentary uncertainty.

Something was happening here on Hivehom. Something of vast and threatening import. It drew him onward while at the same time that damnably persistent part of his brain which had tormented him since birth pushed him from behind. He plunged recklessly, hungrily onward. "What is Sed-Clee?"

"Nothing," the soldier replied solemnly.

"Nothing?" Wuu said.

"Nothing. A great deal of nothing, I think."

"Now you're not only being contradictory, young fellow," the impatient poet muttered, "you're being absurd."

"Not at all, sir," was the respectful reply. "When researching, one occasionally comes across irrelevant but interesting information in the files; 'This information destined for Sed-Clee.' 'That report returned from Sed-Clee.' But never any details, any exposition. Don't you see? Entirely too much nothing comes and goes from what is cataloged as a tiny military outpost. The volume is far larger than a post of such size should warrant, and the information is directed to and dispatched from some of the most esoteric burrows of the military. This one, for example.

"When specifics are absent, an efficient researcher can sometimes glean information from inference. Rumors constantly emerge about the place. The one you study is not the first.

"There is more. I've never encountered a soldier who's actually been there. I've been unable to find anyone who *knows* of anyone who knows anyone who's ever been there."

"Secret military burial chamber," Ryo suggested.

"Not so secret. After all, the existence of Sed-Clee is known," the soldier went on. "It's just that it's so obscured. There's so much formal indifference surrounding the place, not to mention deliberately casual obfuscation, that it makes one wonder if something of real importance is studied there."

"You just called it a place," Ryo pointed out.

"Statistics characterize it somewhat. The hive of Sed-Clee itself is small. Twenty thousand citizens or so supporting a few small industries and a military base, reportedly of modest size. Its exact size is classified above my level. Certainly the known information doesn't point to the installation's being responsible for anything remarkable."

"Yet you believe it may have something to do with the rumors we are tracking?" Wuu asked.

"Pardon if I seem simplistic, sir, but there is nowhere else these rumors can be ascribed to, so it seems to be the logical place to seek out. However, a number of *other* frightening things about Sed-Clee are well known and have nothing to do with rumor.

"I am not able nor personally interested in going there. If the rumors are no more than rumors then it would be a waste of time. If they are true then I especially do not want to go there.

"But since you two are interested, and because of the

admiration I hold for your work, Eint-Master, and the honor you've done me in performing here this day, I have told you all that I know. There is nothing more—save that I will show you what is *known* to be intimidating about Sed-Clee."

They returned to the outer chamber. Under cover of innocuous conversation designed to allay the interest of the soldier's two associates, they proceeded to study his personal desk monitor.

Touches of the keyboard generated a map of Hivehom's northernmost continent. This map was then enlarged and the resolution steadily increased until they found themselves looking at a map of a corner of that continent.

Near its polar crest lay a region of cold where water sometimes never became a liquid, where a Thranx could survive only with environmental protection barely a step simpler than that required for survival in space.

Slightly to the south of the tiny permanent ice cap, just below the thin line of tundra that marked the end of the treeline, lay a tiny hive: Sed-Clee. The military installation it supported was not revealed until the soldier touched several additional keys, whereupon a bright red dot emerged to the north of the hive.

A true destination, at last! Ryo stared at the map, at the source of rumor. "There must be some transportation if it's an integrated, formalized hive."

Other keys were touched. A network of green threads appeared on the map. Only one, so thin it was almost invisible, ran from the northern city of Ghew—through six smaller hives scattered across vast undeveloped plains—to Sed-Clee.

"If I had a secret I wanted to hide, I'd be hard pressed to find a more isolated place," Wuu declared.

The soldier glanced up at him and gestured with his antennae for them to keep their whistles down. The other two operatives were staring curiously at them.

"Yes," the soldier said a little too loudly. "Now, if you're interested in other worlds on the periphery of our current sphere of exploration . . ." The other soldiers returned to their respective tasks.

"I'd agree that this hive," their friend went on more

quietly, "is about as isolated as you can get and still be on Hivehom." He scrambled the map and shut down the monitor. When he returned his attention to them his manner was entirely professional.

"I wish you luck and good hunting in your research, gentlesirs." He turned to gaze appreciatively up at Wuu. "And special thanks to you, sir, for your kindnesses."

"A trifle, my estimable young friend."

They made their own way out.

There was no doubt now where their hunt was going to take them, Ryo mused, but there was a city stop Wuu insisted on making first.

Though they would have no reason to go outside the shielded environs of Sed-Clee, the poet insisted they travel prepared for any eventuality. Even a transport module could break down.

Despite the diversity to be found in the immense hive they still had difficulty locating a firm that sold as exotic an item as cold-climate attire. It took several days.

The purveyor who provided the clothing asked no questions. However perverse, hobbies were the business of none but their adherents. So she simply accepted credit from Wuu and did not inquire what the two oddly matched strangers intended to do with their bizarre purchases.

They checked out of their hotel and took an internal transport to the northernmost main module terminus. From there they traveled for more than an hour in line with hundreds of similar modules, until they reached the outskirts of the metropolis.

Soon they had been switched and were accelerating with perhaps fifty other modules in a train heading due north. At regular intervals modules split off from front or back of the column. Forty, thirty, then twenty-two, according to Ryo's count, were traveling steadily north-northwest.

Some time earlier the transport train had emerged from subterranean concourses to travel on repulsion rails above the surface. The character of the landscape had begun to change. In place of the valley of the Moregeeon and its towering forests of ventilation pipes and air intakes, patches of steamy jungle alternated with cultivated fields and stack clumps marking the location of underground manufacturing facilities.

Hives were scattered more widely as they entered the second day of travel. They had already passed the good-sized cities of Fashmet and Pwelfree and hives were farther apart. Most of the modules they had departed Daret in concert with had split off, but they periodically acquired others and, on balance, the train had shrunken by only half a dozen.

Wuu's considerable resources enabled them to have the luxury of a private long-travel unit, about a third the size of a normal eight-passenger module, with two sleeping lounges and extensive hygienic facilities. The comparatively lush method of travel was something of a risk to their carefully cultivated anonymity, but one that Ryo was glad they'd decided to chance. It was a long way to Sed-Clee.

Though the module was equipped with automated food service, from time to time they varied their diet by pulling out of line to sample the distinctive regional cuisines of hives scattered along the route. Meal concluded, they would slip back to the main track and link up with the next cluster north.

Gradually the stack clusters marking the locations of subterranean industrial complexes gave way to taller, thinner pipes belching treated gases, each above a well-developed mine. Hives became smaller, were set farther apart, and the jungle began to thin out. In clumps and on shady hillsides grew vegetation Ryo did not recognize.

"It makes one appreciate Willow-wane all the more," Wuu observed one day as they sat watching scenery fly past their module's right-side port, "when you realize that the mother world itself is a harsher place."

"I've thought that many times these past several days." Ryo didn't take his eyes from the passing landscape.

Days later found them climbing through a rugged mountain pass. Jungle assaulted the lower elevations, but higher up the rocky slopes they could just discern tall, symmetrical growths. Scrapers, Wuu said they were called. Trees that had thin, sharp excuses for leaves instead of the broad, flat variety they were familiar with. The exteriors of such plants were hard and rough, not like the smooth skin of normal vegetation. The covering was tougher and thicker than the bark enclosing the toughest jungle hardwoods. Vines and creepers turned thin and sickly, though lichens and mosses seemed to thrive. It was very strange.

Three days before endmonth, they came downslope out of the mountains. On their northern flanks the jungle had vanished completely. Plants were still cultivated, but sparsely. Only a few vegetables flourished on the frigid northern plain. Hardship made locally grown vegetables terribly costly, but the price was high enough to encourage their planting.

On endmonth, twenty-two days after leaving Daret, they reached Ghew, the northern hive city. But Ryo and Wuu did not pause; as soon as the transport computer switched them through they were hurrying north toward the first of the six hives that were links in an irregular chain leading to distant Sed-Clee.

It was when they were traveling between Ublack and Erl-o-Iwwex, ascending through a stretch of open hilly country at just forty kilometers an hour, that Ryo woke to the nightmare. He was lying on his right side, preferred for sleeping, near the rear of the module. Only two units traveled in tandem with them now, both ahead of their own. He'd once studied the nightmare he now lived, but the shock of seeing it just outside the window was enough to make him cower on his lounge and pull the cocoon wrap practically over his antennae. "Wuu!" The poet raised himself sleepily and stared across the module at his companion, "What's the trouble? What is? . . ." Then he noticed the direction of Ryo's motionless gaze and turned to stare at the same window.

Wuu climbed down from his sleeping lounge and walked over to the window. He pressed a truhand against it, felt an odd tingling sensation which he didn't identify until he touched the tips of his antennae to the glass. It was Cold. Deep Cold that seeped even through the sealed port.

Moving to the module's self-contained climate controls, he turned up the interior heat and humidity. When the room had warmed further, Ryo, not wishing to appear the larva, slid from his own lounge to join Wuu in inspecting the phenomenon dominating their view.

"It looks like rain," he whispered in amazement. "I remember studying it briefly, long ago. During Learning Time."

"I've seen recordings of clith myself," Wuu said in grim fascination, "but never thought to see in person. It *is* rain. Perfectly ordinary, everyday rain such as falls every morning in Ciccikalk. Except—this is frozen."

"Frozen," Ryo echoed, not savoring the modulation of the strange term.

Little white flakes continued to beat and smear themselves against the module window, reminding Ryo of nothing so much as white blood falling from a cracked and bleeding sky. Cracked wide open like the body of an unwary traveler such as himself, much as he might be if he were trapped outside in such a region for more than a few minutes.

The frozen rain continued to fall. Once the immediate novelty wore off, Wuu rushed to dictate into his recorder, to record several lines that he intended to incorporate into a long narrative poem of delicious horror, to be completed and refined after their return to Willow-wane.

The climb leveled off and soon they were descending. As they did so the frozen rain thinned and blue sky showed through—not the familiar pale blue of home or Ciccikalk or even Daret, but a sharp, terrifyingly brilliant blue that seemed only one step removed from the blackness of empty space.

Oddly enough, Ryo was more afraid of such Deep Cold here, on the surface of the mother world, than he'd been while traveling from Willow-wane to Hivehom. Deep Space was supposed to be deadly. But to see rain—ordinary, friendly lung-moistening rain—falling in hard little chunks on the surface of the center of the Thranx race was far more horrifying than the cold of interstellar space ever could be.

The scraper trees continued to grow tall but not quite as thickly as they had on the other side of the hills; undergrowth was dense and dark. Clinging to branches and accumulating in mounds and drifts was the omnipresent white, frozen rain.

Ryo stood back from the window. Surely, he thought,

even if the rumors are true, even if there is something to the tale of alien monstrosities being held at Sed-Clee, nothing could be more alien or frightening than this awful, sterile, white land.

VIII The fourth hive in the chain of six was well behind them and they soon hummed through the fifth. Then they were alone save for a couple of passengers in the single small module ahead of them.

Eventually, with the frozen rain still falling slowly from the sky, the module mercifully dipped underground again. Ryo was unreasonably thankful for the familiar warmth of confining earth. Lights soon intensified around them and they pulled into the dirtiest terminal he'd ever seen.

Every carrier station he'd ever passed through had centered on a switching circle, a nexus of repulsion rails that fanned out in different directions. Not in Sed-Clee. The track simply curved up against an unloading platform before arcing back the way they'd come.

End of the rail, Ryo thought. No travel, no transport beyond this point. Nothing lay beyond Sed-Clee. He helped Wuu with their bulky baggage, whose contents he fervently hoped would never have to be unpacked. They ambled out of the module into the chill but reasonably comfortable air of the station.

The two who'd occupied the module ahead of them could be seen talking with several other citizens. Other than that the terminal was largely devoid of activity.

As Wuu and Ryo walked past the small module-servicing section Ryo overheard terms and words as unfamiliar as ancient Thranx hieroglyphs. The locals displayed a slowness of movement and an irritability that bordered on the discourteous. That was probably understandable in light of the harsh life they had here. He wondered at the reason for establishing such a hive.

"Experimental perhaps," he suggested to Wuu. "Surely a formal hive isn't required simply to aid in support of the military base."

"I did some research prior to our departure, my boy. A small chromite mine lies nearby, and some cobalt as well. The ore bodies lie directly beneath the town, of course. Both minerals are sufficiently important to justify the establishment of a small hive. Ah, there, you see?" He pointed to his left.

So small was the terminal that the passenger and freight lines ended in the same chamber. Ryo noted the huge hop-

97

per modules, some already loaded with ore. Machines could be heard, working behind the modules, though it was hard for Ryo to imagine operators who could function efficiently under such isolated and depressing conditions.

With considerable effort and much grace they managed to wangle the location of the hive's two small hotels from a passing terminal worker. The one they selected was hardly appealing, but at least they didn't have to worry about attracting attention by choosing accommodations too luxurious—none such were to be had.

The hotel was located on the sixth of the hive's twelve levels. Actually it was the eleventh level because there were five "zero" levels above the first, a phenomenon neither Wuu nor Ryo had ever encountered before. The five were of the same dimensions and were filled not with homes and work areas but with insulation, to help shield the comfortable climate below from the heat-sucking surface.

Upon inquiring, out of morbid curiosity Ryo thought, Wuu was informed that the surface temperature was currently −5° C and that even in midseason summer it rarely rose above 15°.

To Ryo, zero degrees, the solidifying point of water, seemed cold enough to freeze the blood in his body. The idea of being somewhere where the temperature was actually below that was like visiting hell itself.

They settled in, taking the evening meal at the hotel's own small restaurant. The fare was simple, devoid of dressings or gravies. The meat was pungent and tough, but edible. The following morning they started to explore the hive and ask questions.

Seeing no reason to conceal it, Wuu announced himself to be the well-known colonial poet, but was disgusted to learn that none of the citizens they questioned had ever heard of him. "We don't have much time for poetry or any other kind of entertainment here," one informed them. He was a middle-aged male whose body looked like it had been run through the ore crusher a few times. "I'm afraid what few pleasures we have are of the less refined variety."

Ryo had never thought of poetry as being particularly refined. It was just something any moderately aware intelligence paid homage and attention to. But the principal recreation in Sed-Clee appeared to consist of various forms of strenuous physical activity, surprising in light of the hard work required in the two mines.

Several days' indirect questioning failed to elicit the location of the military-complex entrance, so they decided to chance asking one of the citizens directly, rather than risk a formal information terminal.

"The base?" The stunted, old female did not appear suspicious of the question. "It's sixty kilometers north of town, of course."

"Sixty north? . . ." Ryo was momentarily confused. "But the transport line ends here in town—at least, the one we came in on did. Is there a separate, special spur that runs from here to the base?"

The old lady responded with a gesture of second-degree negativity. "No, there's no other transport rail, youth. All traffic to the base moves on the surface, in individual vehicles."

Like my dependable old A24 crawler back home, Ryo thought, but something much tougher. "Isn't there any kind of general transport?"

"The workers and soldiers from the base come into town often enough," she told them. She didn't have to. Both Ryo and Wuu had seen military personnel, circles and stars shining from their shoulders, wandering around the hive since their arrival.

"But they come on military transport at regular intervals. Very few hivefolk ever go out to the base. No one wants to."

"Who does travel out there?" Ryo inquired.

"A few do special work and have permits and special clearance. They use the same military transportation. I don't know why you're so anxious to go out there. You don't look like fools. But if you're determined to try, I can help you a little." She gestured past them, back down the corridor.

"Third cube, second level, is where the information office is located. Go and speak to them. Perhaps someone at the base will be in the mood to indulge idiots. Perhaps you'll be lucky and they'll turn down your request." She cocked her head to one side. "Tell me, why do you want to subject yourselves to such a journey?"

"I'm a poet," Wuu said, not bothering to give his name. "I'm doing a long spiral poem on the military."

"Well, I don't think you'll raise much material out there, if you get that far," she replied. "They're an uncommunicative bunch. Can't say as how I blame 'em. I can't imagine a worse place in the civilized worlds to be stationed. I'd leave here myself if I could, but I've two unmated daughters working in the mines and they're all the family I've got."

Having always been surrounded by family and clanmates, Ryo found her confession particularly touching. "I am sorry."

"We all have our place," she said philosophically.

"So all nonmilitary visitors have to be cleared through this information station?"

"I would think so." She preened at a badly damaged left antenna where some of the feathers were missing, then glanced around and whistled softly. "If you're as determined as you are crazy, however, you might have a flagon of juice in the first-level public eatery and ask for an individual name of Torplublasmet."

"Why—could he help us?" Ryo asked eagerly.

"He could if anyone could."

Wuu made a gesture of wariness mixed with lack of comprehension. "I don't understand. Even if this person were capable of doing so, why should he?"

The ancient one let out a delighted, wheezing whistle. "Because he's crazy too!" And she turned and waddled off down the corridor.

"What do you think?" Ryo asked Wuu as soon as she was out of sight.

The poet considered. "I made up that story about seeking material for a poem to allay any suspicions she might have had and to answer her question as to our purpose, but why should we not continue with that? My credentials can be verified. We are traveling outside official channels because such interference would inhibit artistic inspiration."

Ryo gestured hesitant concurrence. "I accept that, but will the authorities at the base?"

"A poet's palate can accomplish miracles, my boy. And perhaps our friend Torplublasmet—"

"He's not our friend yet."

"—will have a suggestion or two."

They ambled off uplevel and located the eatery, but two days passed before the enigmatic Torplublasmet chose to show himself. As soon as he did, Ryo found ample reason to agree with the old matriarch's assessment of him.

Tor was a solitary trapper, one of the few Thranx courageous or foolhardy enough to brave the howling, arctic wilderness above ground. He wore the skins of dead animals instead of proper clothes, and it was some time before Ryo could face him without experiencing nausea.

Wuu, on the other hand, seemed to find something kindred in this bucolic spirit, and by promising the chance to see something "no one else even suspects may exist," he succeeded in convincing the trapper to convey them to the distant base.

A faintly voiced hope turned out to have substance when the resourceful Tor did indeed propose a reasonable excuse for their presence. They would be fellow trappers, visitors from far-off trapping grounds, come to sound out the opportunities for peddling some merchandise among the isolated citizens of the base.

Days of wandering on the hunter's loosp cart through frozen forest eventually brought them to a place where the last tree shrank to a stunted embarrassment and the land stretched into the windswept horizon, white and completely barren.

It looked like a moonscape to Ryo. He'd never been anywhere plants didn't flourish the year 'round. To find such a blasted landscape here, atop the mother world itself, was shocking.

Before long they could see the familiar silhouettes of ventilators ahead, misty in the cold fog. A fence seemed to spring from the ground before them. It was three meters high and ran to east and west as far as the eye could see. No signs hung from the fence, no identification.

Ryo forgot the cold, the dry, and the desolation as he struggled to recall the cover story that Tor had tried to drill into them during the frigid days of travel from Sed-Clee.

I am a hunter-trapper, he told himself slowly: I've marched over from the western bulge of the Jezra-Jerg to visit my old friend Torplublasmet. My old associate and I usually sell our pelts and rare meats in Levqumu because it lies in warmer territory than Sed-Clee.

We have a few exceptionally fine mossmel skins with us and we might sell them at the base. Our old friend Tor is escorting us over so we can check out the prospects ourselves, as is only right and proper.

Such was the tale that Tor strove to impress on the hapless guard who emerged with great reluctance from the angular entryway. Moist, warm air roared from the opening like the breath of a gleast. After more than a quarter month of dry cold, Ryo nearly swooned when the blast reached him. He was careful, however, to control his reactions lest the guard notice something not in character for a back-country trapper.

After some polite exchanges and minor formalities between Tor and the guard, they were waved inward. "Enough talk of this miserable weather, friends," the guard said disgustedly as they strolled in. "Come inside and moisten your spicules."

As they entered, the door closed quickly behind them, the three triangular sections meeting tightly in the center. The whisper of the outside vanished.

Following Tor's example, Ryo kept his furs on but unstrapped the belly latches and shoved the hollowed-out skull and clith goggles back off his head. He wiggled his newly erect antennae gratefully, glad to faz and smell once again.

The hunter led them down a winding ramp. Before long they exited into a modest, busy avenue. Not far above them lay the frozen, clith-coated wastes of Hivehom's hostile arctic. For the moment, though, it was as if they were back in Daret.

Military personnel scurried everywhere, emerald and crimson insignia sparkling from shoulders and foreheads. Only rarely did they espy a civil worker. The three oddly garbed strangers drew only occasional stares, testament to Tor's frequent visits.

Their guide knew precisely where they were headed. From time to time he stopped to chat briefly with passersby he knew. Soon they stopped for a drink at a concession. From his observation of the crowd and the size of the corridors they'd already traversed, Ryo guessed that the base was much larger than Sed-Clee itself.

Later they strolled down a corridor that paralleled an immense artificial cavern filled with hybrid aircraft and military shuttles. The latter, part of the planetary defense network, were narrow, round-winged craft armed with missiles and energy weapons. To Ryo's amateur eye they looked almost new, and, indeed, none had been flown on anything more strenuous than training flights.

Having lived through an off-world attack, Ryo felt a surge of confidence at the sight of the deadly craft, hibernating peacefully beneath the clith but ready to leap spaceward in defense of the mother world. Everything required to mount such a defense was here, safely underground, except for the ventilators and the forest of electronic receptors that doubtless lay camouflaged somewhere above.

If only we'd had two or three of these warcraft when the AAnn attacked, he thought. Those broken-plated invaders would have received a lot more than a simple diplomatic reprimand!

Dwelling on the past was useless, he reminded himself. There was nothing constructive in retained bitterness. He forced the incident from his thoughts, concentrated on admiring the ranks of gleaming ships. Then they'd passed beyond the hangar and were once more making their way through the warren.

They'd been walking for some time and Ryo's feet were beginning to hurt around the single footpad and trimmed claw, for his feet were still swathed in the fur shoes Tor insisted they wear to complete their hunter's garb. He moved next to Tor. "I know we must be headed somewhere—but where? If this is a tour, I've seen enough."

"It's no tour. Our roundabout course is intentional. So is our walking instead of taking an internal module. Walking can't be traced.

"There are only two sections of this place I've never been into. Three, actually, but one of them is the battle command center and we're not likely to find our answers there. No one's ever told me what goes on inside the other two and I never bothered to go there and inquire for myself. That's what we're going to try today. Surely the best place to hide something that doesn't exist is in a section where no one's allowed to go."

"You say no one's told you what takes place in these two sections," Ryo said. "Does that mean that you've asked?"

"Of course. Even on this visit—and I mentioned the possibility of alien monsters this time. Either my friends are not as friendly as I thought, or their ignorance is genuine. Not one of them professes to know anything about what goes on in the two maximum-security areas. Even officers at the level of Burrow Marshal aren't allowed inside without special permission.

"As to the possibility they harbor captured aliens, the thought was met with derision and laughter."

"Then how are *we* going to learn anything?" Ryo muttered concernedly.

"Let us find the sections first, my impatient friend," the hunter advised him, "and proceed from there."

Gradually foot traffic thinned around them and they came to a turn where the corridor was blocked. No side branches here, only the single dead end.

It was very impressive, in its understated fashion. Bold and effervescent as ever, Tor sauntered unhesitatingly up to the low barrier that blocked the tunnel. A gate was cut into the left side, near the tunnel wall. A single officer was seated behind the barrier. Two emerald stars shone on her shoulder.

There were also two guards, one before the gate, the other behind. They were not resting in saddles but stood stiffly at the ready. To Ryo's amazement, each was armed with a large lethal-looking energy rifle held in firing position, tight in both foothands with a truhand on the trigger stud.

Neither of the guards turned a head to study the new arrivals. They stared in opposite directions, one up the corridor and the other down. It seemed as if their sole purpose in life was to insure that nothing approached the barrier unseen. They reminded Ryo of pictures he'd seen of ancient warriors standing ready, jaws agape, to defend the primitive hive.

The officer saddled behind the barrier, however, looked up readily at Tor's approach and favored him with a greeting movement of her antennae.

"You're Tor the hunter, aren't you?"

"That I am. At your service." He executed a fluid gesture of third-degree obeisance combined with two degrees of sexual admiration.

It did not have any visible effect on the officer. "I've heard of you." She seemed open and friendly. "I am Burrow Tacticianary Marwenewlix, tenth level."

Tor took note of her insignia. "Greetings and warmth to you."

"What may I do for the three of you?" She was eying their pelts with curiosity and none of the disgust Ryo would have expected.

Moving forward, Tor rested his truhands on the barrier as he spoke. "My friends are hunter-trappers, as am I. We deal in the skins and skeletons and corpses of those beasts favored for aesthetic and culinary application, which beasts the hive dwellers would rather avoid while the fearsome things still live."

"I know that," she replied. "I have a byorlesnath thorax muff I bought from a concession in the service corridor. The proprietor told me you were his supplier."

"Fourth booth, level two?" She gestured in the affirmative. "Young Estplehenzin, yes, I remember. I hope you find the muff to your liking."

"It is quite attractive in its barbaric way—and very warm."

"Then you can understand, as an appreciator of such items, why my friends and I are always on the search for similar items with which to supplement our stock."

For the first time she sounded uncertain. "I'm not sure I follow you."

Tor leaned closer, his tone turning conspiratorial. "It's come to our attention that you might be studying some creatures whose pelts would be especially marketable. More than just the usual novelties, if you follow my meaning. Something will have to be done with them when you've finished your studies. We would be glad to handle any post-experiment disposal, with mutual profit to all concerned."

"I've no idea what you're talking about." She added two degrees of politeness and one of puzzlement. "No such creatures exist in this section."

"Come now, tacticianary," he urged softly, "we've all

heard the rumors. Since no such creatures are being studied anywhere else on the base, they have to be back there." He gestured past her, down the corridor. "Or else over to the south in Section W, right? Those are the only two places in the installation tight enough to hold them, as well as the rumors."

"They are not here, nor in Section W, because no such things exist," said the officer. "The cold has weakened your reason while stimulating your imagination, hunter. I can enlighten you no further."

"It's not that I'm doubting your word, tacticianary. It's only that the tales I've been told have been so persistent and inconsistent. If we could have a quick look for ourselves, why then we could leave easy in mind that we're not missing out on a special opportunity. Just a quick look. We wouldn't tell a soul. Don't but rarely meet anyone else to tell anyway, Outside." He forced a laugh.

"I can't allow you past this point." She was not amused. "You know that."

"Well then, what goes on back there, anyway?"

"Research."

"Real secret research, hmm?"

"Come now, sir. Enough badinage. Surely you realize that if I must turn away military personnel I could never let one of you past this station, any more than I am able to relate what kind of research takes place here. I can say that most of the time I do not know myself."

"Then let us pass," Wuu interjected, speaking only because he saw chance slipping rapidly away, "and upon our return we'll enhance your store of knowledge from our own."

She eyed him intently. For a moment Ryo thought that Wuu's instinctively elegant speech had betrayed them.

The officer's mandibles moved and Ryo feared she was about to ask the first of many unanswerable questions, when something *whoomed!* from the far end of the corridor. Even the fossilized guards unbent, whirling with their raised weapons. Flakes of sealant fell from the corridor ceiling.

Tor had clung to the desk for stability. Ryo and Wuu barely managed to keep their own balance.

There was a disquieting pause as the officer took a step

toward the source of the explosion. A second blast shook them. This time smoke and a brief flare of orange flame filled the far end. The flame disappeared, the smoke began to dissipate, and shouts and whistles sounded from unseen Thranx.

Several appeared from behind the smoke, running toward the barrier. They gestured urgently. Without a word the two guards rushed to join them and the little group hurried around the bend that had produced the smoke and fire.

The officer had hesitated before turning back to face her inquisitive visitors.

"I'm afraid I must ask you gentlesirs to return to the central sector, preferably to the concession area." An intercom video console was built into the barrier. The status indicators on it were going berserk. From down the corridor they could hear the shrill blare of warning whistles.

"We won't get in the way," Tor said with admirable calm. "Maybe we can help, if you'll allow us to—" He broke off suddenly, speechless with amazement.

The officer had produced a pistol, which she held in a foothand. It displayed not the civilized snout of a stinger or of an energy weapon, but that of a charged-projectile device whose tiny explosive pellets could blow a person's chiton to splinters. "Please return the way you came," she instructed them brusquely, with maximum-degree assurance, "or I will be compelled to kill you here."

"Kill?" Wuu repeated stupidly. It was the first time Ryo had ever heard the poet at a loss for appropriate words. "We haven't done a thing. We—"

"You have five seconds. One . . . two . . ."

"Enough. We can argue later." Tor turned and started running. Ryo did not need further urging. As he ran he turned to glance back over his shoulder. The officer had resumed her saddle, her hands flying over the console's controls. The ugly projectile weapon lay close at hand atop the barrier.

"Outrageous!" Wuu was muttering. "Whatever trouble they are experiencing is no excuse, no excuse. Such a breach of common courtesy, of farewell custom! They cannot—"

"This is a restricted military installation," Tor interrupted him firmly. "They can do anything they wish."

"Surely she would not have shot us with that thing?" Ryo said wonderingly. They turned down a bend in the tunnel.

"Did you not see her posture or note the inflection in her voice?" Tor asked. "No question in my mind. She would have blown us apart as we stood there gaping at her; bang-bang-bang, one-two-three. Good-bye hunter and his curious friends, just like that."

"But *why*?" Wuu wanted to know. "What trouble could have provoked such a threat? It's unthinkable, a throwback to the primitivism of the hive wars."

"She would have done it because she'd been ordered to," Tor told him. "I can see that neither of you has spent much time around the military. We can consider her reasoning later." He turned sharply to his right.

"We did not come this way, I think." Ryo looked backward again. They were alone now. "Do you think it's possible . . . those explosions . . ."

"I don't give a damn what's possible," snapped their guide. "We're not going to ask questions until they put away projectile weapons and such. I want no part of anything that's got them so jumpy."

"Don't you see, though? This may have something to do with the monsters," Ryo told him.

"And maybe it has something to do with a top-secret weapon that's going haywire," Tor responded. "We'll find out later, when mysterious explosions aren't going off and attractive officers aren't threatening to shoot us. For the moment I think the sensible thing for us to do is follow her advice and relax with the other nonmilitary back in the concession area."

By this time they were running through a particularly narrow corridor laced with conduits and pipes. "Maintenance tunnel," Tor said, stating the obvious. "There's going to be a lot of confusion in the nearby corridors. This way, we'll miss the traffic and come out close to the concession level. I could use a cylinder of hot cider right now, as well as a little calm. If there's been a general mobilization, we'll learn about it just as fast and a lot more comfortably while we're drinking."

"Two explosions," Ryo was muttering. "I heard at least two."

"I also heard them, my boy." Wuu was breathing hard and having trouble keeping up with his younger comrades. "I thought the second closer but smaller than the first."

"I'd give a great deal to know exactly what's going on," Ryo said.

"Perhaps we'll encounter personnel in the concessions who know something and are more willing to talk about it," the poet replied. "Confusion and excitement can loosen the tightest of throats."

Ryo moved on as Tor dropped back to assist the slowing Wuu. Noise sounded from ahead.

"They're probably trying to shut down power and so forth to the affected area," the hunter declared. "Maybe the maintenance workers can tell us something. I may be more cautious, but I'm as curious as either of you as to what's happening."

"I'll ask." Ryo sent a greeting whistle toward the hidden work crew. "Greetings, friends! Do you know what is happening? Did you hear the explosions? Can you tell us? . . ." He turned the corner and stopped.

The work crew he'd expected to find was not there, but something else was.

The horrors that turned to confront him held Thranx energy rifles in pulpy, pale fingers. Ryo could not understand how anything so soft-looking could hold even a drinking tankard. Each of the two upper limbs ended in five digits instead of the normal four, and only one was opposable.

They stared at each other, Thranx and monster equally surprised. Ryo wondered if the two were a mated pair. There were some superficial differences between them, but that was no assurance of mating or even gender. Certainly neither displayed anything like a pair of ovipositors, but then, he reminded himself, most mammals practice live birth.

Despite the presence of fur he couldn't be certain they were mammals. Their bodies were heavily clothed and what fur he could see was restricted to their heads. So startled was he by the unexpected sight, he forgot to sound a warning.

It wasn't necessary. "What is it, boy?" Wuu called. "Is something the matter?"

"Yes, do they know—" Tor pulled to a halt down the corridor. They did not round the bend as Ryo had in his haste, but remained out in the main tunnel.

One of the monsters made a throaty, gargling sound and raised its rifle. Tor and Wuu immediately turned and bolted back the way they'd come.

Whether out of desire to protect the elderly poet or from some unconscious urging (he never really knew), Ryo stepped in front of the rifle and dropped all four arms. The monster glared down at him out of tiny single-lensed eyes and hesitated. Ryo had confused it.

It did not run after the retreating Thranx. Ryo noticed that the energy rifle was similar to those the two barrier guards had wielded. Its tip dropped away from him, but as he took a step backward it came up again.

Ryo stood quietly, staring up at the monster, his antennae working furiously as he examined the creature. There was nothing remarkable about their smell. It was oddly familiar, in fact.

For their part, the monsters seemed puzzled by Ryo's calm. They continued to make the strange gargling noises, clearly their method of communication.

There were other differences besides the amount of fur they displayed. One was slightly larger than the other and they had different shapes. The latter could be due to clothing as much as physiognomy, Ryo reminded himself. They displayed the flexibility of leuks. Their outer skin was mostly bare of fur but was not hard and composed of jointed plates as was that of the AAnn. The softness fascinated him. The creatures had outer coverings as thin as paper.

They seemed to fit no known life grouping. As endoskeletal beings they probably belonged to a lower order, though the AAnn were an exception to that otherwise universal rule. If their physiology followed Thranx norms then the larger of the two should be the female.

They appeared to be tail-less. Their faces were flat and they had external nostrils instead of antennae; it was likely they could not faz. When they conversed they showed only four canines, two upper and two lower. The rest of their teeth seemed relatively flat and blunt. That suggested they were herbivores, but they didn't act like plant-eaters. Omnivorous like us, perhaps, he mused.

Since they were clearly bipedal the lack of a substantial tail puzzled him. Such an arrangement seemed designed for instability, yet they appeared to balance themselves without difficulty in the awkward upright position.

There were only two upper limbs and he wondered if they could double as another pair of legs like the Thranx foothands. He doubted it. Both upper and lower limbs appeared too specialized for such duality of employment.

The energy rifles were designed for use with three hands. The monsters managed by holding the stock of the weapon in the space between arm and body, thus freeing one hand to work the lower grip and the other the trigger. They seemed to know exactly what they were doing and he had no doubt they could fire the weapons whenever necessary.

All these observations registered on his brain in seconds. As he'd hoped, by stepping between their weapons and his companions he'd prevented shooting. Now they were probably trying to decide whether he was sacrificial by nature or merely insane.

They were neither as terrifying nor as familiar as he'd hoped. If it came to physical combat, he thought he had a good chance. They were each twice his mass, but that skin looked terribly fragile. He hoped there would be no bloodshed. It was only a matter of time before they were recaptured anyway. Surely the hunt had already begun.

His thoughts returned to the two explosions and he wondered if anything besides property might have been hurt. As he considered that unnerving possibility the taller monster tried to stand erect, bumped its head hard against the corridor ceiling, and made some loud mouth noises. Its rifle's muzzle dipped and Ryo took a step back.

Immediately the smaller one swung its weapon to cover Ryo. He halted. Clearly this was an escape attempt, and just as clearly it would soon come to an end. Before that happened he hoped to acquire some interesting information.

He was quite calm as the taller monster prodded him with the rifle muzzle. Evidently it desired that he move.

Ryo responded with a second-degree gesture of negativity. Keeping the tremor from his voice, he politely whistled that he had no intention of going anywhere and that it didn't matter because they would be recaptured any moment.

There was no way of telling if the creature understood. In any case it prodded him harder with the rifle and made a loud mouth noise. Not wishing to tempt their instincts further, he turned resignedly and walked in the indicated direction.

The monsters paced him, the larger one taking the lead and the other walking behind Ryo, occasionally glancing over its shoulder for signs of pursuit. There were none as yet.

The maintenance tunnel rambled on and on, but they encountered no one. Ryo used the opportunity to study at close range the monsters' remarkable method of locomotion, marveling continually how they kept their balance on only two legs and with no tail as counterweight. They looked very agile. Being more primitive, they were probably capable of good speed over a short run.

The concealed feet tantalized him. Though larger than his own, the pad design did not seem all that dissimilar, hinting that each foot probably formed a wide base ending in a single claw. That would make them efficient diggers.

They turned still another corner in the dimly lit tunnel and found themselves facing a sloping ramp. Unhesitatingly, the taller monster started up the ramp. Ryo followed, noticing with interest how the creature automatically leaned forward to compensate for the slope.

As they ascended, new noises sounded faintly from far down the corridor. Distant whistles and clicks grew momentarily louder, then faded as a search party turned in a different direction.

Ryo derived perverse pleasure from contemplating the panic that must exist among those responsible for insuring the isolation and security of these creatures. For all their nightmarish appearance they seemed sensible enough. These were not ravening, bloodthirsty beasts.

Still, there was the nagging matter of the two substantial explosions and of how this pair came to be in the possession of a set of energy rifles whose original wielders did not likely surrender them without contest.

The ramp continued to ascend, turning a gradual spiral. Soon the lead monster halted, put out a hand that would have forcibly stopped Ryo had he not slowed willingly.

"I beg your pardon," he said, slightly out of breath, "but this really is a waste of time, you know." At that point the creature did a remarkable thing. Showing that it had done some studying of its own, it reached out with a single flexible hand and clamped all five digits around Ryo's mandibles. Ryo instinctively tried to pull away, but the monster was quite strong and did not loosen its grip.

Slowly the monster released its hold, put one digit across the two soft fleshy mandibles that bordered its mouth. It had no horizontally opposing mouth parts, Ryo noted. He had no idea what the movement signified, but the grip on his own jaws was clear enough. He kept silent.

The creature disappeared ahead, was back in seconds. It made a wonderfully fluid gesture to its companion, who prodded Ryo forward. They emerged from a tiny exit no larger than an enclosed saddle, the monsters barely squeezing their bulks through the opening. Only their astonishing flexibility permitted it.

They were standing in a storage compartment filled with ventilator cleaning material. To the right was an unguarded doorway.

The taller monster moved unhesitatingly to the door and worked the controls with a confidence that hinted at careful preparation. There was a hum. Clith was falling heavily outside. Icy wind poured inward and Ryo instantly flipped down the headpiece of his skin and the protective goggles.

"Surely," he told the smaller monster, "you don't intend for us to go outside? Neither of you has proper clothing." Though extensive, their attire was not nearly as thick as his byorlcsnath pelt, and they had no head covering whatsoever.

The second monster prodder Ryo forward. After a brief pause during which he thought he might prefer a quick, hot death from the energy rifle to a slow, freezing one outside, he opted to survive as long as possible and started into the driving clith.

They staggered through the frozen rain. Ryo did not notice when they crossed the boundary fence. He was certain, though, that they'd left the base well behind because before long they were making a path through the forest.

That they'd been able to slip out undetected did not shock him. After all, the weather was dreadful and as slim as the thought was that someone might try to break into a military base, the concept of breaking out of one verged on the absurd. He had no doubt the search for the escaping monsters was continuing more intensively than ever, just as he had no doubt that it was still confined to the interior of the burrows.

Clearly these creatures were better adapted to cold than his own kind. They moved steadily through temperatures that would have killed an unprotected Thranx in minutes. Or an AAnn, he told himself, taking some encouragement from that thought.

From time to time one would simply wipe accumulated clith from its face, ignoring the freezing liquid that ran down head and neck. This redoubled their alienness in Ryo's eyes.

Yet they were not immune to cold. Onrushing night brought a further drop in the temperature. The clith had ceased falling, which was some relief. At that point the monsters did the first sensible thing since leaving the base. They located a considerable hollow beneath several fallen logs and beckoned him inside. One of them removed a tiny, thin metal tube from its clothing. Ryo did not recognize the tube, but he was familiar with the faint aroma of the particles the monster sprinkled from it.

These fell on a pile of reasonably dry wood, which immediately burst into flame. Ryo edged as close to it as he dared, not wanting his pelt to catch fire. The monsters extended their bare hands toward the warming flames. The cold was deep enough now to trouble even them.

"Listen, I don't know what you intend to do with me," he said softly, "but I won't make you a very valuable hostage."

This brief speech caused them to begin making strange mouth noises at each other. Ryo tried to see how they formed the sounds, and it did not take long to figure out that they employed air from their lungs, or at least from inside their bodies. Modulation probably came from movements of their flexible mandibles and the peculiar fleshy organ soft creatures sometimes possessed inside their mouths. They did not communicate by making word-tones with their mandibles. Soft as the creatures were, that was not surprising.

They made the sounds in their throats, not at the mandibles. He did not have that internal mouth appendage, but he thought he could approximate some of the sounds.

A first try produced a mildy surprising little bark. He was not nearly as startled by the attempt as the monsters were. The smaller one, after a brief pause, looked straight at him and repeated the noise. He tried again, forcing himself to keep his mandibles apart and utilize only moving air.

This had an interesting effect on the creatures, for they once again set to gargling furiously among themselves.

He made the sound a third time. The monster responded with a different one. When Ryo tried to imitate it, he failed completely. His initial confidence evaporated. His mouth-parts simply could not duplicate that volume and pitch.

As an alternative, he responded with a whistle and click of his own. The monsters did not make any more noises. Instead, they huddled close to each other.

Ryo gave a mental shrug and pushed himself into a corner. He lay on his left side, watching them. It was dark outside now. The monsters still cradled their energy rifles, and they watched him intently.

It suddenly occurred to him that *they* might be afraid of *him*. That was a ludicrous thought. They were twice his size, twice his number, and heavily armed. The only thing he had in his defense was the fact that they were strangers on his world.

I suppose that's frightening enough, he thought sadly. Poor monsters. I mean you no harm, and I hope you can feel the same about me.

One of them closed both eyes and he wondered what it might be like to have eyelids. The creature was going to sleep, and it was another relief to learn they had that in common. The taller one remained conscious, watching Ryo.

Watch all you wish, he thought. I am going to sleep myself. He let his vision dim, his thoughts weaken. He was very tired.

He was so tired the dim realization did not rouse him. I thought their smell was half familiar, he thought exhaustedly to himself. Now I remember what it reminds me of.

The aliens smelled very much like the yaryinfs . . . Thranx-eaters.

IX Search parties came close the following day but did not find them. By the third day Ryo and the monsters were so deep into the forest Ryo doubted anyone ever would.

Occasionally, search aircraft would slowly pass overhead. At such times the monsters concealed themselves and their hostage beneath tree roots or overhanging rocks. Once they even buried themselves into the clith, which badly strained the temporary truce between monster and Thranx because the thought of immersing himself in that numbing cold was nearly too much for Ryo to bear. They settled for his remaining motionless against a small rock, trusting to his pelt to camouflage him.

The next day one of the monsters demonstrated its familiarity with the energy rifle by using it to kill a small emlib. The furry herbivore jerked once and was still. Ryo watched with interest as the creature drew a small Thranx knife from a pocket and neatly butchered the carcass, which was then roasted over an open, largely smokeless fire.

The larger monster offered a piece to Ryo. While he normally would have disdained so uncivilized a meal, he knew that if he didn't eat hunger would kill him before the cold did. He accepted the meat, holding it under the head of his pelt as he bit off small chunks with his mandibles and swallowed them whole. Some vegetables would have helped, mixed together with the meat in a proper stew, but he was thankful enough for just the protein.

It was comparatively warm that night. The next day, they crossed ground that was mostly devoid of clith. As they walked Ryo was startled when one of the monsters suddenly began to whistle. There was rhythm but no sense to the sounds. It was very similar to the crude speech of a newly hatched larva.

Perhaps it was simply their mode. He tried imitating the sound, managed to match it almost perfectly the first time. It was simple compared to the monsters' more common communications noises.

The monsters looked pleased and whistled back at him. At that point Ryo wondered if the researchers who'd studied these creatures had concentrated only on trying to learn their guttural language instead of trying to teach them

Thranx. If so, they probably tried to use electromechanical interpreters. And for various reasons the monsters might not have been interested in cooperating with the study.

Stopping, he pointed importantly to the nearest bush. "Slen," he whistled. He gestured again, adding movement indicative of third-degree importance. "Slen." He repeated it several times, much slower than normal, drawing out the whistle comically.

The monsters hesitated. The larger seemed to argue with the smaller. That was only Ryo's impression. For all he knew they might have begun a mating ritual.

Turning to Ryo, the smaller monster hesitated a moment longer, then formed its pair of flexible mandibles into a circular opening. The sight was so disgusting Ryo had to force himself to watch.

But it produced a fine whistle. "Zhlcn," it said, also pointing at the bush.

"No, no," he said. "Try again." He touched the bush. "Slen."

"Zh . . . slen," it said.

Ryo again touched the bush, said "slen," and added the movement for affirmation. The monster repeated the word, but left off the gesture.

At that point Ryo glimpsed part of the trouble and was further amazed. These creatures spoke only with their lungs! They apparently never utilized their whole bodies.

Without thinking, excitement completely overwhelming normal caution, he walked up to the monster and took hold of one of its upper limbs. Both reacted sharply, but the smaller one did not pull away. Ryo pointed to the bush, said "slen," and made the affirmation gesture again.

This time, after the monster repeated the word, Ryo moved its limb in the gesture of affirmation. The limb moved freely, but the feel of it made him a little ill. He fought to retain his composure. If the researchers studying these creatures had thought to try the same thing it would not have surprised him to learn that the larger monster had thrown its inquisitor into the nearest wall.

Sometimes physical contact means more than mental, he mused. Fal had told him that. It was an important rule to remember while teaching larvae.

He let go of the arm, stood back, and made the click

sound signifying "do you understand?" The monster stared at him. He repeated the sound.

The monster slowly made the gesture for "yes," then pointed at the bush and whistled "slen." He was about to try the word for clith when the larger monster, which had been watching intently while keeping the muzzle of the rifle pointed at Ryo, suddenly walked over and touched the bush. It looked at Ryo, made a gargling sound, then pointed at Ryo and used some part of its internal mouth-parts to click, "Do you understand?"

Ryo was so overjoyed he almost forgot to make the gesture of affirmation. Then he said "slen" and tried to imitate the monster's own mouth noise.

At that point the monsters made a whole series of very loud mouth noises accompanied by a great deal of mutual touching.

The whistles, he knew, were produced by forcing air past those soft mandibles. It took him a while and the patience of the smaller monster to discover how they produced their clicks. These sounds were softer than his own. Instead of grinding mandibles together as Thranx did, the monsters apparently utilized their peculiar mouth appendages against the upper parts of their jaws. The resultant words were sloppily executed but, if one paid attention, quite comprehensible.

The point of communication which had eluded them the longest, that of gesturing and posture, turned out to be the simplest for them to duplicate, once they began to understand that civilized speech was more than merely a matter of atmospheric modulation.

By the fifth day Ryo was imitating some of the monsters' terms fairly well. As they marched they all engaged in an orgy of identification, beginning with the bush and working up to more complex terminology. Trouble was had with certain gestures because the monsters were short the correct number of limbs. They solved this by using one of their legs as an arm or sitting down to use all four limbs if a quadruple complicated movement was required.

By midmonth they were carrying on crude conversations. By the end of the month and yet another meal of carbonized emlib Ryo was convinced the authorities had given both him and the monsters up for dead.

The monsters were not members of different species, which was one thought he'd given some credence to. Like the Thranx their kind had two sexes, but the larger turned out to be a male, the smaller a female. Ryo readily accepted this mild perversion of the natural order. They were not, however, a mated pair, but simply members of the same ship's crew. Their name sounds were "loo" and "bonnie." They did not have clan or hive names, only personal and family. Ryo allowed them the unusual familiarity of calling him by his personal name alone, since his full name verged on the unpronounceable for them.

He learned that their skin color and slight difference of eye shape were due to internal racial variations. Other things he already knew by observation, such as the fact that they were omnivorous.

"Our ship," the larger monster Loo was explaining one day, "hurt by other ship." The term hurt required a double click. Ryo took personal pride in the monster's tolerable pronunciation.

"What different . . . other, ship?"

The monster stopped. In damp mud he sketched the outline with one digit. Ryo recognized it immediately. It only confirmed earlier thoughts.

"AAnn ship," he said. As he repeated the word he picked up a rock and threw it forcefully at the drawing, sending mud splattering. That was one gesture that did not require elaboration.

"Bad. Not good," the monster agreed, making a gesture of fifth-degree and maximum affirmation. Clumsy and unsubtle, Ryo thought, but a least they are learning how to get their thoughts across. The monster emitted a long, rippling whistle. "Very bad."

At least we have one thing in common, Ryo mused. Neither of us has any love for the AAnn. These creatures were *not* allies of the Thranx's hereditary enemies.

"Why we imprisoned?" the monster suddenly asked.

Ryo thought, constructed a simple reply. "My people afraid you AAnn-friends."

The monster made a funny noise that Ryo had not learned how to translate. He asked for an explanation.

"Funny. Very funny."

So that was monster laughter, Ryo thought. Most peculiar. "Understand." He then demonstrated the gestures and whistles for first- through fifth-degree amusement. "No like AAnn, my people," he said. "My people afraid you and AAnn friends."

The smaller monster said, "Funny. We afraid you Thranx people and AAnn friends. Very funny."

"Big mistake," Ryo agreed.

"Very big mistake," the larger monster agreed. "All you Thranx people afraid of us people when capture us. Why afraid? Because afraid we AAnn-friends?"

"Partially," Ryo said. That required further explanation. Understanding was coming quicker to both sides now. "Also another reason."

"What reason other?" the monster asked.

"'Other reason,'" Ryo corrected it—no, him, he reminded himself. He hesitated, then decided that if they were offended there wasn't much he could do. It would have to be brought out sooner or later.

"My people, the Thranx, certain type." He tapped the chiton of his thorax, then a leg, then his head. "On this world, on other my people Thranx worlds, many creatures like you." He pointed to each of them in turn. "Such creatures eat Thranx."

It took them a moment to digest this. Ryo had learned to recognize some of their emotions, which were transmitted not by distinctive gestures but by certain positioning of their flexible face parts. He saw that instead of being angry they were confused.

The she-monster said, "On our worlds, my people afraid of creatures like you Thranx people, only much smaller."

"Eat your people?" Ryo wondered.

"Not people. Eat our people food. For long time. Very long time. History."

"Mine also, all history fear of your creature kind."

They walked on in silence. After a while he thought it safe to continue. He touched his antennae with a truhand. "Other things, too. You people smell not good."

The smaller monster made the gesture of apology, without adding degree.

"Not your fault," said Ryo.

"You," she replied, "smell not like little Thranx kind all history trouble our people. You smell very good." She halted, drew in the mud. Ryo did not recognize the species, but the flower outline was unmistakable. "Like that."

"Your color also," the he-monster added. "Very pretty."

"Thank you," he replied. "Your colors not so pretty but not so bad as your smell."

"Your feel . . ." The smaller monster reached out slowly. Ryo flinched, forced himself to hold his ground. He'd touched them while demonstrating proper gestures, but neither of them had touched him since Loo had clamped five massive fingers around Ryo's mandibles.

"Just want to touch," Bonnie said.

Feeling like a museum exhibit, Ryo stood motionless while the monster ran its fingers under the byorlesnath fur and along his body.

"My turn now," he said.

The monster opened its clothing, exposing itself to the air. The sight made Ryo shudder, and he had to remind himself of the creature's extraordinary tolerance for cold. He ran a delicate truhand along the exposed surface, wondering how closely their bodily divisions and internal organs would match up. Too much botany, he told himself, and not enough zoology. Though alien design would not necessarily conform to similar Willow-wane shapes, he reminded himself.

The most remarkable thing about the body was its flexibility. He pressed in lightly. The monster did not complain or pull away. Fascinated, he watched the tip of his finger sink into the flesh. When he pulled his hand away the covering sprang back.

Such a reaction was normal for plastics and artificial fibers. On the exterior of a living creature it was stomach-turning. He pressed again, a little firmer. The exoderm changed color slightly. He could even see bodily fluids moving beneath it. Utterly remarkable, he thought. The more so when one realized that the beings inhabiting that thin envelope were intelligent.

"Strange, so strange," he murmured. "Skeleton inside, flesh outside."

"We find you same," Bonnie said. "Skeleton outside, flesh inside. Very different."

"Yes," he agreed, "very different."

* * *

The monsters ate three times a day instead of twice. As they were finishing their odd midday meal Ryo thought to ask a question that had been lost in the excitement of mutual education.

"Where are you going? What are you going to do?"

They looked at each other. "I do not know, Ryo," Loo said. "We thought you were those who had attacked our ship. We thought you enemies. We were treated like prisoners."

"Remember," Ryo reminded them, "my people think you are allies of the AAnn. How then should they treat you but as enemies?"

"But we're not," Bonnie said. "Especially if you tell truth when you say it was AAnn who attacked our ship."

The challenge to his veracity was cause for combat. He calmed himself. Remember, he told himself, these creatures have but primitive notions of courtesy and common etiquette. They will for some time be as clumsy in their perceptions as they are in their speech.

"Big mistake," he said. "Cosmic mistake. You must do something. Out here," and he gestured at the surrounding forest, "you will die." He did not include himself in that prediction. It was self-evident.

"Better to die here," Loo said roughly, "than in captivity, poked and prodded at like an exhibit in a zoo."

"No need for that," Ryo said encouragingly. "Silly mistake. Silliness in proportion to size. We must go back. I can explain everything. I can interpret for you. When mistake explained by me, will be clear to all. We will be friends, allies. Not enemies."

"I don't know . . ." Loo made a gesture of third-degree indecision. "The way we were treated . . ."

"Were you killed? Are you dead?"

"No, we're not dead. We've been reasonably well fed." He made a face gesture of mild disgust.

"More mistakes. Must return and explain all mistakes." Ryo implored them with gestures. "Trust me. I will explain everything."

"We would wander this place forever to keep our freedom," Loo told him.

"Not a logical end of itself," Ryo countered. "Also another factor." Maybe, he thought, it wasn't self-evident. "I

. . . my people—Thranx—cannot tolerate long cold weather." He'd felt his circulation slowing the past several nights. "I will surely die. Will you kill me to preserve your freedom, which has no logical end of itself?" There, he thought as he leaned back against the log. There is the real test. Now he would learn just how civilized they were.

"Most of what you say is truth," Bonnie declared finally. "We would not like to be responsible for your death. We have been careful not to kill. Yet. You have been friend. There are misunderstandings here, on both sides." She looked up at Loo and for a moment Ryo thought they might also be telepathic.

"Friend speaks truth," she restated. "We'll go back with you."

"Next problem," said Loo. "Can we find our way back?"

"I think so." Ryo gestured skyward. "In any case, if we make our presence known when a search ship flies over, we will be found."

The hoverer set down nearby. There was a tense confrontation between Ryo and a group of net- and stinger-wielding soldiers. Disbelief gave way grudgingly to guarded astonishment. The two monsters were conducted to the base under watchful eyes instead of netting. There they descended via a heavily sealed entryway to a section Ryo had visited before. The gestures of complete amazement performed by the officer who'd previously refused him admittance were lively to behold.

Torplublasmet was not present to greet him, having been questioned and allowed to return to his burrow, but Wuu was. "My boy." He spoke while looking past Ryo at the two monsters towering nearby. "I'd given you up days ago. I've been asked many questions, which I answered sorrowfully and freely. How we came to be here, and why. But you appear whole and healthy. I thought they would have consumed you by now."

"Not at all. That would have been impolite, and these are civilized creatures. They can't help their appearance. Their ship was attacked by the AAnn. They thought we were responsible.

"If we can overcome the unfortunate beginning our respective species have managed to make, they may prove to be strong allies. There has been mutual misunderstanding of colossal proportions."

"What are you saying, Ryo?" Loo asked.

Wuu and the other Thranx looked properly shocked. "By the central burrow, they can talk!"

"Sometimes situation and precedent can combine to blunt, rather than facilitate communication," Ryo explained smoothly. He looked up at Loo. "This friend of mine," and he pronounced the alien name, "is a he, the other a she." He then gestured at Wuuzelansem, gave his name, and tried to explain what a poet was.

The monsters soon deciphered the gestures and clicks. Then they shocked the assembled researchers, guards, and Wuu alike by simultaneously gesturing at the poet with a movement indicative of third-degree respect mixed with mild admiration.

"They may be monsters," Wuu decided, "but they display an unarguable ability to recognize higher intelligence when it is presented to them."

"Come, let's go in," Bonnie said to Ryo. "We want you to meet our companions."

Ryo followed, Wuu hanging back just a trifle. The guards hesitated but the Thranx scientists and researchers in the group gestured them aside.

The party passed through several corridors, the monsters having to bend to clear the ceilings. Eventually they entered a large chamber. The saddles inside appeared unused, for obvious reasons of physiology.

Six monster males and four females lay alone or in small groups on the floor. To Ryo's untrained eye, half of them looked damaged.

As he watched, the aliens suddenly recognized Loo and Bonnie. A great deal of noise and physical contact resulted. Alien greetings, he explained to the enraptured scientists, who stood clustered in the open doorway, recorders running at maximum speed.

When the greetings were concluded, Loo and Bonnie turned to Ryo. "Well, it was good to be outside for a while, anyway," said Loo.

Ryo responded with a gesture of mild negativity. "Good to be back *inside*." He added a whistling laugh while the two monsters made their own laughter noises. It was difficult to tell who was more flabbergasted; the Thranx scientists or the other monsters in the chamber.

"Different preferences," Bonnie said, running a hand through her cranial fur.

"Yes," Ryo agreed. He gestured past her. "How are your friends?"

"Pleased to see us alive," Loo said. "Disappointed that we could not do more. I explained to them that we now have a friend. This they understood, for a friend can often be worth more than freedom."

"I am sure it will be so," Ryo replied confidently. "I will explain all to these authorities." He indicated the rows of busy Thranx crowded around them. "This mistake will be straightened out soonest. There is much to do between our peoples."

"Yes," Bonnie said. "There is nothing like a mutual enemy," and she made the gesture for the AAnn, "to produce understanding among potential friends."

One of the officials was gesturing urgently to Ryo. He turned back to his friends. "They want to talk to me now and I am equally anxious to talk with them. Will you be well?"

"Well enough," Loo replied.

"Then all is calm for now. I will return as soon as I am able. Burrow deep and warm." He inclined his head slightly and extended his antennae.

"Be warm," Bonnie said, reaching out to touch the tips of the delicate organs.

Several of the Thranx guards turned away or otherwise indicated their disgust. Of sterner stuff, the researchers and scientists simply recorded the exchange with cool detachment. Then Ryo turned and joined Wuu and the little cluster of specialists gathering around him. The two aliens rejoined their own companions, who crowded excitedly around them.

Ryo was escorted to a nearby chamber and promptly sat down in a comfortably padded saddle. The scientists who'd packed in around him immediately threw a barrage of questions at him.

"What was it like? . . . What did they do out there? What did they do to *you* out there? . . . How did you learn the language so quickly? . . . How did they learn ours so quickly? . . . How did they avoid the search parties for so long? . . . How? . . . Why? . . . When? . . ."

"Slowly, gentlesirs. I will—" He paused, suddenly dizzy.

Wuu stepped close. "Leave the youth alone for now. Can't you sense his exhaustion? Doubtless he is weak from hunger as well."

Ryo looked gratefully up at the poet, made a third-degree gesture of assent. "I am far from starving, though it would be wonderful to have a good soup. I've had little but meat and raw greens for a month."

"Then they are omnivorous like us?" one scientist inquired anxiously. "It seemed thus because they ate much of what we supplied them, but it is helpful to have it confirmed by nonlaboratory experience."

"I said, no questions," Wuu broke in firmly.

But Ryo gestured his confirmation. "Yes, though they take their meat largely in burnt chunks and not in proper soup or stew."

There was muttering among the assembled researchers at this fresh assurance of alien oddity.

"They don't boil it or cook it with any other liquids?"

"Not that I saw."

"But they eat soups and stews here," another pointed out.

"It may not have been by choice," Ryo told her. "When one is in prison, one eats what is supplied." There, let them ponder that one, he thought.

After a few additional questions Wuu began to shove officials from the chamber. A hot meal was delivered that was among the finest Ryo had ever enjoyed. Upon devouring it he had a second and then a third serving. Following that he lay down on the sleeping lounge provided, the warm feeling induced by the food overpowering his excitement, and fell into a deep sleep from which he did not awaken for over a full day.

After rising and performing hygiene he was ready to face his interrogators. Apparently someone had decided that it would be better not to swamp the unfortunate wanderer with a hundred questioners at once, so only a half-dozen assembled opposite Ryo in the discussion chamber. Each brought audio and video recorder units integrated with autoscrolls. Two were not much older than he, while the other four were clearly experienced elders. Wuu was present at his own insistence.

"It's not necessary," Ryo had argued. "I can handle things."

"If not for me you wouldn't be here," the poet had replied. "I feel it my responsibility to see that you are not intimidated."

"If not for me, *you* wouldn't be here."

"I have acquired sufficient material to keep me composing for the remainder of my life," Wuu declared. "Such heady rhythms and couplets and stanzas as have never been heard. They will shock the civilized worlds. I owe you that. Time enough to work later." He gestured toward the saddled group. "These sirs and ladies wait patiently, yet their brains fester with curiosity." A couple shifted uneasily at the poet's words but waited their turn. "I would not let them wake you."

"For which I am very grateful," Ryo admitted. "I am awake and ready now, so let them ask what they will."

Ryo accepted the questions slowly, sharing his knowledge of the aliens freely and imparting it with as much pleasure as the scientists seemed to feel in receiving it.

"The business of communication came about almost accidentally," he informed them. "Furthermore, if you use lungs, mandibles, and spicules carefully, you can duplicate their language quite well." He demonstrated with a few words that he was especially good at, and was rewarded when a couple of the researchers who'd been inscribing information suddenly looked up as startled as if one of the aliens had just strode into the room.

"Do that again," one of them requested.

They listened while Ryo repeated the phrase and added several others. "It is difficult, but by no means impossible," he said. "They do seem, however, better able to master our
129

language than we theirs. Yet I venture to say it can be done. I've no doubt an experienced linguist such as yourself," and he gestured at the Thranx who'd asked him to repeat the sounds, "could do far better."

"Let me try." The researcher listened. On his second attempt he made the noise comprehensible. It had taken Ryo many more attempts than two to voice the term that clearly, but communication was the elder's specialty. He should have thrown away his machines.

The others had to break in or the discussion would have quickly been monopolized by an impromptu language lesson.

"Pressure of circumstances," the elder commented. "Foolish of us not to realize it."

"They are mammalian," said one of the younger scientists, whose name was Repleangel. "We've already established that. However, they are almost completely bare of fur. Most extraordinary."

"We thought at first," one of the other scientists said, "that it might be due to a seasonal variation."

"I don't think so," Ryo said. "I saw no evidence for it. Devoid of fur or not, their ability to withstand extreme cold is unarguable."

"From our point of view, not necessarily theirs," said Rep.

"They were always cold, but never dangerously so," Ryo continued. "I often saw them remove portions of their extensive clothing to expose their naked, furless bodies to the air while they cleaned themselves. I would guess that the climate they would consider ideal must average some ten to twenty degrees cooler than our own. Furthermore, they seem to have no need whatsoever for moisture in the air. They must therefore find the environment you have produced in their room both overly hot and humid."

"Are you certain of this lack of need for humidity?"

"All I can say is that in this polar region my lungs would have cracked without the moisture pack I wore. The monsters had no such device and seemed to thrive. I still shudder to think of their breathing that untreated air. I venture to say they could even survive on the worlds of the AAnn, which are notoriously dry if pleasantly warm. That is another factor which makes them valuable allies."

As he said the last his gaze went sideways to the sixth questioner. So far the military representative had asked nothing. He did not react visibly to Ryo's last comment any more than he had to any of the previous ones. He simply sat in his saddle and monitored his instruments.

Ryo let it pass. At least the thought had been planted.

The questions went on and on. "How many sexes do they have?"

"Two, like us."

"Male and female?"

"Yes."

"Do they lay eggs or bear their young alive?"

"I have no idea. That wasn't a question that entered into general conversation."

"Do they have sexual taboos?"

"Your line of questioning strikes me as peculiar, elder."

"They cook their meat by burning it over an open fire?"

"Their cooking facilities were restricted. Maybe they require the additional carbon. Or it might be purely a ritual thing. I never asked."

"Is their vision comparable to ours? They utilize only those two simple single-lensed eyes."

"It seems to be. They can see much farther, I think, but not as well up close or in the dark."

Then came the voice of the military observer, speaking for the first time, in a soft whistle. "They took energy rifles from two of the guards."

"Something I meant to ask," Ryo said quickly. "Was anyone injured during their escape?"

"Injured, yes, but fortunately not killed. As you've noticed, they are physically more massive than we. Their balance is unexpectedly good."

"Yes, I noticed that right away," Ryo admitted.

"They are not as vulnerable to a severe blow as we are," the military elder went on, "but they are far more susceptible to damage from cuts and scrapes. Their thin exoderm is incredibly fragile. However, if it is torn it heals far more rapidly than a chiton break. There are pluses and minuses to such a structure."

"Beauty is not one of the pluses," commented one of the two younger scientists, adding a gesture of third-degree disgust.

"The two guards," the tenth-level officer continued, "were merely stunned during the escape, when their rifles were taken. The planning was admirable. They set off two explosions—"

"We heard them both," Wuu said.

"They were set to create a diversion. This was accomplished. Those who misinterpreted the situation have already been disciplined. The creatures took, as I said, two energy rifles, yet did not use them." He shifted in his saddle, putting a little urgency into his tone. "You said you observed them in use?"

"Yes," Ryo replied. "I'm sure they studied the weapons around them before settling on the rifles. Despite having only two arms and hands, they seemed to manage quite well. I have no doubt that had the circumstances required it, they could have employed them against soldiers as efficiently as they did against game."

The officer did not seem surprised at this, simply entered it into his recorder. "Did they talk at all about their home world or about their vessels?"

"Nothing about their planet of origin save that it was colder than Hivehom seemed to be. Little about their ship except that the principles behind its method of propulsion seemed similar to ours. Neither of them is an engineer."

"Anything about weapons, military strength, or posture?"

Ryo had been waiting for that question from the time the officer had taken his saddle. Nevertheless, he was surprised at the resentment he felt when it was finally asked.

"Nothing whatsoever. They are explorers. Their sole concern and principal subject of conversation was survival. Military matters were not mentioned."

The officer mumbled something half audible. ". . . couldn't expect much . . ." Then louder, "For your own information, we found nothing during our study of their ship to hint they are especially advanced militarily. What we have been able to glean of their social structure indicates they are not, for example, organized in a paramilitary society like the AAnn."

"I could have told you that," Ryo said confidently.

"However, they display certain worrisome characteristics of both social and individual temperament."

"I don't understand, elder." Ryo was uncertain how to interpret the officer's last statement. "I've already told you that they thought we were the ones who'd attacked them. They are more than ready—I would, even say anxious—to form an alliance with us against the AAnn. This despite unfortunate differences of shape. They find us only slightly less disconcerting physically than we find them."

"That is difficult to believe," the second young researcher murmured.

One of the elders scolded him. "That is not a scientific attitude, Drin."

"I know it's not, but I cannot so easily wipe out thousands of years of mental conditioning. They are mammals, no matter how similar their minds might be. Soft of exterior and flexible of form. My insides turn whenever I have to look at them." He swiveled to eye Ryo.

"I understand you actually engaged in physical contact with them, even to the point of extending formal farewells."

"They are not at all that repulsive," Ryo insisted. "It's merely a matter of seeing them as people. As I've mentioned, they feel the same way about the tiny arthropods on their own worlds. We are each the stuff of the other's nightmares. Those are primitive attitudes that both races must fight to overcome. There is no logic to them."

"All of which I understand," Drin admitted without offense. "Still, thousands of years of nightmare . . . We are professionals here, used to dealing with the incredible and outré." He surveyed his colleagues. "How do you think the populace will react to the existence of these beings? And if what you say is true," he said to Ryo, "these monsters will have similar problems on their own world of Earth."

"Odd," one of the elders commented, "that they should name their home planet after the ground when in fact they live above it, exposed to the open sky—or so you tell us." He turned to Ryo.

"There are many such fascinations awaiting us," Ryo told her confidently, "as soon as formal contact is opened." The words of the officer returned to haunt him. "You said certain characteristics worried you. What characteristics?"

Silence reigned in the chamber. Ryo studied his questioners curiously. "They are allies, you know. Or will be soon."

More silence. Several of the scientists looked away. The others did not.

"We can never let them leave here, of course," one of the elders said finally. "Surely you realize that."

"I do not. That's absurd. How do we open negotiations with them if they are not allowed to return home to begin discussions and make introductions.?"

"There will be no introductions," the military observer remarked quietly. "Not for a long time. Not with this group."

"But . . . these are the people who can make us so strong the AAnn will not dare prowl among our colonies. Their presence here is indication enough they are a technologically advanced race."

"Of that we never had the least doubt," the officer informed him. "That is one of the things that troubles us."

"You *have* to let them go. It's indecent to keep imprisoned those who've done you no harm. I've talked with them—two of them, anyway. I know them. They are ready to be friends."

"So they have told you," said the elders. "Are you a qualified xenopsych then, that you can positively interpret their motives?"

"They were telling me the truth." Ryo struggled to contain his anger and frustration. What was wrong with these elders? At least two of them wore the black star of Eint. Did that stand for nothing here? "They had no reason to lie to me."

"No reason by your reasoning, perhaps, but what of their own?"

"I spent quarter months with them, in a difficult survival situation. Once communication was opened they were no more than cautious toward me. There was no continuing hostility. After a while there was honest friendship. So much so that they allowed me to persuade them to return."

"We are aware of that," Drin said, "and very grateful to you for doing so. Not only was their escape scientifically disruptive, but had you somehow made your way south into more populated regions, your companions could have precipitated a panic."

"I still don't see what you're all so afraid of."

"We've had a chance to study them for some time, in a

closed environment," the elder spokesman said. "The results," he hesitated significantly, "do not hold out much promise for interspecies cooperation."

The military observer was more direct. "When they were first settled here and placed under continuous observation, it was immediately evident their social relationships are—well, disturbing."

"What would you expect," Ryo argued. "They thought you were the ones who'd attacked their ship."

The officer made a gesture of denial. "We treated them kindly, realizing they might not be allies of the AAnn. It was their reaction to one another that was so unexpected, not their reaction toward us." His tone filled with remembered amazement.

"They fought among themselves. It's still hard to believe. Here they were, twelve aliens trapped by possibly hostile creatures, yet their anger was vented not so much toward us as each other. Though we could not understand their language, battering a companion into unconsciousness can only be interpreted in one way.

"One actually damaged a companion so badly that it required medical treatment. When that was provided their attitude toward us softened visibly, but they continued to act in an unrelentingly hostile manner toward one another.

"It is the opinion of the behavioral psychs who have had them under surveillance that their actions suggest a racial paranoia of heretofore unimagined dimensions. Compared to these creatures, the AAnn are models of harmonious cooperation. Do we really want to ally ourselves closely with such a race?"

"But they showed no such tendencies with me," Ryo said, bewildered.

"It is a fact that certain mammals act far differently in clusters than they do when isolated," Drin said somberly. "They are rather like subcritical fission masses—harmless when kept apart, explosive when brought together. We do not know what the mental 'critical mass' of these creatures might be, but I would not like to be around when it is reached."

"It is the considered opinion of the xenospsych staff that the entire race may be collectively psychotic," the elder spokesman said.

"There may be other explanations," Ryo protested. "The pressure they've been under as prisoners, their confinement underground when they prefer the surface . . ."

Drin was making a gesture of negativity. "We've allowed for that. The signs are still there."

"You see now," the officer said gently, "why we cannot possibly let them go. They now know the location of Hivehom. These are a sophisticated, space-traversing folk. This group is composed of specialists in exploration. Surely some of them would be able to find their way back here. We cannot possibly let so dangerous and volatile a race return home knowing the location of our mother world while we know nothing of theirs. They destroyed all their records and charts during the AAnn attack, you see. Further evidence of their paranoia."

"No more so than you've just admitted to," Ryo noted.

"Perhaps." The officer was not offended.

"But I tell you, gentlesirs, that I *know* these people."

"You know two of them," Drin pointed out. "That is hardly sufficient evidence by which to classify an entire race."

"Maybe not. I'm no statistician. But I know true friendship when it is offered to me, and I have received that from two of these beings. I can probably gain the confidence of the rest of them if you'll give me some freedom with them."

"I would hope so," the elder spokesman said. "We earnestly desire your help, Ryozenzuzex. Your companion," and he indicated Wuu, "has explained your history."

"Better to provide voluntarily what will become known anyway," the poet said. Ryo saw no reason to argue that.

"We can notify your family and clan," the elder continued. "It will be explained that you are working on a government project of great importance. No lies will be told. We will merely exercise judicious concealment. They should be quite satisfied. Meanwhile, you will be given as free an antenna as possible to work among these creatures."

"Then why not let me tell them they can return home?" Ryo wondered.

"I am interested in a species of carnivore called the produbia," one of the elders said. "It lives in the jungles of

Colophon. While I am fascinated by its eating habits I have no desire to explore its method of digestion from the inside. We will remain friendly with these creatures, but cautious."

"I would rather," the military observer interrupted, "risk the loss of a potential new ally than expose Hivehom to the attentions of a race that cannot even control its most primitive instincts."

Ryo's initial reaction to these comments was barely controlled fury. This gave way gradually to rationalization. The attitude of the government, as represented by the six questioners in the chamber, was dreadfully wrongheaded. But there was nothing he, Ryo, could do about it. The aliens would never be allowed to leave.

That would mean that the Thranx would not gain the benefits of interspecies cooperation. Neither would the monsters. As to the business about their being subject to racial paranoia and homicidal tendencies, he simply refused to believe it. The xenopsychs were misinterpreting their data. Machines again, he thought bitterly. Statistics.

No readout would ever convince him that the time he'd spent in the wilderness with Bonnie and Loo had been filled with deceiving data. But for now all he could do was be patient and try to make friends with their associates.

"Yes, I'll help you. It's my duty, of course."

"We knew that would be your reaction." The elder spokesman was most gratified as he checked his chronometer. "I had not realized we'd been so long. We do not wish to strain you."

"I am fine," Ryo admitted honestly.

"No. Enough for now," one of the other elders said. "We can reconvene tomorrow."

"I need to meet the other monsters," Ryo said.

"Of course. As soon as you wish," Drin told him. "Quarters have been prepared for you. You will have all the assistance you need. I envy you. I too would like to be able to study these creatures and interact with them at first hand. For now, however, we have to rely on you to interpret."

Not only because I can communicate with them so well, but because I'm the only one they trust, Ryo thought bitterly.

* * *

That evening, Wuu discovered him resting on his sleeping lounge in front of a viewer. The poet had been working hard and had filled nearly a whole chip with prepoetry. His pleasure was dampened by something in Ryo's attitude. He'd come to know the young agronomist quite well during their travels and he was concerned about him. He'd been subjected to unusual pressures for one of barely midage and those pressures would intensify in the months to come.

"Greetings, Wuu." Ryo looked over as he switched off the viewer. "How is your composing coming?"

"Extraordinarily well. The guild will be well pleased. And what of you, my young friend? I worry about you. You have been thrown into a situation few are prepared to cope with."

"I seem to thrive on it," Ryo replied, "although at first contact I think I reacted much as a larva would."

The poet slid onto a saddle opposite the lounge and sighed deeply, the air whistling out his spicules in a long gasp. "I will remain if you wish me to, although they have no need of me here."

"I would like that. I need someone familiar nearby, for a while, at least."

"That is understandable. These scientists are a little better than bureaucrats, but not much. I suppose the nature of their positions does not encourage individualistic thought."

"It certainly doesn't," Ryo agreed. "For example, anyone with a modicum of hive sense would see that we have to let these people return to their home world so that formal exchanges between us may begin. Don't you agree?"

The old poet stared back at him. "Certainly not, and it's about time you started purging your own head of such addled notions. They are the major reason I worry about you."

For a moment Ryo simply could not reply. "But . . . these will become our allies, our friends against the AAnn."

"Did you not hear the findings of the researchers, the opinion of that officer?" Wuu asked. "As an individualist, I can empathize somewhat with these creatures. Naturally they would like to return home. I would want the same were I in their position, I would also understand our position." He leaned out of the saddle and added a gesture of fourth-degree emphasis. "The safety of our entire race is at stake here, Ryo. These are a powerful and dangerous people."

"I'm sure the AAnn will think so."

"Are you such a master diplomat?" Wuu snapped. "Are you then completely confident they would ally themselves with us because of a single incident involving one ship and its crew?"

"There is always some risk in such a situation," Ryo admitted, "but it must be chanced. We cannot hide ourselves from them forever. Eventually contact will be established. If we take the initiative now we can avoid a potentially disastrous misunderstanding. Future contacts might not begin so auspiciously.

"And what of the AAnn? They are as masterful at diplomacy as they are at slaughter. What if they were to realize their error in attacking this first ship and contact these people before us and instead of attacking them again, forge an alliance with them against us? What would be our position then?"

"All unlikely and all a problem for the future," Wuu replied, though it was obvious the scenario Ryo presented concerned him. "For all we know they may lie on the other side of the galaxy and we may never encounter them again. The universe, my boy, is vast."

"If, as the military observer says, their ship's propulsive system is not very different from ours then they cannot dwell very far, in interstellar terms, from Hivehom."

"We know nothing of their life spans," the poet pointed out. "Indeed, we still know little about them. That ignorance is yet another reason why we cannot let them leave."

"Such a position is morally indefensible," Ryo insisted.

"I beg to differ with you, my earnest young friend. It is eminently defensible, from a moral as well as military standpoint. You would feel differently if you had seen them fighting among themselves, much as our distant ancestors used to do. A group of Thranx placed in a similar position would be mutually supportive and calm, not hysterical and violently combative." He made a gesture of disbelief. "It is quite unbelievable. They possess dominant-internal traits they are not even aware of. Such ritualized combat is a part of their basic nature. How could we possibly be allies? Mentally as well as physically we are nothing alike."

"Don't you see," Ryo argued, "doesn't anyone see that that is precisely what makes such a union worthwhile? The differences would complement each other. What is there to be gained from mating with someone exactly like yourself? There is never anything new, never any surprises."

"Surprises are delightful," the poet agreed, "in art and music. Surprises are wonderful in science. When the destiny and survival of your entire race are at stake, I am not so sure that surprise is welcome. Even were what you say to be so, what of their psychoses?"

"Every race has its distinctive problems," Ryo admitted. "We are not perfect, either."

"No, but neither are we inherently homicidal, as these creatures appear to be. While they might act quite sanely as individuals or even in small groups, it is en masse that we would deal with them through treaties. There is simply too much at stake to take such a chance.

"Besides, I disagree with you when you say they have something worthwhile to offer us. From what I have seen, an alliance between us would work largely to their advantage. They are a clumsy, primitive people whose technological achievements have outstripped their moral evolution."

"They are being treated as prisoners, looked upon by many with disgust. That is hardly an atmosphere conducive to cultural understanding," Ryo argued. "They must have all sorts of things to offer us, from the arts through the sciences. This in addition to military alliance against the AAnn."

"I am sorry, my boy. The only thing I've noticed about them that has made much of an impression on me so far is their violence and their smell, both of which I believe we could survive without. I am surprised you cannot see this."

"Perhaps—perhaps you're right. Perhaps I've been deluding myself. The days out there in the clith . . ."

"The strain is quite understandable," Wuu said sympathetically. "You have nothing to apologize for."

"I guess you're right. Surely all the specialists cannot be wrong. I need . . . just some time. The excitement of the moment of contact, of mutual supportiveness out there . . ."

"I know it is discouraging, but this is the time for calm consideration of all the facts, not just those you may have been exposed to personally, my boy. You were not alone in your thinking, by the way. Many of the scientific study group favored expanding contact with these people. But at the last, when time came to make the actual decision, they too realized it was better to err on the side of caution. Enthusiasm always gives way under the assault of reason and good judgment.

"You have come a long way from the fields of Paszex. It must be discouraging to see the adventure come to an end, but eventually youthful enthusiasms must give way to reality. The reality is that such contact is not regarded as advantageous by the majority of elders here. I am pleased you have matured sufficiently to realize the truth of this."

"What you say about my enthusiasm is undeniably true," Ryo quietly confessed. He sighed and his thorax pulsed. "At least I will be permitted to remain to study these fascinating creatures further."

"It is not a question of permission, as you well know. The authorities actively solicit your assistance. It is conceivable that had you not agreed to do so, they might have invoked security edicts to keep you here. Your experiences are unique, as is your relationship with the monsters.

"At least you will have one nongovernment friend here while I remain, though flexible and ingratiating as you are, I've no doubt you will soon have many friends among the staff."

"It will be comforting to know you are around," Ryo told him. "Such discussion as we have just concluded is exhilarating as well as enlightening."

"For me as well. More material for the massive volume I intend to compile that will detail our entire journey. An arduous work, but one which I look forward to completing. It will be a monument."

They continued the discussion, arguing animatedly and enjoyably, as they made their way down the corridors. Their rooms were located close to the large chamber where the aliens were being kept.

As Ryo learned more of the layout of what was called X Section he was able to see how the authorities had managed to conceal the aliens. The xenology section was completely independent of the main installation. It had its own supply and power facilities, its own staff, even its own entrances and exits.

Only three narrow corridors connected it with the rest of the base, which had been built as part of the planetary defense system. Those Thranx who staffed the latter prepared for an attack that they hoped would never come, blissfully ignorant of the sensitive research being carried out close at hand.

Ryo relaxed in the hygienic corner of his comparatively luxurious quarters and cleaned himself with the damp scented cloth.

Wuu had immediately accepted Ryo's conversion to the majority opinion. The old poet was clever, even brilliant, but his brilliance did not make him a master of deception. Ryo was certain others were assigned to watch him.

Poor Wuu, he thought. A composer of the Eint order. For all his imagination and abilities he could see no further than his own specialty. Wuu was a poet, and a masterful one. He was also an elder whose thinking had become as predictable as the midseason rains. Petrification of the imagination seemed to have infected everyone of any authority. Ryo was coming to believe he was the only one able to spark a new thought, a fresh idea.

That was only natural. That had been his talent since larvahood. Yes, *that's* my profession, he thought excitedly. *That's* what I was intended to do—to initiate newness, to break convention. All this time, all these years, he'd sublimated his real profession by breaking jungle ground, when the topography he should have been attacking was that of conventional wisdom.

If Wuu was convinced Ryo had come around to the accepted way of thinking, then there was no reason to suppose the staff scientists would think otherwise. But Ryo would still have to be patient, would have to bide his time. He smiled inwardly. I've done that before. This time, however, the unknown territory I have to cross is somewhat greater then the distance between Paszex and Daret.

This time he would also not be fleeing by himself.

XI Arranging a private conversation with Loo and Bonnie was less difficult than he'd imagined. When the monsters understood what was wanted they simply organized a group singalong. The rest of the monsters generated sufficient noise to drown out the most sensitive directional pickup. In addition, the new phenomenon of collective sound kept the fascinated researchers busy at their instrumentation. The volume was much greater than an equal number of Thranx could have produced.

"This is a tremendous burden you've taken on yourself," Loo told Ryo softly. "You're going against the considered opinion of all your superiors."

"They're not my superiors."

"Your elders then," Bonnie said. She looked away from him, a gesture he'd learned indicated general uncertainty of approximately the third degree. "It may be, Ryo, that they are correct. I realize I'm hurting our own cause by saying that, but this is not the time for prevarication. Throughout human history, we've often questioned our own motives for fighting among ourselves. Many times we cannot come up with satisfactory explanations for what we do. It may be that, as your psychtechs insist, we are inherently homicidal."

"Then this alliance will be of more benefit to you than you can imagine," Ryo told her. "We Thranx are not very excitable. We are very good at reasoning things through and seeing to the heart of misunderstandings. Perhaps what you've always needed are friends who will not fight with you, but who are ever available to explain and to soothe."

"Perhaps." She looked back at him. "I do know one thing. Regardless of what our governments decide to do, we three have consummated our own little alliance." She reached out a hand to touch one of Ryo's truhands.

He grasped it firmly, having learned the significance of the gesture many days ago. There was considerably more power in her fingers than in his, though with a foothand he could have matched her grip. She was careful not to bruise the more delicate upper digits.

"Our ship," Loo whispered, "is still functioning. It's in a synchronous orbit above us right now."

"How do you know that?" Ryo asked, a little startled.

143

"Because while Bonnie and I were free, they ferried some of our friends to it to answer questions about design and function. Certain queries were answered. Others were not. There was no coercion."

"Naturally not." Ryo was upset at the very thought.

"Our people are different," Loo murmured. "Anyway, our shipmates report no dismantling of components. Not yet, anyway. We'd nearly completed repair of the damage the AAnn had done to the drive when your own exploration ship stumbled into us. Our engineers are confident they can finish the few repairs remaining in sufficiently short time to make an escape feasible."

"How are we to reach your ship? I'm an agricultural expert. I know nothing of astrophysical matters."

"But that's not a problem!" Bonnie told him excitedly. "They wanted to study our mechanics and design with advanced diagnostic equipment, so they induced Alexis and Elvira," she pointed to two of the wailing monsters, "to bring one of our shuttles down. It's right here, in the base."

"Separate hangar," Ryo muttered, "to conceal it from the general personnel."

"Our friends argued about it. Eventually Alexis agreed because they threatened to take the shuttle apart inside our ship. Getting to the shuttle will be the problem. I'm sure it must be under heavy guard."

"Not necessarily."

Loo made the frown gesture with his rubbery mouthparts. "I don't understand. Why wouldn't it be?"

"What reason is there to guard a shuttle? There is only need to guard its pilots. You are here, the ship is elsewhere. Keeping you apart is security enough. No Thranx, of course, would think of assisting a bunch of monsters."

"Thanks," Loo said drily. "Except you, of course."

"And I am possibly mad. By helping you, I will become something of a monster to my own people." He paused reflectively, added in a different tone, "You realize, of course, that if there is no resultant alliance, that if friendship does not materialize between our races, then I will be effectively dead."

Neither of them said anything.

"Excuse me," he said apologetically. "That was impolite.

Those are not thoughts to be inflicted on others. This is my own free decision. Nothing compels me to do this.

"I demand only one thing in return for my assistance. That if our escape should be opposed, under no circumstances will you or any of your hivemates kill to facilitate it."

They looked uncomfortable. "We can promise for ourselves," Bonnie agreed, "but I don't know about the others. If we're close to making it back to the *Seeker*, I'm not sure one or two would not hesitate to use any method to insure our successful boarding."

"Precisely such traits," Ryo noted solemnly, "have convinced Thranx scientists that it would be unwise to expand contact between us. You *must* impress this on your companions. Opinion is still uncertain among some members of the research staff. Killing would forever solidify the feelings against you and would make further contact impossible."

"We'll do our best," Loo assured him. "We'll try and convince the others."

"Who is clanmother among you?" He made a quick gesture of embarrassment. "I am sorry. I forgot. You have neither clan nor hive organization. You go from family to some sort of loose tribal federation. It must make you feel very alone sometimes. I think that may be part of your problem."

"Maybe we are loners compared to the Thranx," Loo said, "but I think we have more individual freedom. Your own experiences are proof of that."

"From this undisciplined freedom comes perhaps your tendencies to—but enough philosophy." He was concerned that their long conversation might attract the attention of the hidden researchers.

"I shall try to divine the location of your shuttlecraft, ascertain the difficulties involved in reaching it, and decide on a propitious time to attempt an escape. Since your first successful attempt, security measures have been strengthened, I am told. You are all closely and constantly watched. It will be more difficult this time."

"That's only to be expected," Loo noted, "but we didn't have an ally working for us outside before, either."

"Very true." A strange feeling rippled through Ryo, a combination of the way both monsters had stared at him out of their vitreous single-lensed eyes and the way Loo had pronounced the word "ally."

Days passed, stretched inexorably into months. Eventually Ryo was allowed to communicate freely with his family. From Fal to sire to clanmates, all were pleased but puzzled. They'd been told that he was engaged in very important, serious work for the government. This had been openly accepted.

For his part Ryo was pleased to learn that his initial perfidy in ignoring family and clan directives had been put aside. All were content to accept that he was doing useful work and that he would return home when feasible.

As the days rolled on and the monsters were more tranquil and cooperative, the authorities relaxed their surveillance somewhat, but not even Ryo's continued assurances that the monsters had come to terms with their fate was enough to convince every member of the observation-and-study staff.

Most of the monsters could now speak some Thranx. A few Thranx were struggling to acquire fluency in monster speech, though this was deliberately and subtly discouraged on Loo and Bonnie's orders.

Ryo was given a formal position with the research team and the title of assistant consultant. The income momentarily took his breath away. It was considerably more than he accumulated as board member for the Inmot Company's Paszex operations. He felt guilt at accepting such position and compensation when he was spending most of his time planning to contravene everything he was being paid to do, but he accepted it all with apparent gratefulness.

A time came when even Wuu was ready to return to Willow-wane. The old poet assured Ryo that once his affairs were back to normal he would take the time to travel to Paszex so he could meet with Ryo's family and assure them of his good health in person.

In addition to his research work and mastering the human language Ryo also casually acquired a thorough knowledge of X Section and all security measures. The monsters' shuttlecraft was located in a small hangar nearby. It was subject to intense study by Thranx engineers. Occasionally several closely guarded monsters would be allowed aboard to explain design functions and Ryo would accompany them as interpreter.

During such visits security surrounding and on board the shuttle quadrupled. Given such precautions, it took Ryo some time to formulate a plan promising even a slight chance of success.

The fugitives would ignore the corridors save for one. Since Loo and Bonnie's escape, everything larger than a water pipe was constantly monitored. This time, all would flee quickly topside, then cross to another exit and use it to reenter the base as close as possible to the hangar. Ryo hoped the authorities wouldn't consider the possibility that once outside, the aliens would then try to escape back *inside*.

It was difficult to be patient. Ryo's pleas for time were backed up by the burrow master—"Captain"—of the aliens, Elvirasanchez. She did not talk much, but her words were listened to.

Eventually Fourth Season came to an end with the festival of Teirquelot, a cause for celebration among the base personnel. At an outpost as dreary as Scd-Clee, holidays were taken seriously.

Cannisters of sleep gas had been installed by security personnel around the aliens' chamber, which precaution was intended to prevent any alien rampage. Ryo planned to turn the security measure to his friends' advantage.

Many months had passed since Loo and Bonnie's escape. Relaxed security combined with the holiday allowed Ryo to slip from room to room without question. No one saw him readjust the cannister control valves, even though several timeparts of nerve-racking activity were required to complete the job. Now, when the cannisters were activated, they would spew their soporific contents not into the monsters' quarters but into the surrounding areas.

Only one corridor was to be left ungassed because it led to an emergency escape ramp that ascended to the surface. Ryo worried some about the aliens' tolerance, but the humans assured him even Deep Cold would not prevent their making the short run to the next exitway.

Using ventilation towers, Ryo had triangulated the position of the hangar holding the monsters' shuttlecraft, then he selected the closest exit port visible. Once inside again, their precise location would determine their next moves. To his unpracticed eye, the exit port seemed quite near to the shuttle hangar.

He would wait until the guard had been reduced to its minimum, which would probably coincide with the height of celebration. The monsters would feign sound sleep inside their chamber. Then, appropriately masked, Ryo would circle the surrounding rooms, opening the gas cannisters everywhere except in the chosen corridor.

If standard procedure held, two guards would be stationed in that corridor, and Ryo would somehow have to neutralize them. It should be easy, for they would not be expecting trouble. But it was still the part of the plan that worried him most.

Once he'd bypassed the instruments that monitored the monsters' body heat, oxygen consumption, and so forth, the escapees would race to the ramp, shut down the warning unit that would indicate it was in use, exit, and run across the frozen landscape to the exit above the hangar. There they would descend, overwhelm whatever guards might be present, and power up their shuttle. The hangar doors would be programmed to open and several minutes after entering the hangar they would lift clear.

At least, that was how the escape was envisioned. Ryo and his friends studied it repeatedly, refining movements, trying to shorten the necessary time. Whether the plan would work or not remained to be seen. There could be no trial run.

It was a particularly dark and cold night. Ryo hurriedly retreated from the observation post, though his presence did not surprise the indifferent guard, who attended to his fiction chips and ignored the consultant. Ryo's peculiar affection for the surface was well known throughout X Section, confirmed by those who'd researched his past.

Omoick, the larger moon, was new and black. Omuick, the smaller, was only half full. That should aid concealment as they made the dangerous run from one exit to the next.

He made his way back toward the study sector, occasionally greeting cheery celebrants. Not all of them were drunk, but all were involved in season-end celebration and little else. A quality that may not facilitate intellectual advancement, he mused, but one which both races shared.

No one questioned Ryo's presence as he ambled from room to room checking instrumentation. Most of the study chambers were empty. A few were temporarily occupied. He waited in those until their inhabitants departed, then quickly activated the altered cannister controls. The sleep gas was odorless and colorless. If you knew it was present you had seconds in which to flee. If not, you quietly succumbed.

He did not have to use the small filter mask he carried in his vest except once when he thought to check a room originally empty.

A young researcher was preparing a report on the conjectured premating nocturnal habits of the monsters. She was having a difficult time because the aliens were not cooperating much in that area. Ryo watched from the corridor as she started to enter her observation room, halted, swayed for an instant, then toppled onto her right side.

Retreating, he closed a corridor barrier, shoved several wads of expanding plastic against it to insure a tight seal. He repeated this with doorways on the opposite side of the corridor. Then he hurried inward, steeling himself.

Only a single guard was mounted where he'd expected two, but this advantage was mitigated when the guard turned and recognized him.

"Good evening, Consultant."

"Good evening." Ryo fought to recall the guard's name. Time was ticking away. "How are they behaving, Eush?"

"Quiet, as always." The guard held his energy rifle loosely as he looked past Ryo. Was some half-gassed scientist staggering down the corridor toward them, waving frantic alarm gestures at the guard?

The corridor was deserted save for the two of them. The guard was gazing longingly, not specifically. "Sounds like everyone else is having a fine time."

"An energetic celebration," Ryo agreed tensely.

"I wish I could join them."

"Why don't you? I've nothing to do this evening. This far from clan and friends I don't feel much like celebrating. I'm qualified to assume watch for you."

"That's very gracious of you." The guard wavered. "But it would be my star for deserting my post. I couldn't possibly, not even on the permission of one so highly regarded as yourself. I thank you, however, for your generous offer."

"As you wish. A shame." He stepped past the guard. Just ahead lay the monsters' holding chamber and the barrier with its multiple-sensor locks. Behind it, twelve monsters feigned sleep. They retained their personal chronometers. Though their time markings and splits differed from normal time, they had been able to coordinate them sufficiently with Ryo's for them to be stirring uneasily by now.

"Those two lovely females waiting back there, for example," Ryo said smoothly, "have accompanied me this far and are anxious for celebratory companionship. See them whispering, the one with the turquoise chiton and her companion of the gilded ovipositors?"

"Where?" The guard stepped cautiously to one side and tried hard to see up the darkened corridor. "Perhaps they might join us here? Nothing was said about my not celebrating at my own post."

"Hello," he called out. "My name is Eushminyowot, friends of the consultant!" He said nothing more because of the weighted cloth that Ryo brought down hard against the back of his skull. The guard fell as silently as those who'd inhaled the sleep gas. His chiton whacked sharply on the hard floor.

"Rest and celebrate in your dreams," Ryo said. Then he hurried the last steps down the passageway and ran the combination of the sensor locks. For a few seconds nothing happened and he wondered frantically if someone had changed the combination without notifying him. Then the door slid slowly into the wall. Standing behind it were a dozen anxious aliens.

For just an instant the sight of their horribly flexible masks looming over him in the dim light sent a stab of fear through Ryo. Then the inherited fears faded as Loo and Elvira stepped out into the corridor, bending low to clear the ceiling. A couple of the monsters exchanged words when they saw the motionless body of the guard.

"Quickly now, we've no time to waste," Ryo said urgently.

"Lead the way. We'll be right behind you." The captain was tall even for a human, Ryo noted.

As they emerged silently into the corridor, Ryo noticed the aliens had armed themselves with pieces of furniture. He said nothing about this because there was no time for arguing.

Ryo staggered slightly as they passed one of the doorways he'd hurriedly sealed. Sleep gas was seeping from behind it despite his work. His head cleared as they rushed past. The monsters did not seem to notice it at all A much stronger dose was required to affect them.

Another couple of turns, up two levels, and they were at the emergency exit. They met no one. Blessed be the celebrants, Ryo thought gratefully, for they shall remain pure in spirit and devoid of knowledge.

It took him a minute to bypass the warning unit. He could only hope that no backup alarm sounded a warning on the central security console as the first was disconnected.

The hatch flipped up and out. There was a soft *flump* as it landed on accumulated clith. Then the party was on the eerie treeless surface that roofed the base. In the distance the treeline was visible, its ghostly ranks marching silently away in the half-light. Only a single shadow marked his emergence. Clith crystals sparkled like gems in the light of Omuick.

Ryo marked their position and pointed the way. The monsters said nothing as they started for the correct exit marker. The hangar lay a modest distance away.

They were perhaps halfway there when the obvious suddenly intruded on Ryo. They had prepared for so many things; speed of progress, the sleep gas, the holiday night, the phases of the moons—he'd forgotten only one thing. His cold-weather gear!

He slowed, the numbness already beginning to overcome him. "You go on," he told Bonnie and Loo as they hung back with him. "You know where the hangar entrance is now and I've told you how to program the cover. I'll wait here."

"Permanently? Not a chance, Consultant," Loo said.

"We need you, Ryo," Bonnie added.

The two massive creatures bent and lifted him between them; they ran with an extraordinary jouncing motion, and he thought for certain he would be sick. His body felt like a vibrating spring by the end of the short run.

They set him down next to the hangar exit. Despite the increasing numbness in his hands he managed to set the second bypass.

If the alarm had been raised it had not yet reached above ground. No high-intensity lights swept the frozen surface in search of them. The hatch cover clicked and flipped open. With the monsters flattened against the ground and watching him, he started down.

The smaller hangar was dimly lit. Ryo paused at the bottom of the ramp and let his dangerously chilled body soak up the warmth. When he was comfortable again he moved forward and peered cautiously around the opening at the end of the ramp. Nothing moved inside the hangar, but he thought he could discern voices far away. They must be on the far side of the hangar, he thought. That meant they could not see anything at this end.

Ahead of him stretched ranks of planetary defense craft. The hangar was a miniature of the vast cavern located in the main base. Armed shuttlecraft were visible farther away. To his right, just beyond the first of the aircraft, was a bulky, awkward shape that had to be the monsters' shuttle.

Hurrying back up the ramp, he confronted a circle of anxious alien faces.

"There are guards about, but so far away I can only hear them. Your shuttle is close by. From what little I could see it seems intact."

"Be our luck," grumbled one of the monsters, "we'll get down safely, get aboard and be all set to blow, and find out they've defueled the engines."

"Relax," Loo advised him. "You said they broke the chemical makeup of the solid fuel components a month ago. They know the stuff's inert until ignition. They've no reason to disassemble anything."

"I'm not talking about reason," the pessimistic monster continued, "I'm talking about luck. We're going to need both to get out of this."

"Let's move," Bonnie said sharply. She started down the ramp.

Ryo caught up and passed her, halted once more at the bottom. There was still no one in sight, but he fretted because the idle voices seemed slightly louder. "I will go first," he announced. He noticed how tightly the monsters were gripping their makeshift weapons. One carried Bush's energy rifle. "And please, no violence."

"Did you tell that to the guard in the corridor," said the engineer named Alexis, "before you clobbered him?"

"It was a careful blow, intended only to incapacitate, not to kill." His tone was sharp, but the engineer was not offended.

Ryo stepped into the open and walked around the single aircraft. Up close, the monsters' shuttle was clearly larger than a comparable Thranx craft, but not unduly so. It fit with room to spare beneath the vaulting ceiling of the hangar.

At first he could find nothing amiss. It was near the end of his check that he discovered a large metal plate dangling from the vessel's stern. Returning to the rampway, he related what he'd seen.

"Sounds like they've been studying the coordinated feed and firing controls," said Javier the engineer. She was a diminutive female not much taller than Ryo.

"We'll just have to fix whatever's been tampered with," Elvira added huskily. "Hopefully it's not serious. We've come this far." She eyed the hangar opening hungrily. "We're not going back to that cage."

Murmurs of assent rose around her.

"I concur. We must take our chances now," Ryo agreed. He led them silently onto the floor.

The boarding ramp was down. Most of the monsters started up but a few technicians, led by Javier, hurried toward the stern where they began working inside the open hatch.

Ryo nervously stood guard nearby. The voices came nearer still, then began to fade again. After what seemed like an eternity a loud metallic *click* sounded from behind him. The monsters had finished their work and were closing up the hatch. Loo and Bonnie waited to greet them at the base of the entry ramp.

"All set," Javier whispered softly. "It looked like they'd just been testing. Nothing seemed out of place." She shrugged, another gesture Ryo had come to recognize. The monsters were incorrect in stating they communicated only with their voices. "We'll have to try it anyhow. We don't have the time to run a detailed inspection."

"Right. Get aboard."

The three monsters climbed the ramp. Loo turned uncomfortably to Ryo. "We don't know how to thank you. You know that. There's really nothing appropriate any of us could say."

"You haven't even reached your ship yet and you're a long way from jumping to Space Plus. It's premature to think of thanking me."

"No, even if this is as far as we get we owe you more than can be put in the words of either language. We'll be standing by for the overheads to open. Are you certain you won't be harmed? You told me it would take them a while to determine for certain that it was you who reset the sleep-gas cannisters, but that guard recognized you."

"It doesn't matter anyway," Ryo replied. "I'm coming with you. The overhead doors have already been programmed. I did that when I first checked your ship for damage." He indicated a nearby computer terminal. "There's no lock or guard on them. No one would expose himself to the air here without orders."

Loo and Bonnie were momentarily speechless.

"Why should I not go with you?" He fought hard to contain his excitement and his nervousness. "My entire life something has pushed me onward, to seek extremes, to learn the unknown. It pushed me into extending friendship to the both of you and then to your companions. It has pushed me to commiting an act of Eint-denial. Why should I not carry it to its next extreme as something inside is forcing me to do?"

"I don't know." Loo looked uncertainly at Bonnie. "I don't have the authority. I . . ."

"Talk to your captain, Elvirasanchez. It will take only a

moment. We have no formal contract, but it might be said that you owe me this."

"I'm still not sure—"

A piercing whistle punctured the resulting silence. Single- and multiple-lensed eyes turned. Three guards stood between an air-defense ship and a shuttle. They were gesturing frantically while whistling and clicking at the top of their range.

Lights winked on inside the monsters' shuttlecraft, blinked several times. A slow whine started from its stern. Somewhere a horn hooted violently and confused whistles rose from all around the hangar.

No time remained for argument. Loo made a gesture Ryo did not recognize, then shouted, "Come on! We'll argue about it later!"

Even as they hurried up the boarding ramp, it was starting to retract. Inside, everything was confused and out of place to Ryo's eyes. Monsters moved rapidly around him, through corridors far too high and narrow. Everything seemed backward, distorted, an imager's nightmare vision of what a real ship should look like.

He stayed close to Loo and Bonnie, afraid of losing himself in that distorted interior. Loo threw himself into one of the tiny saddles and began exchanging complex words with another monster seated nearby. Despite months of study the phrases' meaning eluded Ryo.

"They've just seen us," the other monster told Loo after concluding the barrage of technical talk. "What about the hangar doors?"

"No time!" came the word from over the internal communicator. Ryo recognized the captain's tone.

Alien words flew around the chamber. "What's the bug doing here? . . . Wants to come with us . . . What, but why? . . . Wants to . . . worry about it later . . . No time . . . How do we get out of here? . . . One way, hang on! . . . Open and closed! . . ." And other exclamations Ryo had neither the wherewithal nor the time to translate.

Thunder rattled the shuttle and Ryo found himself thrown to the deck. The sudden movement was not taken out of disregard for his safety; several monsters were likewise dumped on their abdomens.

Something under Ryo's feet went *rhooom!* and for a moment every light in the chamber went out. He fought to regain his balance. It sounded like the ship had been hit. In fact, the opposite was true.

The guard in the fringe tower had reacted to the base-wide alarm, but no one had bothered to tell him what the alarm was about. He thought it likely to be another drill.

This illusion was violently and unexpectedly dispelled by the geyser of metal and plastic fragments that erupted from the far side of the base. Without warning, a ship hung in the center of the falling shower of splinters. It was bigger than any shuttle he'd ever seen and showed only two wings. A bright glow emanated from one end.

Then the roar reached him and that at least was familiar. The ship jumped as if kicked, rising skyward at an extreme angle. So stunned and enthralled was he by the sight that he forgot to activate his own alarm. Sometimes it is not planning but inspired confusion that is the best aid to escape.

The light of half a moon shining down on it, the *Seeker*'s shuttle rapidly accelerated into the cold, cloudy night air of Hivehom.

XII There was nothing aboard like the acceleration saddles he'd lain in on the shuttles that had lifted him from Willow-wane and dropped him down to Hivchom. Human saddles were short and angled in on themselves. He could not possibly straddle one.

The monsters were hastily strapping themselves into their own units except for one who staggered forward. Forgotten, Ryo chose a place on the deck where two walls joined and spread himself as flat as he could. With foothands he grasped the support pylons of two monsters' saddles.

He worried overmuch. No radical maneuvers were performed and the steady acceleration was not difficult to bear. Soon the shuttle was coasting in free space.

That did present some problems. The monsters' shuttle-craft was not large enough to retain artificial gravity, so Ryo went floating past several of the securely strapped-in crew. Loo unbuckled his upper torso and reached up to grab one of Ryo's flailing hind legs, then pulled him down to where he could obtain a grip on the back of the monster's saddle with all four hands. From there he was able to manage reasonably well.

The voices of the pilots reached them via the communicators. Again Ryo recognized that of the captain.

"I don't see a thing," she said. She paused, then, "There's nothing up here. Not a damn thing, not even a shuttle."

"What about the *Seeker?*" an unseen questioner asked.

"Coming up on her." A longer pause, broken by a third voice.

"She looks untouched. I don't think they've tried taking her apart."

"Why should they?" Elvira responded. "For all they knew it could be booby-trapped."

"I don't know," the second voice began. "They don't strike me as a suspicious people. Though I don't see how they could be anything else after years of sparring with the AAnn." A brief silence. "God, she's beautiful. I never thought I'd call her that."

"I never thought you'd call anything that if it wasn't female," Elvira responded. This was followed by human laughter.

I must begin thinking of them as "humans" and not as monsters, he told himself firmly. Diplomacy must be done.

"Hey, I wonder if any of them are on board?"

"I don't know," the third voice commented. "We'll find out soon enough. In any case, we've got our weapons system back now. I'm sure as hell not going peacefully back to that hellhole. If they try and stop us there'll be bug juice over half the stellar objects between here and Centaurus space."

Ryo stiffened mentally, forced himself to shrug the comment off. The speaker doubtless did not know Ryo was on board. Nevertheless the viciousness in the human's statement unsettled him. He began to wonder if he might not have overreached himself. Perhaps these creatures were as duplicitous as the AAnn. Morally he was still confident he'd done the right thing. However, there were a few concerns that overrode even morality.

There was a dull thump. Hanging as he was, Ryo could not obtain a decent view through one of the indecently rounded ports, but humans were unstrapping themselves. Using guidelines, they pulled themselves toward the rear airlock. With his four hands Ryo was able to maneuver on the guidelines even better than his companions. Bonnie complimented him on his agility.

"I've only been in space twice before," he told her as they pulled themselves down the narrow, circular docking tube toward increasing gravity and the alien mother ship, "but I've always been dexterous."

"I've often wished for an extra pair of hands," Loo remarked from ahead of them, "but I think I'd settle for a few more brains and a lot more luck."

"There is no such thing as luck, according to the philosophers," Ryo replied. "They insist it is an outmoded mythological concept."

"We'll debate that one later," Bonnie said, interrupting them. "We're still not out of it."

" 'Out of it'?" Ryo murmured. "I misunderstand."

"Safely away. I don't think your presence on board would be enough to prevent your government's attacking us if they decide on that course of action, do you?"

"Most certainly not. The contrary might be true."

Then he was in the alien ship. The humans were vanishing to different posts like so many milla-bugs. Someone called from a distance, "Detection reports nobody on board. Not a guard in sight."

"Why should there be?" another, more distant voice yelled. "Who's going to try and steal it? Besides, they haven't been able to figure out how to run it yet."

The final checks Bonnie had spoken of took even less time than Ryo had expected. Then all of a sudden he was standing in the corridor all by himself. Loo and Bonnie had rushed to their stations. In the haste to complete final repairs the crew of the *Seeker* had forgotten there was an alien in their midst.

That was fine with Ryo. He strolled around the peculiar vessel unchallenged, touching nothing because nothing was familiar. The corridors were generally identical; high, narrow rectangles instead of the comforting low triangles or arches. It was most disconcerting, as if his whole world of perceptions had suddenly been squeezed from both sides.

Some of the chambers he inspected were evidently living quarters. Their contents remained a mystery to him. All except a single item of furniture that, save for being higher and longer, closely resembled a proper lounge. He wondered if they were intended for sleeping or some as yet unknown function.

Since no one was around to stop him he tested one— overly soft with a slightly irritating mushy movement to its insides, but otherwise quite suitable for resting. He had to haul himself onto it. Once there and as soon as he got used to the rolling sensation, he succeeded in making himself comfortable for the first time since they'd boarded.

"What do you think, Captain?" The cocontroller was studying the activated screens that showed the green-white mass of Hivehom and the space surrounding it. Several moons appeared as graphic representations, as did moving points of light too large to be dust and too near to be satellites.

"Ships," Sanchez noted tersely. "Have to be. Orbital. No, *there's* one moving." She checked a readout, announced with satisfaction, "Moving away from us. Standard commercial traffic. It squares with what the bug told us. This is a busy world."

"His name is Ryo," Bonnie announced from the other side of the cabin.

"All right—it squares with what Ryo told us. This is their capital world. Traffic's to be expected. I don't think we could mask ourselves with it, though. Ship signature is too different."

"I'm sure they're marking us right now," said Taourit, the cocontroller. "They've kept us well away from the other ships. Probably a restricted area."

Sanchez nodded, spoke toward her pickup. "Engineering? Status?"

The speaker replied. "Engineering checks okay."

"Thanks, Alexis. We're set, then."

Bonnie leaned a little closer to one screen. "Lights coming up," she declared. "Small mass, moving fast. Too small for a ship. Military shuttle maybe."

"That was fast," Taourit murmured. "Somebody down there's good at deduction."

"And so we bid farewell to the vacation world of Hivehom," Sanchez muttered. "Our stay was pleasant but overlong, I think. Let's get out of here."

A slight vibration ran through the room and the *Seeker* began to move. It was still too close to the world below for the Supralight drive to be engaged. In normal space the tiny shuttle coming up behind would be just as fast. For a while it seemed to be gaining.

Eventually the captain issued additional commands. Far out in front of the ship a deep-purple glow appeared, the visual manifestation of the immensely concentrated artificial gravity field generated by the ship's projectors.

The *Seeker* leaped outward. As it did so it pushed the growing field, which pulled the ship, which pushed the field. Acceleration was rapid. There was a moment of nausea and utter disorientation. The field and the ship within passed the speed of light and entered the abstract universe known as Space Plus. Stars went wavy and streaked around the ship.

Everyone was about to relax when Bonnie's screens displayed three new marks, behind and to one side of the *Seeker*'s course through Space Plus.

The *Seeker*'s computer went to work. Bonnie studied the resultant readout, but did not try to conceal a sigh of relief.

"Not a chance of intercept—not unless they're a lot faster than we are. Of course, they could track us all the way back to Centaurus, but I don't think they'll risk that."

Still, one of the pursuing vessels continued to follow as its companions dropped from the screens.

"Maybe they think they're faster than we are."

Bonnie shook her head. "If anything, the reverse is true—unless they've tried to fool us into thinking that."

"Anderson, you're a detection specialist, not a psychologist," Taourit observed.

"We all have our hobbies."

The computer interrupted to announce the result of studies begun when they'd reentered the ship. It declared that the air was breathable, gravity was operational, and in general all was right within the enclosed metal globe that was the *Seeker*.

The single light on Bonnie's console continued to hold position as if its crew was determined to follow all the way across the galaxy, if need be. Twice it dropped from the screen, only to crawl slowly back into view. Once it made up some distance on its quarry.

"What do you make of that?" Sanchez asked the cocontroller.

Taourit studied the monitors and readouts, punched a query into the computer, and received fresh information. "They're fiddling with their drive. Probably pushing it to the limit." He looked over at her. "It would be detrimental to future relations if this bunch were to blow themselves up trying to catch us."

"We can't be held responsible for that," the captain replied calmly. "We made no hostile gestures toward them and they still kept us prisoners—would have kept us permanently if we hadn't escaped, according to this Ryo individual."

"Yes, according to it," agreed Taourit.

"It's a him," Bonnie reminded them.

They both turned to glance at her, then resumed their conversation. "According to him, and exactly who is 'him'? Could he be a cleverly planted spy?" the cocontroller wondered.

"I don't think so," Sanchez said. "Our escape clearly was not engineered by them."

"You sure?" Taourit asked. "Maybe they felt they'd learned as much about the ship and about us as they could." He gestured around the room. "Just because everything's in place doesn't mean they mightn't have taken the *Seeker* apart and put it back together again. I'd bet they could. Did you notice those upper hands, the ones they call truhands? They can do detail work finer than the best human artisan.

"So why couldn't they also have engineered our escape? Not one of their people was harmed. That could be due to surprise—or complete lack of it. I don't think there's any surveillance equipment on board. Our diagnostics would have found it by now and it could hardly report back over interstellar distances, anyway. But they've got a better recording instrument on board in this Ryo."

"Farfetched. How could he get his information back home?"

"I don't know, Captain. But then, there's quite a lot we don't know about these bugs. Sure, it's farfetched—but not impossible."

"No, not impossible," she admitted.

"Maybe they were right," Bonnie put in from across the control room.

"Right about what?" Taourit asked.

"About our racial paranoia. Our history supports them about as much as your current conversation."

"It's only a possibility that ought to be considered," Sanchez argued. But she did not resume the discussion with the cocontroller. The implications of the detector's words were unpleasant.

They were twelve hours out and a good distance from Hivehom, and Alexis Antonovich was exhausted. He had been glued to his drive monitors since they'd retaken the *Seeker*. The ship was performing beautifully. The repairs continued to hold and there wasn't a hint of oscillation in the field. She shot through Space Plus snugly wrapped in her convoying envelope of mathematical distortion. Now the engineer just wanted to rest.

He stopped in front of the door to his compartment, touched the switch that slid it aside. Bleary-eyed, he moved to the wash basin. After cleaning his face he felt much better. A glance in the mirror showed a scraggly growth of beard that had accumulated on the bug world. Depilatory cream was one of many items they hadn't had time to bring down from the orbiting *Seeker*.

Something else was reflected in the mirror: a pair of bulbous, gleaming, multicolored eyes stared at his reflection. Whirling, he was confronted by the sight of a five-foot-long arthropod lying on its left side on his bed. It held his pillow in one blue-green armored hand.

"Self-inspection," it commented in whispery but quite understandable Terranglo. "That's interesting." It gestured with the pillow. "Perhaps you can explain the function of this soft device to me?"

"It's called a pillow," Alexis responded automatically to the polite question. "We rest our heads on it while we sleep."

"But why would you need something else to rest your head upon," the Thranx inquired, examining the pillow closely, "when this lounge is already too soft?"

"That's because—" Alexis broke off the reply, suddenly conscious of what was happening. He moved quickly to the wall communicator, activated it, and talked without taking his gaze from the creature on his bed.

"Captain, Alexis here. I just went off duty. I'm in my cabin. I think perhaps there are some matters we have to clarify."

Despite Taourit's suspicions, Ryo was given the run of the ship. He was full of questions that he knew sometimes irritated his human hosts, who were concerned only with their own safe return. Though he was still learning about facial expression, a radical new concept to a being with an inflexible exoskeleton, he was convinced some of them looked at him in a less than friendly manner. That disturbed him, but he told himself firmly that it was only natural.

His first request for access to the *Seeker*'s computer bank was turned down. Only when the last, persistent Thranx ship finally faded from the screens did the captain relent. Ryo could find nothing harmful without special coding. The general files were more entertaining than dangerous and Ryo's desire to learn more about his hosts seemed devoid of ulterior motive.

He was also able to study the crew at their stations. Of the twelve surviving members of the *Seeker*'s crew, at least four were openly, even enthusiastically friendly—Loo and Bonnie, the engineer named Alexis, and the ship's environmental monitor. Another six, including Captain Elvirasanchez, were politely neutral. Only two remained overtly hostile, despite Sanchez's orders for them to act courteous in Ryo's presence.

Their hostility troubled him. After several unsuccessful attempts to win them over—one even became physically ill in his presence—he decided not to press the matter and simply avoided them whenever possible.

A study of human history revealed an antiarthropod bias exceeding the hereditary Thranx fear of mammals and other soft-bodies. In addition to groundless but very persistent phobias, actual events such as plague and the massive destruction of food supplies lent support to such a bias.

Small arthropods such as insects sometimes ate Thranx food, but not to the degree they had devastated human supplies throughout history. It was not surprising, then, that in unguarded moments even Loo and Bonnie looked at him with unconscious expressions of fear and disgust. It was hard for them to overcome a lifetime's conditioning.

As it was for him. Their warm, smelly bodies pressed constantly around him and he had to struggle to suppress his own instinctive reactions.

At least that was not a reciprocal problem. Even the two who actively disliked him confessed that his natural odor resembled a cross between lemon and lilacs, whatever they were. More than once he caught a crew member inhaling with obvious pleasure in his presence. Their sense of smell was located in twin openings located just above their mouths, which struck Ryo as a particularly impractical arrangement.

How odd it would be, he thought amusedly, if understanding should be reached between our species not on the basis of mutual interests or intellectual discourse, but because one of us smells good to the other.

He spent the days in Space Plus devouring everything the computer would feed him. Its controls were unnecessarily

bulky and easy to manipulate. His knowledge of monster—
of human language and customs increased.

The engineer Alexis had shown Ryo how to use the terminal in his burrow. Then he moved in with a companion
so his living quarters could be given over to the Thranx.
Since each burrow had individual climate controls Ryo was
able to alter temperature and humidity to suit his own temperament. As the humans found the hot, sticky climate in
the room distinctly uncomfortable, he had a good deal of
privacy in which to pursue his studies.

Few visited him except for Loo and Bonnie and, after a
while, the captain. Sanchez did not warm to Ryo as they
had, but her conversation was always absorbing. Ryo knew
she was in a difficult official position because, as she saw it,
the Thranx were the first intelligent race mankind had encountered and the circumstances under which contact had
been made were not covered by official procedure.

"No," he corrected her. "We're the second intelligent
race you've encountered." Ryo then gave her a complete
rundown on the AAnn, admitting from the first that it
would be biased. The *Seeker*'s remaining science staff was
brought in and they listened raptly to the lecture.

The atmosphere on the *Seeker* was never completely relaxed. No one knew if her repairs would hold to the end of
the journey. If the drive were to fail, their sublight engines
could still get them back to Centaurus in a couple of
hundred years or so. Her arrival would be of interest, but
not to the desiccated corpses crewing her.

But the repairs continued to hold and the drive continued to function. The air grew foul and thin for several
days, but that was as close as internal elements came to a
serious breakdown.

Activity intensified on the day designated for emergence
into normal space. The countdown commenced with no
more than the usual tension, the familiar wrenching sensation was felt, several of the crew lost the contents of their
stomachs, and then it was done.

Ryo moved hurriedly to the main port in the ship's control room. A planet drifted below and, above it, a distant
and to him very dim sun. Though no astronomer, he
thought the world beneath must be far too cold and harsh
to support life. Surely it was not their intended destination.

"You're right," the cocontroller informed him, without taking his eyes from his instrumentation. "There are eight planets in this system, of which the third and fifth have been colonized." He smiled. "Mistakenly, too. The colonists who first arrived here thought they'd reached an entirely different star."

"If this is not our destination, then why are we stopping here?"

"Standard precautions regulating returning exploration craft," Taourit told him. He pointed to the port. "See that bright spot just ahead? That's where we're going."

The orbital station circling Centaurus' seventh planet was an enormous wheeled complex, mankind's farthest outpost. It impressed Ryo. The world it circled was cold and dead.

A large and, Ryo thought, too well-armed cluster of humans met him and his companions when they emerged from the station airlock. They were polite, but he could read emotions other than welcome in some of the faces.

The official who made the short speech and greeted him in a mildly patronizing manner was courteous enough, however. Ryo was conducted to a spacious burrow on the skin of the station. A sweeping port offered a view of the stars and the icy globe rotating below.

The temperature and humidity had been set to his specifications, and plants had been provided to give the burrow a homelike atmosphere. Someone had gone to a great deal of effort to insure his comfort.

After the expected argument he was allowed a computer terminal, one slightly more complicated than the one he'd used on the *Seeker*. The engineer who instructed him in its use watched with more than a little envy as Ryo utilized sixteen digits and four hands to input requests far more rapidly than any human could have managed.

Days of conversation followed. As long as the station authorities allowed him access to information, Ryo was reasonably happy. The percentages of humans who openly liked him, were uncertain, or unremittingly inimical remained about the same as on board the *Seeker*. But his visitors were mostly scientists and researchers, he reminded himself. He doubted he would be as well accepted among the general populace.

Occasionally he was visited by members of the *Seeker*'s crew. They were undergoing debriefing elsewhere on the station and did not try to conceal their pleasure at once more being with their own kind.

Ryo's guests included one group of three that spent an inordinate amount of time with him. There was one large elderly male and a smaller elderly female who both sported white fur. The third member of this team was a considerably younger male.

At the moment Ryo was stretched out flat on a saddle that the station shop had hastily cobbled together for him. The alien fabric was gently gripping against his abdomen and thorax, the head brace decently curved. He crossed his hands over his front and let his legs droop lazily over the sides of the saddle. In addition to the three scientists, Loo was present, not to act as interpreter, since Ryo's mastery of the human language was now extensive, but simply to be a familiar go-between should the need arise.

After several hours of discussion concerning Thranx cultural habits, Ryo had a question of his own.

"You know, I have an interesting proposal I would like to make. I've given it a good deal of thought." He studied his visitors as they waited for him to continue.

On the right was the elder male named Rijseen. Ryo had decided he was the equivalent of an Eint, for he was often deferred to by other inquirers. Next to him sat the elder female Kibwezi, whose skin was nearly as dark as the space surrounding the station. Nearby was the youngest of the three, the diminutive male called Bhadravati.

Since they'd first come to question him many changes had been made in Ryo's burrow, at his request. The ceiling had been lowered nearly a meter. A human of more than average height was therefore compelled to stoop when walking. All the right angles had been removed through the addition of sprayed polyfoam. The lighting had been reduced. The heat and humidity remained at Willow-wane normal.

By way of partial compensation a changing room had been installed between the station corridor and the burrow proper. There visitors could discard whatever clothing they wished so they might speak with their alien guest in comparative comfort.

Despite the fact that he was sitting practically naked, the sweat was pouring from Rijseen's face. His companions seemed more at home in the tropical climate of Ryo's quarters.

The phenomenon of sweat fascinated Ryo, but he led his thoughts away from it to the question he intended to ask. "During my studies I have learned that there are regions on several of the worlds you have settled which you make little or no use of. This includes your home world of Earth."

"You aren't supposed to know details like that," the younger man interrupted sharply. Then he blinked as if he'd mentioned something *he* wasn't supposed to. The woman threw him a look of reproach. It didn't pass Ryo, who'd become adept at recognizing the meaning of such flexings. He let out a short whistle of amusement.

"When a society becomes sufficiently advanced technologically it becomes very hard to conceal something from someone who knows how to ask the right questions. While we are considerably different in shape, our information machines generally obey the same laws. Do not be surprised that I have circumvented certain restraints. I do so out of curiosity, not malice.

"On your Earth there are areas such as the Malay peninsula, the Congo region of the continent called Africa, and in particular the Amazon basin that are to this day thinly inhabited and inefficiently utilized, though you have made extensive efforts to exploit them."

"They're likely to remain that way," Kibwezi commented.

"That is not necessary. For example, you have left the Amazon basin largely untouched because it was found some time ago that extensive development of the region would result in catastrophic deforestation. This would upset the production of oxygen and possibly unbalance your atmosphere.

"We are not only experienced at making use of such areas, we prefer to live beneath them. The humidity and temperature would be like home to me. We can tunnel through and live in almost any kind of ground, the result of thousands of years of sophisticated excavating. Although it is a little cool during certain seasons, my people could live quite contentedly in such a place, which can be only forever inhospitable to your kind." He hurried on.

"Lest you think me making a subtle suggestion of invasion, I must also tell you that there are comparable regions on our own worlds that you would find quite pleasant, though I would not live in them for all the credit in the universe. Some of them are greater in proportion to their planets' surface areas than this Amazon basin is to your Earth's.

"For example, the extreme polar regions of our capital world of Hivehom are lethally cold to us, yet according to my studies no worse than much of your northern hemisphere continents." He gestured at Loo. "Those who were held there can attest to its climate during our coldest season.

"There is also an extensive plateau that rises two thousand meters above its surrounding country. Many of the trees you call softwoods thrive up there. Rainfall is moderate by your standards and temperatures too cool for Thranx comfort. There are no mineral resources but the soil is suitable for the kinds of farming I have studied." A little pride crept into his tone. "Of that I can promise you.

"I would guess that the climate there approximates what is average around your Mediterranean Sea. So you see, we could greatly benefit each other by trading off such territories. Development of these regions could proceed easily, since they are located not on new worlds but on highly developed ones. All would benefit."

"We are hardly empowered—" Rijseen began apologetically.

The female took over for him. "You must understand, Ryo, that we are simply scientists, observers. We are here to study and learn and to teach. We do not set policy, though we may make recommendations.

"I am not a bureaucrat, but I think I can say with confidence that your proposal is more than simply premature. There has not been even preliminary formal contact initiated between our species. Yet you sit there and calmly propose not a mere alliance or expression of friendship, but an actual exchange of territory and colonists."

"Let me try and put it more graphically," the younger man said, "and excuse me if I use terminology that seems indelicate. The idea of perhaps a million of your own kind, a million giant, armor-plated, glow-eyed bugs, actually settling down on Earth, is one that would be very hard for its general population to accept."

"No more so," Ryo responded, having anticipated the objection, "than it would be for the people of the Hive of Chitteranx, who dwell directly below the plateau I told you of, to gaze every day up its cliffs knowing that hundreds of thousands of giant, fleshy, flexible aliens were building machines and lives up there."

"Then you are as subject to the racial paranoia your psychtechs accused us of as we may be," said Kibwezi.

"Not at all. We are discussing now deeply ingrained cultural fears and ancestral emotions. You may loathe my appearance, my people may loathe yours, but unlike you, we do not loathe each other's. We have not fought among ourselves for thousands of years. Your history, which I have studied, is full of devastating internal conflicts of appallingly recent date."

"We're getting away from your proposal," Rijseen put in. "I don't see how—"

Ryo risked censure by interrupting, though, he reminded himself, that did not carry the disapproval here that it would have among his own people. "Think of the knowledge to be gained by both sides, the advances that would surely be made, not to mention the necessity of striking a military alliance against the AAnn."

"That may not be as vital as you seem to believe," Bhadravati noted. "You insist it was an AAnn vessel that attacked the *Seeker*, but we have no way of confirming that. You could be trying to smooth over a mistake by your own government."

"The AAnn exist. They attacked your ship and killed your people and are every bit as dangerous as I've told you."

"You've told us that these AAnn once attacked your own home town," Kibwezi said softly. "That they killed your friends and relatives."

"That is also truth."

"Then your own personal—not to mention racial—bias against the AAnn would naturally induce you to seek an alliance against them. Even if they did attack the *Seeker*, it may have been in error. They might, for example, have thought it a new design of your own. Why should we ally ourselves with you against them when we might be friends with them as well as with the Thranx?"

"A neat trick," Ryo replied, controlling his temper. "There is one difficulty. The AAnn believe they are a chosen species, designated to rule the entire galaxy. Other, inferior races are to be exterminated or enslaved. They are very patient and careful to conceal such feelings in the presence of diplomats. This patience makes them all the more dangerous."

"So you say," Bhadravati responded.

Ryo's composure slipped just a little. "What reason would I have to lie to you?"

"I just enumerated," began the woman, but Ryo hardly heard her now.

He had innocently thought his carefully prepared proposal would be accepted instantly and approved. Its logic was unassailable. Instead, it had been casually brushed aside as unworkable and premature. Another aspect of human behavior to be filed for later dissection.

"They might indeed offer you apologies and alliance," he told them. "Deceit is their refined weapon, deception their most prized characteristic. These attributes are supported by an advanced technology and militaristic society."

"So you say," the younger man repeated with infuriating self-assurance.

"We digress again," Rijseen pointed out. He tried to reestablish the atmosphere of cordiality with which they'd begun the questioning.

"As you've heard, we are only researchers. We can only pass your proposal along—as we do all information—to others better positioned to act on it."

"You will do that for me?" Ryo asked.

"Of course. We are collectors of information, not interpreters. Now tell us again," he said eagerly, "about the higher implications of the filian ceremony."

Ryo sighed inwardly, determined to raise the issue again and again at future meetings until he received some kind of positive response.

XIII A quarter-month later Ryo had an informal visit from Bonnie and Loo. Like the rest of the *Seeker*'s crew, they were still sequestered at the station, subject to medical as well as mental study. They were answering nearly as many questions as was Ryo.

Neither human was as uncomfortable as Ryo's questioners. They were more accustomed to the climate of his burrow. The low ceiling and rounded corners did not trouble them at all. They had endured such surroundings for months on Hivehom.

Conversation consisted largely of pleasantries and reminiscences. Eventually the matter that had troubled Ryo for some days could be ignored no longer. He escorted them to the wall where his private terminal had been installed.

Since the meeting with Rijseen and his two companions he'd found that tighter blocks had been placed on certain channels of inquiry. Nothing had been said about it and the computer had been programmed to be evasive rather than specific, but he recognized the establishment of channel locks.

He'd discovered the other almost on a whim, in a moment of boredom. It presented a challenge and he attacked it more for the entertainment it offered than out of any desire or need to know its contents. They had turned out to be something other than entertaining, however.

"I was working here several days ago," he explained to them, sliding into the saddle, "trying to research your contacts with other life."

"I thought you were an agricultural specialist," Bonnie said, staring over his shoulder as the screen ran information.

"So I am, but the question of other intelligences has intrigued me since larvahood. If it were not for that I doubt we three would ever have met."

"That would have been a loss," Loo said with a smile.

"Yes." Ryo worked the keyboard with two hands. In addition to the central screen the two peripherals on its right promptly winked to life. Patterns flashed across the glass. "It was while hunting for evidence of such contacts that I stumbled into a block. I'm used to that now. Normally I file their location and ignore them. That is the polite thing

173

to do, since your superiors evidently feel there is certain material I should not have access to."

Both humans looked a little uncomfortable despite Ryo's admission that such blocks did not bother him.

"We have no control over such matters," Bonnie said finally.

"I am aware of that. I was not accusing you. This block, however, tempted me to try to circumvent it, since it concealed information of particular relevance to me. I have come to believe the block was placed not specifically against me but to prevent general access by the majority of the staff at this station.

"In my years as member of my Company's local council I have had ample opportunity to make use of information-retrieval technology. Though your system differs from ours, I have applied myself both on the *Seeker* and while here, and have succeeded in learning a great deal. Also, Thranx are naturally proficient at logic and aesthetic inference.

"Briefly then, I managed to bypass the block that had been placed on this particular line of questioning. I was in fact surprised that a stronger block had not been placed on it. Sometimes in their eagerness to conceal vital information bureaucrats may overlook the trivial."

He returned to the console and his fingers moved across the keys. The flow of information on the three screens slowed, stabilized. The words MAXECRET—ALIEN CONTACT and THRANX appeared. Demand was made for a second input, which Ryo supplied.

The words vanished, were replaced by a computer-generated diagram of Ryo's body. On the peripheral screens information began to unroll, accompanied by smaller diagrams and appropriate commentary.

"That's your file!" Loo blurted in surprise.

"Indeed," Ryo replied. Behind him the two humans leaned closer. Evidently neither had seen the information now appearing on the screens.

Ryo let it unspool at its own leisurely pace for a while, then touched a control. The text and graphics became a multicolored blur on the screens. A beep sounded from somewhere inside the console and the information slowed to a near crawl.

"This is the section I would like you to pay attention to," he said drily. "I found it most interesting."

Bonnie's eyes traveled through the paragraphs, slowed at a particular line. ". . . and it is therefore concluded, that additional questioning beyond the prescribed date can generate only minimal new information. Urgent requests continue outstanding from Xenophysiology and other bureaus for further material on internal construction and in particular cerebral makeup and capability of the specimen in question."

Behind Ryo, Bonnie flinched at the last phrase. The information continued to roll up the screen.

"The military branches in particular are interested in all aspects of the aforementioned with view toward future methodology for confusing such functions as vision and feel. Particular inquiry is desired into the physiology of the *faz* sense, which is not duplicated in humans and which presents unique military difficulties of its own.

"It has therefore been decided by a vote of twelve to ten by the senior planners of Project Thranx that, since the specimen in question appears to occupy only a minimal status among his own hierarchy and that since his whereabouts are in any case unknown to them, postmortem internal studies should commence on the date indicated.

"Psych Staff sees no problem in creating suitable excuse to explain the specimen's demise should the need arise. This also supported by a vote of 12–10 by the senior planners.

"Note is made of the closeness of the decision and the vehemence of those voting in opposition. Revote reconfirms the decision to proceed with the aforementioned. Euthanasia will be performed the evening prior to the announced date and dissection and study will commence following. Sig.Per.Proc. See tables MEDICAL, THRANX PROJ."

Fresh information continued to appear. Neither Bonnie nor Loo paid any attention to it. Their single lenses seemed slightly glazed. While he recognized the phenomenon, Ryo could not interpret it sufficiently to correlate it with his companions' feelings.

"Did I not tell you it was most interesting?" he finally said into the silence. "Apparently your superiors are so busy keeping knowledge of my presence here unknown to the station personnel, they neglected to guard it sufficiently from me."

"It's monstrous," Loo muttered. "They want to cut you up to see what makes you tick."

"They have no grounds, no reason . . ." Bonnie began, so angry she could hardly speak.

Ryo's reply was couched in philosophical tones. "There is no more knowledge they feel they can gain from my aliveness, and much from my death. I have already made my peace with eternity. I am prepared to accept the inevitable."

"It's not inevitable," Loo objected.

"Is it not?" Ryo turned the saddle and stared up at him. His ommatidia sparkled in the light from the console. "Among my people such a situation calls for resignation. I can sympathize with the desires of your superiors. They wish only to further their knowledge."

"There are some things more important than furthering knowledge," Bonnie countered.

"I would disagree with you, Bonnie."

"Don't," she snapped. "You may be willing to go calmly to your death, but I'll be damned if I'm willing to let you do it." Precipitation oozed from the corners of her eyes, another human phenomenon Ryo found fascinating. It was astonishing that any creature could generate precipitation in so many different ways and for so many different reasons.

"What could you do?" Ryo murmured. "The decision has been made."

"Only on a local level," Loo noted. "The order could be countermanded by higher scientific bodies on Earth. I'm sure that's why they've set the date so soon, so they can commence their little vivisection party before any response could be returned. Oh, they know what they're about, all right. They're very clever." He seemed to slump in on himself.

"We can bloody well go to the council and offer our own objections," Bonnie said.

"Yes, and you know how much weight they'll give to that."

"They have to listen to us," she objected. "Contact and follow-up is our profession."

Loo was nodding. "They'll tell us we did a marvelous job. That our work is finished. We'll all be promoted and given huge bonuses." The irony in his tone was clear even to Ryo.

"We've got to try." Loo's relentless reasoning had reduced her initial angry determination to a hopeful whisper.

"I cannot say that I do not wish you luck," Ryo admitted, adding a gesture of mild amusement. "You did find the information interesting, as I thought you would. Don't worry about me. I am content.

"I have learned that intelligence exists in yet another corner of this stellar forest we call our galaxy. That is sufficient revelation to die for. I shall return my component elements to Nature, with dissolution already begun." The attempt at humor evidently failed; neither human responded as he'd hoped.

Something soft and pulpy was caressing his neck. The burrow was eerily silent. At the same time his antennae twitched at the presence of a malignant, musky odor close by.

He awoke with a start, terribly frightened, wondering where Fal was and if the monster that was gazing down at him had already devoured her.

"Be quiet," urged the monster in a quiet, familiar voice. "I don't think we've set off any alarms yet. There may not be any to set off. After all, there's nowhere for you to escape to, is there?"

Slowly his sleepy mind cleared, recognized the fragmented shape of Bonnie standing over him. He lifted his head and looked past her. Several other human silhouettes stood in his burrow. Others were outlined by the light of the distant corridor, visible through the open entryway.

"What's wrong?" he muttered. "What's the trouble?" He was still too sleep-drenched to think in Terranglo.

Bonnie's Low Thranx answered him. "Some of us retain fragments of civilization." Her tone was bitter. "We owe allegiance to standards not incorporated in official manuals."

"I believe I understand what you are saying." He slid off the lounge and fumbled for his neck pouch and vest.

"What I am saying is that a good friend is not a candidate for the butcher block."

"It's not at all like that," Ryo protested. "As a question of scientific expansion of knowledge—"

"As a question of scientific expansion of knowledge," she interrupted in Terranglo, "it sucks. Have you got all your things?"

He closed the last snap on his neck pouch. "I think so."

"Then let's go." She started for the doorway. He followed automatically, still drowsy and increasingly bewildered.

"Where are we going? This is not a planet. You cannot hide me on this station for more than a short time."

"We have no intention of trying to hide you on the station."

They were out in the corridor. Ryo dimmed his perception to compensate for the bright human lighting. Loo was waiting for them, and Elvirasanchez. With them were the cocontroller Taourit, the engineer Alexis, and someone Ryo didn't recognize as a member of the *Seeker*'s crew. Six in all. Greetings were exchanged quietly and in haste.

"We're all committed to this," Sanchez informed him solemnly. "You risked your life for something you believed in, believed in enough to risk condemnation from your entire people. Well, there are a few of us who are capable of equally strong beliefs."

"The shortsighted will always be among us," Ryo replied philosophically. "Those who try to reach out with their minds are more often restrained from behind than from ahead."

"I know." The captain gestured around her. "These are the only ones who agreed."

"Will the others not betray you?"

Sanchez smiled. "They're convinced we're all talk and no action." She looked past him. "I think you know Dr. Bhadravati."

Ryo turned, was surprised to find the young scientist who had questioned him so many times. He had considered him the least friendly of the three and confessed his astonishment at seeing him now.

"I'm not here because I think this is reasoningly or legally the right thing to do," the young human said, "but morally I don't see how I can do anything else. I believe that you are one of God's creatures, that you have a soul, and that what they intend doing to you is wrong both in the eyes of man and of God. I don't know if the term is one you've learned, but prior to my matriculation as a xenologist I was a theology student. I draw support for these actions tonight from the Bible, the Rig-Veda, and the teachings of Buddha. What I do here now is part of my journey down the noble Eightfold Path."

"I do not understand all of what you say," Ryo replied, "but I welcome the result of your reasoning. I believe you would consider me a Theravadist."

"That is impossible to reconcile with belief in—"

Sanchez stepped between them, spoke to Bhadravati. "You can try converting him later. Our searches turned up no monitors, but sooner or later someone's going to make a personal check of our guest's condition."

They hurried down the corridor. The station was big and the *Seeker* was docked a considerable distance away. It was general sleeptime for the humans.

I have done this before, on a more familiar world, Ryo mused suddenly. It seems I am destined forever to be escaping to someplace or from somewhere.

They were running down a narrow serviceway where the light was subdued and Ryo was grateful for the respite from the usual glare.

"That's far enough!"

The humans running ahead of Ryo came to a halt. He peered around Sanchez. Blocking the corridor was a single human male. Ryo recognized the object he was holding as a weapon. After a moment Ryo recognized the figure. It was one of the *Seeker*'s crew. One of the two who'd sneaked hostile glances in Ryo's direction when he thought no one else was looking.

"Hello, Weldon," Sanchez said easily. "I had a hunch you might have suspected. You always were a sharp one."

"Shove it, Captain." Sweat was pouring down his cheeks and his thinning hair was in disarray. "It wasn't hard to figure that you were planning something. So I listened." He smiled, but there was no humor in it. "I listen well."

"Okay, so you listen well. What are you going to do, turn us in?"

"I don't care what you do. I don't have anything against you, Captain. Against any of you. You've been under a strain. We all have. It's clouded your vision, but not mine. Not Renstaad's, either, but she isn't up to this. Someone's got to do it."

"Do what?" Sanchez.

"What needs to be done. My God, don't you people realize what's happened here? What these filthy creatures portend? We always knew it might come, but not with such subtlety, not with such deviousness."

"What might come, Weldon?"

"The invasion, of course. All these centuries they've been watching us, waiting. Now they've duped us into bringing one of 'em back with us. He's the advance scout. Somehow he's even managed to hypnotize you all into taking him back. Back with the vital information they need. Centaurus will be the first. After that, they'll probably go straight for Earth itself."

"Weldon, you just said yourself we've all been under a strain. Ryo is—"

"Don't call it that!" he screamed. "Don't give it a name. Things don't have names!"

"He's a friend. We're the ones threatening him, not the other way around." She took a step toward him and the muzzle of the gun moved ever so slightly to one side.

"Don't try it, Captain. I said I've got nothing against you, and I don't, but by Heaven I'll shoot every one of you down to save the rest of us if you force me to." His gaze, wild and fanatic, turned to the one who'd been standing behind her.

"It will only take a second." His finger started to tighten on the trigger. "Messier than a spray, but just as effective—"

"Don't do it, Weldon!" Loo stepped sideways, waving his hands. "We can!—"

The gun made a slight hissing sound. Something struck Loo in the chest and knocked him backward. His arms, already disconnecting from his brain, flopped loosely in the air. Bonnie screamed. Taourit pulled something from his jacket pocket. Weldon turned to face him, brought his pistol around as the dart from the little gun struck him in the forehead. His eyes glazed instantly and his body went as rigid as if he'd been frozen. He made a loud thump when his head hit the floor.

Bonnie was kneeling next to Loo. She was not crying. Alexis was pulling at her.

"Come on. It's too late." He put a hand over the man's chest. There was a very large hole in it. "It's too late, Bonnie." The others were looking down at them.

Ryo touched his antennae to the back of Bonnie's neck. She jerked at the airy caress, looked back at the sharp mandibles, the great faceted eyes.

"I am sorrowed, friend Bonnie. He was my friend too. The minute of lastlife is gone and cannot be recaptured."

For a moment sanity left her gaze. Then reason and reality flooded back in. "We're wasting time here." She stood, disdaining Alexis' offer of assistance. "Let's not waste everything."

They started up the serviceway, stepping over the still rigid body of the man named Weldon. No one stood guard over the airlock leading to the *Seeker*. People did not steal Supralight-drive ships. It was almost comically easy. No one was in a humorous mood, however.

The hatches were unsealed. For a second time the crew of the *Seeker* prepared to flee with their ship. Only this time they were running not from another people but from their own. How Wuu would love this situation, Ryo mused, thinking fondly of the old poet and wishing he were present to offer advice and companionship.

I had two equally fine human companions, he reminded himself. Only now one of them is dead, because of me.

It was true there were no alarms to set off, no traps to trigger. But when the *Seeker*'s maneuvering engines were engaged and the umbilicals connecting it to the station power system were jettisoned, portions of the orbiting city's instrumentation came alive rapidly.

Ryo stood in the control room, watching his friends. Bonnie threw herself into her work, becoming an emotionless appendage of her station. Dr. Bhadravati paced and fidgeted as if he did not know what to do with his manipulating digits. Not being a member of the crew, he was at that moment as useless as Ryo. Unlike Ryo, however, he was dying to do *something*.

From the first, there was nothing ordinary about the inquiries that sounded over the console speakers. "You there, aboard DSR *Seeker*, acknowledge! You have disengaged and your engines are functioning. DSR *Seeker* is not authorized to disengage. Who is aboard, please? Acknowledge, DSR *Seeker!*"

"This is Captain Elvira Manuela de loa de Sanchez. I acknowledge for DSR *Seeker*. Received and acknowledge orders to check out sublight engines and life-support prior to boost to C-III for overhaul prior to next EX flight. All okay here. Sorry about any confusion." She clicked off. "That ought to keep them busy for a while."

Indeed, by the time the speakers squawked again the station was just a disk against the reflective side of Centaurus VII. The voice that came this time was deeper and more emphatic than that of the station's duty communicator.

"*Seeker*, this is Colonel G.R. Davis, Centaurus Station commander. You are ordered to return to base forthwith. We have checked with both station command computer and EX Control on C-V. The *Seeker* is not due for overhaul for another six weeks."

"I know," Sanchez replied calmly. "We thought we'd start her out early and bring her in slow so we could give her systems a thorough run-through in case there are any on-the-verge problems. I'm anxious to be rid of her."

"You will be rid of her permanently—and all other possible commands if you don't return her to dock immediately." Voices could be heard arguing in the background.

Another voice came over the speaker. Ryo recognized this one as belonging to the Eint elder human.

"*Seeker*, this is Dr. Rijseen, in charge of the direct contact branch of the special xenology project here at the station. We have discovered that the alien is absent from his quarters. A thorough search has been made of the station. While it may be that he is hiding somewhere, we have every reason to believe that he is on the *Seeker*, and not as a stowaway. We will continue to operate on that assumption unless we can be persuaded otherwise."

The young xenologist moved forward. Sanchez gave him

a stare, then nodded slowly. Bhadravati spoke toward the pickup.

"Ryozenzuzex is aboard, Maarten."

"Jahan, is that you? I wondered where the hell you got to when the alarms went off. What's going on?"

"Well, you know, it's a funny thing," the young researcher began. Ryo could see that he was very nervous and uncertain. No hint of this surfaced in his voice, but it was evident in his posture and movements, to which Ryo was more sensitive than most humans. "But the bug, as many refer to him, once saved the lives of every crew member on this ship."

"All that's well known. What has it to do with the crew's unauthorized action?" The elder spoke with feigned ignorance that would have been admirable to an AAnn, Ryo thought.

Taourit looked over at the captain. "There's a ship detaching from the station."

"Supralight?"

The cocontroller shook his head. "Too small. Intersystem capability only."

She nodded once, listened as Bhadravati replied to Rijseen's question.

"It's not right to dissect an intelligent being, no matter that he might be understanding about it. That's the remarkable thing about this, you know. Ryo sympathizes with the staff's majority viewpoint. He knows about your intentions, you see."

"You didn't have to tell him that," Davis' voice said.

Bhadravati laughed. "You're quite right, Colonel. We didn't. He already knew. Found his file in the station bank."

"That's impossible!" The colonel sounded upset.

"You didn't put a strong enough block on it. He was rummaging through and came across it himself, did the necessary bypass all by his lonesome. The Thranx are superb logicians and excellent with computers. That's in his records too."

The channel was silent for a while. When Davis responded it was in a gentler, more reasoning tone. "Bhadravati, there is more at stake here than you know. I admit that this Ryo individual seems friendly enough, but you cannot positively deny the possibility that his 'escape' from his home world might simply have been a ploy to get him to a human system."

"If it's a ploy, Colonel," Sanchez said into the pickup, "it's working damn well. Better than yours."

"Captain Sanchez, you and everyone operating alongside you will be completely pardoned if you will just return the *Seeker* to dock. Otherwise you will be classed as criminals, and treated as such."

"Ship is beginning to move outward, straight for us," Taourit whispered.

She nodded again, her attention on the pickup. "Don't threaten me, Colonel. I react real nervously to threats."

"Where do you think you're taking that ship?" Davis demanded. "Centaurus V? Three? Earth, maybe? The word will precede you. The services will be looking for the *Seeker* at every established station and every shuttleport on all the civilized worlds."

"Not all the civilized worlds," Sanchez informed him assuredly. "We considered every alternative before embarking on this, Colonel. If we're compelled to, we'll take Ryo home."

"Then what?" Davis' voice was more curious than threatening. "Once you return him to his world, where do you expect you can return to?"

"We don't expect to," was the quiet reply.

Dead silence came from the speaker. It was matched by the atmosphere in the control room. Since the colonel apparently could not think of a suitable response, it was Rijseen who finally resumed the conversation.

"Very well, then. We will drop the plans for the dissection. The vote was close enough to allow that. Guarantees will be drawn up so that no one can override. Not even the military."

Davis' voice, in the background: "You don't have that authority, Dr. Rijseen."

"If you will check your records," the distant voice of the staff head advised him, "you will find that I am in complete control of this project, sir. That authority extends to anything below a direct military threat to the civilized worlds. Human civilized worlds," he added, with just a tinge of amusement. "I do not regard one isolated and avowedly friendly alien as constituting such a threat."

"How do we know you'll do what you say?" asked Sanchez.

"Ask Dr. Bhadravati."

"Obviously, Dr. Rijseen and I have disagreed on a number of matters. Or I wouldn't be here at this moment." Bhadravati flashed a bright smile. "I believe he is trustworthy. I have never known him to break his word. I believe it once cost him a substantial scientific prize and accompanying honors. He is one of the few scientists I know whose word is as sound as his studies."

Bonnie spoke toward her own console pickup. "I believe you, sir. If Dr. Bhadravati trusts you, then I'm willing to trust you. But can you vouch for your associates? And can you guarantee the cooperation of Colonel what's-his-name?"

Muffled sounds issued from the speaker. Then, "I will go along with whatever Dr. Rijseen and the science staff advise. My sole concern is for the safety of the civ—of the human-inhabited worlds, and for government property, of which you are presently in unlawful possession. If that is returned undamaged, then I am perfectly willing to stay out of this." His voice dropped to an irritated rumble. "I would far *rather* stay out of this. Would you people please make up your minds?"

"I believe you, Colonel," Bonnie continued. "There's just one problem. We're not dealing solely with scientific decisions anymore." She glanced at Sanchez, who returned a comforting smile.

Bonnie took a deep breath. Her voice trembled slightly. "In Service Corridor Two-Four Dee you'll find . . . you'll find . . ." She hesitated, forced herself to go on. "You'll find the bodies of Loo Hua-sung and *Seeker* maintenance consultant Richard Weldon."

Rijseen's voice did not change as he asked, "Bodies? Both dead?"

"Yes, sir."

"Weren't you and engineer Hua-sung engaged to be married at one time?"

"There was—we talked about it, yes."

Ryo was staring at her. Finally he understood the relationship that had existed between his two closest human friends. They were, not quite premated, but living in similar status. It explained a great many things.

"Weldon suspected our intentions," Bonnie rushed on. "He managed to follow one of us, maybe more. I don't know."

"I wonder why he didn't sound the alarm, if he knew," said Colonel Davis.

"He had other plans," Bonnie told him. "Plans of his own. You know how restricted access was to Ryo. Of the *Seeker*'s crew, generally only Loo and I were allowed to see him once he'd been established in his own burrow—his quarters.

"When Weldon became suspicious of our actions, he bided his time. He was waiting for us in the service corridor. He didn't have the slightest interest in stopping us. All he wanted was to kill Ryo. Loo—Loo stepped between them."

"Cocontroller Taourit here," said the man on Sanchez's right. "I'm the one who shot Weldon. For the record." He said it proudly.

"I don't understand," Davis was muttering. "Two men dead. Why did this Weldon want to kill the alien?"

"Because to Weldon, Ryo was an ugly, stinking, hard-shelled, smelly slimy bug. That's why, Colonel. That's the attitude we're going to have to contend with and that's why we have to be allowed to establish formal contact with Ryo's race before word of their existence is leaked to the general populace.

"By the way, you ought to put a seal on environmental specialist Mila Renstaad. She felt the same way as Weldon and could cause trouble."

"I'll handle that," Davis said curtly.

"If we don't make successful, friendly contact," she went on, "then any chance our two peoples have for understanding each other will be drowned by the initial outpouring of visceral, ancestral loathing for creatures of Ryo's appearance." She broke off suddenly, as if amazed at the length and passion of her unintended polemic.

"That's all I have to say about it, sir. I've already lost

a—a very good friend. As you said, two men are dead. That's only a portent of what could come."

"No disrespect intended, Colonel Davis," Sanchez said, "but you can only speak for your immediate staff. The same is true for you, Dr. Rijseen."

"I will enter the revised staff recommendation in the computer," Rijseen said, not offended. "You can check it, through your on-board system. All points about keeping this quiet are well taken and will be properly acted upon.

"As to whether this incident will be followed by your suggested establishment of formal contact with the Thranx, that remains to be discussed. On that I really do *not* have the authority to make promises. Such a decision requires the blessings of at least three of the five acting members of the ruling board of the Terran Society for the Advancement of Science and Exploration, plus permission from the appropriate governmental agencies and elected authorities. The political ramifications are explosive."

"Then if you cannot promise, you can at least promise to try," Sanchez said.

"I will do my best. Of course, if you do not return there can be no discussion. What do you say?"

"It's not for me to make the decision." She looked back at the large arthropod who was carefully preening his left antenna.

"Ryo, I don't know you as well as I'd like to. Not as well as Bonnie does, or Loo did. This is your choice to make. If you insist, we'll move out to five planetary diameters and head for your home. I know what awaits you there, but it's up to you to decide." She didn't smile. She rarely did. "I wouldn't blame you after all this for wanting to return to your own kind."

"I really am not sure what to do. I am an agricultural expert, not one prepared to determine the course of future relations between two species."

"Like it or not," Bonnie said, "you've been put in that position."

"Put your trust in God," Bhadravati urged him.

"Yours or mine?"

"There's only one God, by whatever name you call him," the scientist said.

"Theology student, yes? I can see that you and I are going to have many long conversations, Dr. Bhadravati. There is a friend of mine—at least, I left him as a friend—whom I think you would enjoy talking to more than me, but he is not with us right now. I hope someday you have the privilege of meeting him."

"So do I. Like everything else, though, that's up to you."

So while the humans waited and watched their instruments, Ryo thought. Of Fal waiting on Willow-wane. Or was she? Of his comfortable and unpressured position with the Inmot, which had once seemed so dull and pointless and which now seemed unbearably inviting. Of his sisters and their families.

What would Ilvenzuteck advise me to do? he wondered. What would the hivemother say? He wished desperately he could consult with both those wise matriarchs. But there was no one to consult; not a clanmother, not a poet, not a larva. He stood alone in an alien ship, surrounded by five monsters who meant him well and who would do his bidding.

That trust was not to be exploited. And what of the human Loo who had died protecting him? Which would be the best way to insure that no additional deaths would result? Which way, which way, to allay the mindless hate that festered among the less intelligent members of both species?

Sanchez was right. He badly wanted to return home. But to what? To prison and reconditioning? His own kind had left him with no promises. Here at least he had gained something of a commitment. As to whether that commitment would be honored, well . . . If he returned home, five humans whom he'd come to like very much would return here to suffer. If he remained to work and cajole and fight for contact, only he could lose.

As so many things did, it came down to simple mathematics.

Captain Sanchez's hand was poised over the control console, he noticed. A screen showed the small ship that was coming toward them from the station.

He executed a multiple gesture indicative of fifth-degree sardonicism, with fourth-degree resignation and just a flavoring of irony. No one, including Bonnie, was sufficiently well versed yet in Thranx to interpret it. Perhaps someday they would be.

"Let us return. If all of you are willing to trust this Dr. Rijseen, then so am I."

"I'll be sure to tell him that," Bhadravati said. "I'll make it a point to tell him to his face."

"You can tell him yourself, Ryo." Sanchez's fingers danced on the controls.

The *Seeker* pirouetted gracefully on its latitudinal axis. Systemwise it was facing inward once again. The thoughts and spirits of its inhabitants were soaring in a different direction entirely.

XIV

"You don't change the destiny of an entire people that quickly. It takes time."

The man in the azure jumpsuit was waving his hands as he spoke. Ryo thought he could be very fluent in Low Thranx. The human was short and corpulent. His hair was completely white. It descended in waves down his collar. His pink forehead gleamed in the light, almost shiny enough to pass for stained chiton. If I were to press on it, Ryo reminded himself, my finger would not slide off as is normal but would move inward until encountering bone. He shuddered slightly and doubted he would ever grow used to the idea of wearing one's body outside one's skeleton.

Though he possessed only half the requisite number of limbs, in his metallic attire the man looked very much like a Thranx. He was a part of the hierarchy of the human government, a Secretary of something. His position was not as high as they'd hoped for, but Sanchez and Bonnie had assured Ryo that it was substanial enough. His arrival on Centaurus V, though at night and in comparative secret, had caused something of a stir on that world.

Several others had come with him or ahead of him, traveling the long way from distant Earth to C-V and then out to the system border station slowly orbiting C-VII. From there they had been escorted by shuttle to the wardroom of the *Seeker*. Sanchez and her associates, despite repeated assurances of noninterference from Davis and Dr. Rijseen, had chosen to remain on board and in free space. It helped, the captain explained, their peace of mind.

Rijseen was also present. So were Sanchez and Bonnie. The others were monitoring ship functions—and other items of interest. Outside the observation port that dominated the wardroom lay the cold dark mass of Centaurus VII, the faint disk of the station itself, and two much smaller spots of light that Sanchez and Taourit had assured Ryo were warships.

They did not seem to worry the *Seeker*'s captain, who was confident the ship could engage its Supralight drive before either of those motionless warcraft could do her any damage. The warcraft were present mostly to make an impression, though whether on Ryo, his human friends, or the visiting dignitaries was hard to say. They could not engage their own drives in their present position without destroying the C-VII station and its five thousand inhabitants.

Debate proceeded in the wardroom of the *Seeker* in an atmosphere of cordial uncertainty.

"Of course, I have no authority to commit my people to any kind of formal treaty," Ryo was saying. "I admit that as a representative of my species I stand here unappointed and unanointed. But from all I have observed, all I have experienced, I believe an alliance between our peoples not merely to be desirable but vital."

One of the human officials spoke up. He was ordinarily silent and said very little. Nor did he seem gifted with unusual intelligence. Yet his comments were always relevant and to the point.

"I can understand your use of the term desirable. But 'vital'? I've been informed that your command of our language is quite good, and from what I've seen so far I wouldn't dispute that. But are you sure of your use of the word?"

"Yes. Vital." Ryo added a gesture of maximum emphasis that was lost on his attentive listeners. "Vital for our survival because of the increasing depredations of the AAnn and because our culture badly needs a kick in its gestalt, vital to you for your mental stability."

Several of the officials stirred uneasily, but the white-haired man in their midst only laughed. "I've studied the claims you've made for your psychtechs. Alliances are not made by psychologists."

"Maybe that wouldn't be such a bad change," Sanchez suggested softly.

The man glared at her. "I understand Mr. Ryoz—ryiez . . ."

"Just Ryo," the Thranx said.

"I understand your reasoning." He bent to examine papers on the table in front of him, spoke while reading. "It is your contention that a close alliance between and association of our peoples would be beneficial to the mental health of the human species."

"I have reasons to believe that to be so," admitted Ryo.

"So you think you're better than we?"

"Not better, just different. As I just stated, I believe there are many things you have to offer in return, though doubtless many officials of the government of Hivehom would dispute that."

"You mentioned a 'kick' of some kind," put in another official.

"Our culture is immensely successful. We have enjoyed interspecies peace for thousands of years. This stability has bred technological success. It has also led to sterility in other areas. Many of your art forms, for example, I find delightful. Your music, your forms of recreation . . . there is great energy there, reflective of your racial hysteria. These are outlets for your cerebral furies. We could be another. It would benefit us both."

"Then you want to channel us?" the fat man said dangerously.

"No, no!" Ryo struggled to convey his exasperation as best he could in human terms, without the use of gestures. It was a constant struggle to talk only with air and not with your limbs and body. "I don't want to channel you, don't want to see you directed. There is nothing of dominance in this. I don't want us to do anything for you, or to you. Only *with* you."

"With us." The official considered. "A fine sentiment, but by your own admission it will be difficult to convince your own people of that."

"They will be frightened of you at first, as they were of the crew of this ship. As I was. We must overcome old emotions, all of us. Shape must not interfere with reason. Nor must your psychotic tendencies."

"We do not have psychotic tendencies." The official was uncomfortable.

"Talk to your own consultants," Sanchez advised him. "Study human history. We should not be afraid of admitting that we are what we are."

"Consider your own state of mind right this minute," Rijseen added, "Then look at this alien across from you. He is far from home and among what are to him creatures of surpassing ugliness. See how calm he is, how relaxed and at ease."

That wasn't entirely true, Ryo thought, but he wasn't about to step on the scientist's hypothesis.

"Would a human placed in the same situation react this way? We know he wouldn't. We know it because Captain

Sanchez and her people did not, and they were trained for such confrontation. They kicked and screamed and acted like—well, like humans. From my studies I am convinced that Ryo's mental stability is the result not of racial or individual weakness or fatalism, but of a better understanding of himself."

"I can see that he's convinced you, at least," the official said.

"Facts," Bhadravati said softly, "can be most persuasive, sir."

The official rose and walked toward the large port. He stood and stared silently at the vast dead world below. The star Centaurus (that was not Alpha because of a great mistake) was a dim, distant point of light. Ryo could see his fingers twisting and entwining in some secret ritual.

"It's difficult," the man murmured, "very difficult. For example, we have only your word for the supposedly relentless hostility of these AAnn."

"They'll give you ample proof themselves soon enough," Ryo noted.

"Our records show that the ship that attacked us is different from any Thranx vessel we saw," Sanchez told him. "If half of what Ryo says about them is true, they will present a real danger."

Ryo tried to divine the man's mood by looking at him, but failed utterly. He tried to believe that the continued silence was a sign that the man's indecision was weakening, that despite his uncertainties he was coming around to the side of reason.

He turned, his fingers still working, silhouetted by a dead world. "I mean no offense—damn, I don't know how to put this. There are problems here that logic will not solve. It's simply that—"

"That if I were of a different ancestry," Ryo told him, "everything would be simpler. If I did not look like a big, icky, crawly insect."

The Secretary looked distinctly uncomfortable as Ryo continued. "I have had ample time to study the phobia most humans have regarding my tiny relatives on your world. We are not properly insects, by your classification system."

"The general public," the Secretary replied, "is not interested in scientific niceties. You look like something out of many of their worst nightmares."

"And what about you, Mr. Secretary?" Ryo slid off his saddle and approached. "How do I look to you?" He reached up with both tru- and foothands and grasped the lower edge of the man's shirt.

"Does my touch make your skin crawl? An intriguing phenomenon, by the way. Do I make you want to vomit? Does my smell make you ill?" He let loose of the material. The Secretary hadn't moved.

"As a matter of fact," he replied calmly, "your smell, of which I was apprised prior to my arrival, is quite as lovely as reported. However, our media systems are not sufficiently advanced to convey odiferous stimuli. Only sight and sound. I'm afraid that when it comes to the question of contact, sight will predominate in determining responses."

Ryo had turned and retaken his saddle. "So you are not optimistic."

"You have already had an unfortunate encounter with one fanatic, I understand?"

"Yes. It cost the life of a very dear human friend of mine. I believe the incident proves not the adverse reactions my people might provoke, but the opposite. A human has sacrificed his life for mine, grotesque quasi-insect though I am."

"A singular, isolated example involving a man who was a trained explorer. The same reaction cannot be expected from the average human."

"Or for that matter, the average Thranx," Ryo admitted. "Somehow a solution must be found."

"I can't see one." The Secretary was not encouraging. "We would have to demonstrate beyond a doubt that our two species could live side by side in harmony and understanding despite thousands of years of mutual conditioning to the contrary.

"The best I can realistically offer is a chance to open tentative communications via Deep Space transmissions. Even then I'll have to combat the bigots and paranoids in my own department. But if we exercise caution, with luck and some social maturation we might during the next couple of hundred years—"

"Apologies for interruption, sir." Ryo cut him off

sharply. "The AAnn will not wait a couple of hundred years. They will extend their mischief-making to include your people. They know just how far they can push, how deeply they can wound. They will try to bleed you to death. When you are weak enough, they will attack. Each day they grow more powerful, more confident. For the sake of both our species we must strike an alliance *now*. That cannot be done through cautious, long-range transmissions."

A successful politician knows when to be tactful and when to be truthful. The Secretary was very successful.

"Unfortunately, the facts exist. We cannot alter our shape any more than you can alter yours. I can see no quick way to prove species compatibility."

"I have given much thought to the problem," Ryo replied. "I had hoped not to have to make the proposal I will now lay before you all. It is a bit—well, theatrical. My friend Wuuzelansem would approve the form if not the content. It is all I can think of, however. It will settle the question of compatibility permanently, I should think.

"If the operation becomes known, it will be condemned with many expressions of outrage and horror by both our peoples. I fully expect all of you," and he gestured around the room, "to react in similar fashion as I explain. I entreat you to let me finish, and to consider what I say calmly and reasoningly. I ask you to put instinctive passions aside while considering the larger issues we are dealing with here. With success will come admiration and vindication. Failure would mean dishonor and much worse for all involved."

"I don't like choices that offer only extremes. I prefer to remain in the middle," the Secretary murmured.

"There is no middle here, sir. Are you not risk-takers? Do you humans not like to dance with the laws of chance?"

"We've been known to do so now and then," one of the other government officials commented drily.

"Then I shall detail my thoughts. I request only that you do not reject until I have finished." At least, he thought, I have gained their full attention. Having acquired considerable wisdom during the past years, however, he was not sanguine about the chances for acceptance.

"Now then," he began briskly, "if I have studied your

customs efficiently I believe I am not wrong in saying that you look unfavorably upon kidnaping and infanticide . . ."

The world that hove into view on the screen was so achingly familiar that Ryo found himself shaking.

"Are you all right, Ryo?" Bonnie stared back at him from her seat.

"I am. It's only that I hadn't expected so powerful a reaction." As he stared the misty white-green globe swelled to fill the entire screen. They were diving at it very fast, as was planned. "I thought myself sufficiently detached, removed to a point where such mundane instincts would not affect me. That is clearly not the case. I feel rather numbed."

"I understand." She watched him sympathetically. "We are subject to the same emotions. We call it homesickness." She lifted her gaze to the small screen. They were in Ryo's quarters on board the heavily screened *Seeker*. She wiped the ever-present sweat from her forehead. She'd been sitting with him for over an hour now and her clothing was soaked. "It's a beautiful world, your Willow-wane. Your home."

"Yes. Most of the settlement is on the opposite hemisphere."

"Don't worry, Elvira knows what to do. She'll hold this dive and veer back to Space Plus range at the first sign of a probe. Though if what you say is true, that's unlikely to happen."

"I think we will be all right. The additional screening equipment your people installed should give us the electronic appearance of a tiny meteor temporarily drawn into low orbit. Inside five pd's of Hivehom or Warm Nursery we would soon be detected, but there are many dead zones above Willow-wane. I believe the *Seeker* will be able to orbit undetected long enough to allow us to ferry our material to the surface."

The door admit chimed and Ryo called, "Enter, please." It slid aside and a gust of cold air from the corridor beyond momentarily chilled him. Bonnie moved her arms gratefully in the brief breeze.

A small human walked into the room. Ryo studied it

with his usual fascination. Humans knew no larval stage, did not experience the terror and wonder and glory of metamorphosis. Like many mammals, they were born into the shape they would have for their whole life.

They did not have the benefit of an extended learning period in which to rest and absorb knowledge. Instead they were thrust immediately into a highly competitive adult environment. Though no psychtech, Ryo believed this unhappy arrangement had much to do with the species' paranoia and belligerence.

The larva—no, he corrected himself, the male child—was named Matthew. He stopped next to Bonnie, lifted his hand instinctively. She took it in her own.

"Is that where we're going, Ms. Thorpe?" Ryo noted that though he held his other hand in his mouth he was not using his mandibles to clean the fingers. The habit, he'd been told, had a psychological rather than practical purpose.

"Yes, that's where we're going, Matthew. Isn't it pretty?" She bent over to put her face at his level. Both regarded the viewscreen.

"It looks kinda like home," he said.

"Most inhabitable planets look alike."

"What's 'inhabitibitible' mean?"

"Inha*bit*able," she corrected him. "It means we can usually live there."

"It looks like a lime sundae. How long will we be there?"

"Not so very long."

Matthew thought a moment, squinted at the screen. "When will I see Mommy and Daddy again?"

Bonnie hesitated, then smiled maternally. "After school is finished. They know you're away, you know."

"Yeah, sure."

"Do you like this school so far?"

"Oh, yeah!" Sudden excitement suffused his face. "There's lots of neat things to do and tapes to study and neat food and friends! I like it a lot better than my old school. And it's on a starship, too." He screwed his face into a thoughtful frown. "Too many girls, though."

Bonnie smiled.

"But it's lots of fun. I never thought school could be so

much fun. I'd like to go outside, though. 'Course, I know I can't do that in space, and I don't have a envirosuit."

"We'll be landing real soon now," she informed him, "and you'll be able to play outside. You'll have new lessons to learn."

"Oh, that's okay. I don't mind studying. I like school."

"I know you do, Matthew." She reached out, rumpled his brown curls. "That's one reason why you were chosen to come on the ship for this special term."

"Yeah. It's sure fun." He studied the lime sundae a while longer. Then his attention shifted to the figure sprawled on its right side on the high bed. He still held onto Bonnie's hand but his other fingers were no longer in his mouth. That was a baby habit, he knew, and he wasn't a baby anymore. He was determined to stop it.

"Hi, Ryo."

"Hello, Matthew."

"Will you wordwhistle for me again?"

"Anytime," and he made the Thranx word for happy.

Matthew's brows drew together. His face twisted and his mandibles pursed tight. At first nothing happened when he blew through them. The second time a soft whistling emerged. He smiled. "How's that?"

"Very good, but it needs to be higher at the end. That's the whistleword for happy."

"I know that. You think I'm stupid or somethin'?" He tried again. The sound floated through the room, louder this time.

"That's better. Much better. Want to try the word for sun-up-morning?"

"Naw, not now." He looked up at Bonnie, then back to the figure on the bed. It was a funny bed, he thought, but then Ryo was funny-shaped, so he supposed it matched up okay.

"Want to play horsey?"

"Sure." Ryo slid off the lounge. Horsey was a young-human game, in which one partner assumed the part of a domesticated animal. It was all part of a much greater and far more dangerous game.

He immediately lowered himself to the floor so the boy could climb aboard. It embarrassed him whenever one of the children asked to play the horse.

XV

It doesn't matter who or what you are, Ryo mused. Wherever home is, there is something about its smell that distinguishes it from any other world.

He inhaled deeply, his thorax expanding with a rush as he gazed around the little clearing. Off to his left, muldringia vine grew thick and close until the unscreened sunlight turned them pale and weak at the clearing's edge. Tall grass wore a corona of bright little yellow flowers. Snuff bugs whizzed through the morning air. His antennae waved through the pollen recently dispersed by an overripe bombush. The heady aroma threatened to upset his balance on the ramp.

"My home." He turned to the open lock and those standing there. "Is it not wonderful?"

Liquid was already materializing on Bonnie's exposed skin. Bhadravati and several other friends crowded around her, testing the air.

"Very lush," Bhadravati agreed. "But to us, very hot and terribly humid."

"A mild second-season day," Ryo noted. "I doubt the humidity is much more than 80 percent. With luck it will top a comfortable 90 by midday eve."

"With luck," Elvira Sanchez muttered gloomily as she leaned through the lock and gazed across the treetops. Her concern was for what might appear from the clouds.

"If we had been detected on approach," a voice said from inside the ship, "search craft would be overflying this area by now."

"I know. I'm just a natural worrier," the captain called over a shoulder. Hands on hips, she turned to look past Ryo. "A good place to lose weight, anyway."

Ryo made a gesture of puzzlement. "Why would you want to lose weight—and how?"

"Cosmetic reasons," she replied. "When we move around in very hot weather, our bodies sweat water and we can lose weight."

"Extraordinary." Ryo shook his head to indicate amazement, a gesture he had picked up from the human physical vocabulary. "Being constrained by our exoskeletons we are considerably less flexible in such matters."

201

"A world without obesity," Bonnie murmured. "That would be enough to induce some humans to visit here."

"But not enough of them." Bhadravati squinted into the heat. "Hence our illegal visit."

Highly illegal. The Secretary had provided covert assistance and laundered funds, but had made it quite clear that if the project was discovered he would denounce it as vociferously as anyone else in the government. Only tremendous pressure from members of the scientific community, incited by Rijseen and Bhadravati, had enabled the expedition to literally get off the ground at all.

Clattering and shouts sounded from below the ramp, where humans and their machines were wrestling with the contents of the shuttle's hold.

"We should have the first portion of the shelter set up by the time you return," Bonnie told Ryo. "Of course, if you're not back within the prescribed time period—"

"I know. You'll disappear, leaving me with quite a lot of explaining to do. Assuming I am given time to explain."

"I thought you said your people were highly civilized about such matters."

"Fear of the unknown, while exaggerated among *Homo sapiens,* is not completely unknown among the Thranx," he responded. "It is such attitudes we are battling to overcome."

"I hope you're back in time." She reached out to touch one of his antennae. "Don't get yourself blown apart. You're important. It's not the Thranx we're friends with, yet. It's you."

"I will endeavor most strenuously to preserve myself," he assured her as he started down the ramp. Bonnie and the others followed to the bottom. There they turned to aid in the unloading and setting up.

Peering up at the shuttle he could see numerous faces pressed against the glass of the tiny ports. Some of the faces were smaller and less well defined than others. Soon, Matthew, he thought at the faces. Soon you'll be able to come out and play. Soon I hope to have a new game for you and your friends.

Moving through the jungle on foot was slow and awkward, even though he remembered the area reasonably well. That was one of the principal reasons it had been selected. And he had made his way through far wilder and more hostile flora. Oh, so long ago!

Days passed. Anxiously he kept watch on the frond-shrouded sky for signs of search craft. After a half-month had passed he was finally convinced the shuttle had set down unnoticed.

Before much more time passed, Ryo found himself standing among the first row of tettoq trees. Across the orchard to his left should be the machine shop where broken field equipment was repaired. He'd emerged from the jungle slightly to the south of the Inmot holdings, but he still recognized the landscape. The jungle had not been pushed back *that* far since his hurried departure so long ago.

It was very hard to remain concealed in the trees at the jungle's edge. He wanted more than anything to skitter shouting and yelling down the nearest entryway, but that was not to be, not this night and not for some time, if ever again.

He waited until sleeptime was well along and the stars were high up behind the cloud cover before leaving the shelter of the jungle. Somehow, as he made his cautious way through the carefully cultivated vegetation, he expected things to be more different then they were. In actuality he hadn't been away that long. Mentally, he'd been absent for years.

There were no patrols to avoid, since there was nothing to patrol against. Twice he encountered premates or curious youngsters out for a nocturnal stroll. No one recognized him. That was fortunate, because only total darkness would have been sufficient to hide his movements completely.

It would be simpler if they were humans, he thought as he increased his pace after successfully slipping past the most recent pair. Humans were practically blind in weak light. They really are an amazing species, he mused. Consider what they have accomplished with poor vision, poor hearing, a weak sense of smell, no faz ability at all, and half the sensible number of limbs. Not to mention the burden of wearing their skeletons inside out. Quite remarkable.

He knew that a great deal was riding on his little night-time stroll. He hurried on a little faster.

The machine shop had not been moved. No one was guarding the tools or heavy equipment parked outside. Theft was not unknown in the larger hives, but bulky material was quite safe in a community the size of Paszex because there was no place to steal it to.

Such trust did not extend to leaving the ignition controls activated, however. Foolishness was present among the irreverent in Paszex in proportion to the population. Ryo had a busy half-hour jimmying the controls of one harvester so it could be started with ease.

The machine was used to transport bulk loads from fields to processing chutes. With the familiarity of long practice he started the engine. The harvester slid smoothly forward on triple rows of balloon wheels.

There was an awkward moment when he parked the harvester outside the particular entryway he intended to use, for some night stroller might think to question the presence of the big machine so far from any agricultural station. No one appeared, however.

After altering the internal temperature of the harvester's cargo bay to suit his intentions he slid from the control cab and entered the hive. Nothing unfamiliar assaulted his senses. Yet he didn't feel quite as at home as he'd thought he would. Nothing was different, nothing had been changed. He'd spent most of his life in the very corridors he was now walking. Yet there was a difference, and he feared it was permanent.

Most of the citizenry were asleep, but some were still hard at work. The regular maintenance crews, for example, were preparing the corridors for the next workday. He had to exercise a little care.

He descended several levels, turned at a familiar corner, then into his destination. Workers were busier here than just about anywhere else in Paszex. That was no surprise. He knew it would be so, but he could not avoid it.

"Good evening, sir," the monitor said.

"Good evening."

"It's very late, sir."

"I know, but I had difficulty sleeping and thought I would admire our new cagin." Thranx did not have nieces and nephews. A new birth was relative to all in his clan. The relationship was sufficiently general that Ryo believed he could gain admittance merely by claiming it. Every clan had a new cagin or two in the Nursery.

The monitor did not question him. "Very well, but be quiet. They are all sleeping soundly."

"I know. I will be."

He entered the Nursery proper. The long rows of curved study saddles lay in two orderly rows against the glazed walls. Partitions formed individual cubicles. About three-fourths of the saddles were occupied by larvae in various stages of maturation.

How many years ago had he lain in one such saddle? he thought. Immobile, thirsting for knowledge and food, whiling away the days in idle study with his Nurserymates while anticipating metamorphosis.

Now he was in the Nursery again, with a different purpose. A glance from the doorway showed only three Nurses present. Even that seemed cause for concern. They moved busily about their tasks.

None of them disturbed him or thought to question his presence as he made his way casually down the central aisle. The saddle designs had not been altered in his lifetime. All were portable, each equipped with a tiny motor enabling it to be easily moved should an occupant require a shift to surgery or another department.

He pretended to gaze admiringly at an infant near the end of the aisle. The emergency exit should be nearby. These were not simple holdovers from ancient times when every Thranx Nursery possessed them, but served as important escape routes in case of fire.

The exit should lead to a ramp at the outskirts of the hive. One who used such a passageway for nonemergency purpose was subject to substantial penalties, but then, so was a kidnaper. The confluence of crimes and antisocial behavior in general among human and Thranx is one of our less obvious similarities, he mused.

The larvae he chose were neither newborns nor those on the verge of metamorphosis. All were approximately at midlarval stage.

His patience was rewarded when not one but two of the Nurses working up the aisle made their way out of the

Nursery. When they did not return he quietly started work. Two, three, five of the saddles were linked by couplers. All could now be steered by a single Nurse. Or anyone else. A glance up the aisle showed that the last attendant had disappeared. The cubicle partitions concealed him reasonably well and would do so until he had to move his little train out into the open for the short dash to the emergency exitway. He would be quite satisfied if he could slip them through without being noticed. He did not have time to worry about how long he would have until they were missed.

He was linking the sixth and final saddle to the others when a shockingly familiar scent reached his antennae. They jerked backward in reaction. The scent was followed by a querulous and equally familiar voice.

"Ryo?" He turned. It was Fal.

She wore her uniform vest and neck pouch and was staring at him. How much she'd observed he didn't know, not that it mattered now. She raised all four hands and gestured at the little line of linked saddles. Their motors whispered, their occupants slept on, oblivious.

"Where did you come from and what do you think you're doing?"

Ryo discovered that he was breathing in quick, short gasps. His gaze went past her to the Nursery entrance. The other two Nurses still hadn't returned but he daren't count on their absence much longer.

"I haven't time to explain," he told her. "You must help me get these children out of the Nursery and up to the surface. Everything depends on speed now."

She took a step away from him. "I don't understand you. You told me you were involved in some kind of government project. Then that same agency told us you'd turned criminal." She made a gesture of considerable confusion and uncertainty. "I don't know who or what to believe anymore."

"Everything you were told is true, in its fashion," he said, unfailingly honest. "To a point. I *was* working on a government project and I *am* now something of a lawbreaker. Probably worse than that, according to some. In the opinion of others, I am doubtless regarded as a grand hero. Actually, I'm neither. I'm just me, doing what I think necessary. You can make your own decision, Fal. But I don't have time to explain things. Not now."

He touched a control and the line of saddles moved toward the emergency corridor. She hurried around to block the lead saddle.

"I don't know where you've been, Ryo, or why you haven't been in touch with me or what you've been doing. I don't much care. I do care to see you again. It's good, I think, in spite of what you did. We have many things to talk about. In the meantime and for whatever personal reasons of yours, these larvae are going nowhere. This is the Nursery. This is where they belong and this is where they remain. Unless you *can* explain what you're doing, which I sincerely doubt."

"I doubt it myself," he told her, stepping close. "It's more complicated than you can imagine. I love you, Fal. You are a wonderful, intelligent, insightful, enjoyable female and my opinion of you will never change regardless of what you come to think of me and I hope you will excuse this," and he brought down two fists with what he fervently hoped was carefully gauged strength between her antennae.

She did not even have time to gasp. Her arms went out in a gesture of shock and she collapsed to the floor. He bent quickly over her. A glance up the aisle showed a still empty Nursery. His luck continued.

Her thorax pulsed slowly but steadily as he lifted her onto an empty saddle and linked it to the other six. She would be unconscious for a long time while her body healed the cerebral bruise.

The kidnaping would confront the Hive Council with a great mystery. It would be natural for them to concentrate on Fal's background in the hunt for motives. With luck they might never make the connection between a cluster of missing larvae and a long-absent mental defective named Ryozenzuzex. If the humans had done their part and thoroughly camouflaged their shuttle and the new structures, they might have a great deal of time before the alarm was raised and anyone thought to do some studious deduction.

With less luck and preparation he might be very dead in a day or two, along with the six innocent larvae, Fal, and all his human friends. He preferred not to think about that. In any case, now was not the time.

He met no one in the emergency corridor. No one challenged him when he emerged on the surface with his unlikely cargo in tow.

Getting the seven saddles and their occupants into the harvester was difficult work even with the aid of the machine's autoloading apparatus. Still he was not interrupted. When the last saddle had been positioned and locked in place inside the climate-controlled hold he mounted the cab and gunned the engine. The harvester rumbled off down the nearest access path.

He was careful to stay on the designated roads, even though it cost him some time. The last thing he wanted was to leave a clear track behind him. Soon he was in among the jungle trees, however, and he had to program the harvesting equipment to carefully replace the vegetation the machine bashed through. In a few hours the sun would be up and a preliminary search of Paszex and its immediate environs would be under way.

Confusion would be his most effective shield. They would inspect the immediate belt of jungle surrounding the hive fields, but since there was no reason for the missing Nurse to take her charges farther afield he didn't think a deep hunt would commence for several days. By that time he would be well beyond any sensible search pattern.

He'd entered the missing harvester into the machine-shop program as off-line, on its way to Zirenba for extensive overhaul. Months would pass before anyone thought to check on its status.

Fal presented a more substantial problem. He did not think she would remain calm at the sight of his horrific human companions. If she awoke it might be best to keep her sedated. He would worry about that later. If the project failed her opinion of him would not matter. If by some chance it succeeded—well, he would worry about their relationship at that time only.

When the sun rose, so would his young charges. Ryo had spent time in the Nursery only as an occupant. Very shortly he would have to deal with six confused, unhappy, and hungry youngsters. He didn't know exactly how he was going to cope with that, although the past month had taught him something of handling youngsters and their needs. If he could manage infants of another species, surely he could deal with those of his own kind.

He managed to do so. The presence of the "sleeping" Nurse, whom they all recognized, helped to calm them. When she didn't wake up there might be new problems, but Ryo was grateful for the respite.

The harvester continued to perform admirably, sloshing its way through the rain forest while automatically covering its own tracks. To assist it he tried to choose paths that were particularly watery, but he was positive he must be leaving a trail behind him wide enough for a dozen Servitors to scan.

His only confrontation, however, came not from an angry cluster of Servitors or any of the jungle's omnipresent carnivores, but from several armed humans who materialized magically from among the trees and surrounded the harvester. It was interesting to note that they had shed the majority of their clothing.

Greetings were exchanged and weapons lowered. A couple of the humans gazed dumbly back into the jungle along the path restored by the harvester. They could not believe Ryo had brought off the most difficult part of the experiment.

"You're sure no one's following you?" a beefy male asked. His body fur was black and full of tight curls.

"It proceeded with admirable smoothness," Ryo said. He was glad no one challenged him. He was not ready to explain about Fal. That incident was still painful to recall.

They escorted him to the glade. As the harvester emerged from the trees Ryo had to struggle before locating the exquisitely hidden shuttle. It seemed to have sprouted grass, bushes, and yellow flowers.

Other hills marked the sites of the portable buildings the expedition had brought with them. There would be the section for housing his six immobile charges, there one for their human counterparts. Most of the adults would bivouac aboard the shuttle.

Since shuttle and structures were nearly invisible from the ground, Ryo had no doubt that from the air the illusion would be complete. In addition to confusing any visual search, the humans also possessed sophisticated instruments for harmlessly dispersing heat and restricting sound. They would have privacy and time. That was more than he'd hoped for.

A violent squalling in the form of a rising and falling whistle sounded from the rear of the harvester. Ryo brought it to a halt. Several other humans had joined the intercepting forest guards and were peering into the cargo hold.

Ryo nearly broke a leg as he rushed to get there. In the excitement of the moment the humans had not considered the effect their appearance might have on his intelligent and impressionable passengers.

He had not intended that the children confront their nightmares so soon.

Matthew remembered the first times.

He wasn't sure why he'd been chosen, but he was glad that he had been. The world they were visiting was a neat place, full of brightly colored bugs and flying things, and interesting creepy-crawlies to poke sticks at through the clear surfaces of shallow ponds.

He didn't have much time to do that, since they kept him and the others playing with the funny-shaped kids. They were nice, so he didn't mind not being allowed outside so much.

Bonnie and the big bug, Ryo, had told him that his new friends were children just like him, only of Ryo's people. But they didn't look anything like little Ryos at all. In fact, when Matthew first saw them his initial reaction and that of his friends had been one of pity. They had no arms or legs. How could anyone play without arms or legs?

They had huge wormlike bodies. That was kind of icky at first, but they also had pale colors running just under their skins that were awful pretty. It was funny to see these colors change from green to blue, from red to yellow and back again. Matthew wished he could change color like that.

They smelled real nice, too. Like a field of cut grass, or the hem of his mother's dress, or the laundry when it was new. The grown-ups were afraid at first that he and his friends would be frightened of the larvae, as they called them. That was silly. How could anyone be afraid of someone who smelled so nice and didn't have arms to hit you with or legs to kick you with? The larvae, like his best friend Moul, were a lot more afraid of Matthew and the other human children than the human children were of them.

On the ship he'd learned to recognize a lot of the funny whistlewords and click-talk. That was good, because the Thranx kids didn't know any real speech at all. Matthew was the best of the bunch and he was proud when the other kids asked him to translate. As the weeks went by, however, both groups learned from their counterparts. Because the larvae had flexible mandibles, it turned out they could talk human even better than Ryo.

This seemed to surprise the grown-ups as much as it pleased them. Matthew shook his head. Some grown-ups were just plain *dumb*. After all, a stick is a stick whether you call it a stick or a whistleword.

It surprised him to learn that Moul and the other larvae felt sorry for him. Sure, Moul didn't have arms and legs, but he didn't run into things, either, or stick himself with thorns. That embarrassed Matthew and made him a little bit angry. Sometimes he thought of hitting Moul to show him what hands were good for.

But no matter what he said or how he said it, neither Moul nor his companions ever seemed to get mad. Pouty sometimes, but never mad. You couldn't go around hitting someone like that. And when Moul explained things to him, Matthew lost a lot of his own mads, too. It was funny the things grown-ups got excited about.

Matthew had lots of friends back in school on Earth. A couple of them had also qualified for the trip. One was a bigger boy named Werner, and Matthew couldn't understand how *he'd* made it. He'd beaten Matthew up a couple of times.

Moul was sorry to hear that when Matthew told him about it.

"I betcha Werner wouldn't try and beat *you* up," he told Moul one day as they were sitting in what the grown-ups called the Interaction Room. "You're too big."

"For now," Moul agreed, "but as he matures he'll outgrow me, and after metamorphosis I'll be slightly smaller than I am now."

"That's weird," Matthew said. "Getting smaller as you become a grown-up. But getting a whole new body; that sounds neat. I wish I could metamorphose." He added another magnetic span to the building he and Moul were designing. It was a curved one this time. Moul might not have any hands, but his suggestions were swell.

"Anyway," Moul wondered aloud, "if Werner is bigger and stronger than you, then why does he feel the need to beat you up? If he's bigger he ought to be smarter and realize how counterproductive such antisocial activity is."

"Yeah, well," Matthew muttered, "just once I'd like to pop him back a good one." He brought one fist into an open palm to produce a smacking sound.

"But why would you want to do that?" the studious Moul asked.

"To get even with him." Sometimes even Moul could say the dumbest things.

"For what?"

"For beating me up." Matthew put his hands on his hips and then made the Thranx sign for mild exasperation. "Boy, you're awfully smart most of the time, Moul; but now and then you're awful stupid, too."

"I'm sorry," the larva replied. "I'm just ignorant of your ways. It all seems so silly to me. Wouldn't it be better for the two of you to be friends?"

"Well, sure it would, I guess," Matthew reluctantly admitted, "but Werner is a bully. He likes to beat people up."

"Larvae who are smarter than he?"

"Well," the boy thought a moment, "yeah, I think so."

"That's what a 'bully' is—someone who beats up someone physically weaker than himself?"

"That's right, I guess." Actually Matthew hadn't given the subject much consideration. To him, a bully was someone who beat Matthew Bonner up. The definition need extend no further than that.

"Then he doesn't seem very big to me at all. It sounds to me like he has a very small mind."

"Yeah, I guess he must. Yes, that's it." Matthew smiled hugely. "A small mind. A small mind." He burst into delighted laughter at having discovered a gratifying corollary. At the same time he picked up another span.

"No, not a curved one this time," Moul advised him. "A

double-straight. It will give more support to the tower there."

Matthew studied the growing monument only briefly. Moul was rarely wrong. "I think you're right." He set the span in place, watched as it annealed to the nearby side panels. The structure was over a meter high and still growing. The two youngsters had been working on it off and on for several days. The adults found it most interesting.

He selected a ridge ellipsoid, moved to emplace it.

"Also on the top, don't you think?" Moul asked.

This time Matthew objected, holding it over the windowpanes two-thirds of the way up the left-hand tower. "Don't you think it would look better here?"

"Look better." Moul considered. He envied his friend's ability to see in colors more than he envied him his limbs. "Yes. Yes, I think you are right, Mattheeew. That is a most intriguing composition."

"We can use two of them." The boy chose a second, matching ellipsoid. "One here and one up top, where you suggested."

"An excellent suggestion, Mattheeew. Then I really think we'd better start working on the other side again or we'll overbalance the towers."

"Yeah, that's right." Then he frowned and set the two units back in their box.

"Is something wrong?"

"I'm bored," Matthew announced, sighing deeply. "I wish they'd let us go outside by ourselves. I get tired of having grown-ups around."

"I don't," said Moul. "In any case, you know I couldn't go out with you."

"Why not? Oh yeah, your skin would burn."

"During the day it would," the larva admitted mournfully. "Anyway, I think the adults don't want us to go outside much."

"They sure don't. I wonder why."

"I'm not sure," Moul said thoughtfully. "I respect adults, of course, but sometimes it seems to me they are capable of mistakes as obvious as our own."

"Yeah, they're not as smart as they think. I bet I could get you outside at night." His voice fell to a conspiratorial whisper. "We could fool 'em. Your skin wouldn't burn at night."

"No, it wouldn't," Moul agreed. "I can't get around by myself very well, though."

"Aw, we'd figure something out. I'd help you."

"And I'd help you. I can see almost as well at night as I can during the day," the larva told him. "I was informed that you cannot."

"You can see in the *dark?*" Matthew's eyes went wide.

"Quite well. Not as well as my ancestors, but well enough."

"Wow." Matthew could not conceal his awe. "I sure wish I could. Sometimes back home I wake up at night and can't find the light panels in the floor and bump around in the dark trying to find the bathroom."

"Bathroom?" Moul echoed, and the conversation shifted easily from the aesthetics of architecture and plans for nocturnal excursions to another tack altogether.

Weeks passed. The adults were delighted at the children's progress, much of which originated with the experimental subjects themselves.

"Want to play Cowboys and Indians?" Matthew asked his friend. It was raining hard outside the Interaction Room. There could be no thought of venturing outside, even by oneself.

"I don't know," Moul said curiously. "What's 'Cowboys and Indians?' "

"Well, once upon a time on Earth there was a noble, intelligent, handsome, and just generally sort of neat people called Indians." Matthew enjoyed being the one to explain for a change. He didn't for a moment doubt that Moul was smarter than he was, but somehow the usual resentment he felt toward smarter kids didn't apply to the larva. After all, Moul had received a lot more education and was perhaps a Terran year older than he.

"Anyway, their lands were invaded one day by a bunch of people called the Cowboys. The Cowboys were real nasty. They burned and slaughtered and stole and lied and all kinds of bad things until finally there were only a few Indians left. Eventually, though, the Indians got even because times changed and the life force that kept the Cowboys going faded away from their economy and they all died out. But the Indians kept their traditions and beliefs and lived happily ever after in the end."

"That doesn't sound like a very nice story," murmured Moul doubtfully, "despite the happy ending. I'm not sure I want to play . . . but if you really want to . . ."

"Yeah, sure." Matthew climbed to his feet.

Moul rippled back from the human. "It sounds awfully violent, Matthew. I don't like violent games."

"It won't be bad," the boy assured him. "Now, I'm going to be the Indians and you can be the Cowboys."

Moul considered. "I think I'd prefer to be the Indians."

"No. I suggested the game," Matthew was a mite belligerent, "and I'm going to be the Indians."

"All right. You can be the Indians."

Matthew frowned at him. "What do you mean, I can be the Indians? Just like that?"

"Well, of course. Why not?"

"But you said you wanted to be the Indians."

"I do," Moul admitted, "but you obviously want to be them more than I do. Therefore, it is only sensible to let you be the Indians."

Matthew mulled over this development, which tumbled around in his brain like a rough gem in a polishing unit. "No," he finally decided, "you can be the Indians."

"No, no. I understand thoroughly your desire, Mattheeew. You can be the Indians. I'll be the Cowboys."

"I've got an idea," the boy said suddenly. "Why don't we *both* of us be the Indians?"

"Then who'll be the Cowboys?"

Matthew turned and called across the room. "Hey Janie, Ahling, Chuck, Yer!!"

They entered into involved negotiations, but it developed that no one really wanted to be the Cowboys. They all wanted to be Indians.

In the observation booth behind the one-way, Dr. Jahan Bhadravati turned to his companions, who at that moment included Bonnie, Captain Sanchez of the *Seeker*, and a leading representative of Earth's government. Handshakes were exchanged all around, but the children in the room beyond would have found the adults' enthusiasm at a display of the commonplace very puzzling.

XVI

Bonnie was chatting with Ryo as they strolled from the shuttle toward the laboratory complex when the first rising thunder reached the camp from overhead. It arose in the north and grew steadily louder until a pair of quadruple-winged ships roared by, rattling the trees fringing the glade and scaring hell out of the arboreals.

The two walkers pressed themselves back beneath a canopy of chamelocloth. So did the other humans who'd been out in the comparative cool of early morning.

After a decent wait Bonnie leaned out to squint toward the southwest. "Think they saw us?"

"I don't know," said one of the shuttle's crew from beneath the overhanging limbs of a nearby tree. He too was staring worriedly southward. "They were awfully low and moving damn fast." He emerged from concealment. "I'd better get to my station, just in case."

Bonnie was about to join him when she felt restraining pressure on her arm.

"I do not think we were observed," Ryo told her. "You see, I am almost positive they were not looking for us."

"Then what were they doing out here, at that altitude?" She noticed his oddly rigid posture. "Is something else wrong?"

"Very wrong." Memories rose up, threatened to submerge all other thoughts. Fear and anger mixed inside him. "Those weren't Thranx ships. Those were AAnn warshuttles. I know, because I've seen them before."

"We've got to help." Sanchez glared around at the hastily assembled conference. They were in the shuttle's cargo hold, which had been converted to a conference chamber, among other things.

"It's not our business to get involved in local squabbles," the military attaché reminded them perfunctorily. "We're here uninvited. Our presence constitutes a dangerous provocation to the Thranx government. There is also the Project to consider. We could not assist the local colonists without revealing our presence, and that in turn would surely spell an end to our highly promising experiments here." He gazed coolly down toward Ryo.

"Personal feelings must not be allowed to divert us from

217

our principal reason for being here. We have no formal relations with the Thranx. The same is true for the AAnn. I have no basis for initiating hostilities against a neutral and uncontacted alien race."

"You'll pardon me if I disagree with that." Sanchez gave him a wan smile. "I've established to my satisfaction that it was the AAnn who, deliberately and unprovoked, attacked the *Seeker*. I had many killed and several wounded. I'd call that ample provocation for, at the minimum, an instructive reprisal."

"The attack on your ship could have arisen from misunderstanding," the attaché argued. He didn't enjoy the position he was forced to take, but he defended it admirably. "We could be jeopardizing any future relationships with the AAnn race."

"Your pardon, sir." One of the xenologists at the far end of the room raised a timorous hand. "If these AAnn conform to the psychosocial pattern diagrammed by my programming, then we stand the best chance of making a peace with them by showing a willingness to fight."

"That's crazy," the attaché snapped.

"An apt AAnn adjective," said Ryo, whose knowledge of Terranglo speech had progressed to an appreciation of alliteration.

"Their profile fits, however," the quiet specialist said with some conviction.

The attaché, outgunned, withdrew into silence.

"You must, of course, make your own decision based on the knowledge you have and your own customs," Ryo said gently. "I am under no such restraints. I must take my harvester and render whatever assistance I can, regardless of personal risk. Besides, there is little you could accomplish. For one thing, you have no satisfactory ground transportation. For another, you do not have—"

"I'm afraid that we do, Ryo," Sanchez informed him. The Thranx made an instinctive gesture of fourth-degree astonishment.

"I know this was designed to be a wholly peaceful mission," she continued, "and it should remain so with regard to human-Thranx relations. But considering our former imprisonment, surely you can understand that we wouldn't set down on a Thranx planet unarmed."

"No." Ryo tried to conceal his considerable upset. "I do not understand that."

The captain shrugged. "I'm sorry. Regardless, it remains that we have weapons." She gazed around the room. "I propose that we use them to demonstrate our mental constitution to the AAnn, and to aid our newfound friends. Informally, it would seem." She focused her attention on the attaché. "Of course, I cannot give the order to release weaponry for use here."

The attaché drummed his fingers on the arm of his chair. "I still haven't heard a strong enough reason. It's insane to take up arms against one race on behalf of another that we have no relations with."

"The whole experiment sounded insane when Ryo first proposed it," Bonnie reminded him. "There's something else you haven't thought of. None of you." Her gaze included Sanchez. "What of the larvae we've borrowed from the Paszex Nursery? Their parents and clanmates are all back there. If they're killed we'll have relations of a different sort to deal with, far more complicated relations.

"Also, by assisting the locals we have a chance to insinuate ourselves into their good graces. That would greatly aid the Project." She looked hard at the attaché. "Not hinder or finish it, as you claim. I feel it's time to take the next step, according to the Project programming. We can't stay hidden here forever."

"A most succinct summation." Bhadravati smiled pleasantly at the attaché. "I should very much like to have a gun, please. In the interest of furthering the Project." This sentiment was echoed strongly by most of the others in the chamber.

Ryo's feelings were confused. It was marvelous finally to have committed the humans against the AAnn. He would rather have accomplished it under different circumstances, in a different place, but the web of existence had dictated it be in Paszex. He would cope.

At the same time, the presence of weapons on board the shuttle was a discomfiting revelation. Not one had see fit to come forward to tell him about it. Perhaps, he mused, because my reaction was anticipated.

In spite of the successes and accomplishments of the past months, had Wuu in the final analysis been right all along?

Were these strange bipeds he had befriended really incurably warlike and violent? Or was the presence of arms here merely an understandable human reaction and precaution?

Dissection of philosophies would have to wait. All that mattered now was getting to Paszex as rapidly as possible. The harvester could rush there faster than the humans' shuttle, which had been made a part of the landscape.

Of course, the AAnn ships might not be heading for Paszex. That would spare him a lot of trouble.

Perhaps three dozen armed humans were ready and it was impossible to fit them all inside the harvester. The excess sat on top, clung to the sides. Ryo thoughtfully set the interior thermostat at near freezing, which his passengers found delightfully refreshing.

How long ago had he rumbled through the jungle in a survey crawler on a similar mission, to try and disrupt an AAnn attack on his home? Surely, if the AAnn were intent on Paszex again they would remember and post guards around their shuttles. But they would be expecting only a possible charge by agricultural machinery, not a heavily armed force of aliens.

The military attaché was present with his several associates. As trained soldiers, they easily and immediately assumed command. Ryo noticed how alert they appeared, how intense in posture and speech. That worried him as much as the presence of weapons had.

He'd observed humans in a warlike state months ago, when Bonnie and the lamented Loo had escaped from their military prison on northern Hivehom. That he could understand. Then they'd been motivated by fear. He wasn't sure what was motivating the humans now.

With the humans on top and sides hanging on tightly, Ryo gently put the versatile harvester on *lift*. There was no point in trying to hug the earth now, and they didn't have days in which to slog through the jungle. On full hover he set the craft for Paszex.

They set down into the trees at a sufficient distance to keep them off AAnn detection equipment. It took as long to negotiate the final short stretch of jungle separating them from the hive fields as it had to hover all the way from the glade.

The invaders had set down in a different orchard. As in

the previous nightmare, smoke was rising from ruined ventilators and intakes. For some perverse reason the AAnn seemed to have selected Paszex as a test hive for their inimical soirées. Ryo had no idea how many small, isolated hives on Willow-wane and other colony worlds had suffered similar repeated attacks, but it was obvious that an alliance with the humans was more necessary than his own government was willing to admit.

Distant explosions sounded from the direction of the hive. "We will approach stealthily at first," Ryo was telling the military attaché, "and try to slip close to them. I found that if you threaten their shuttles' engines they will—"

But the attaché was already making loud mouth noises which even the knowledgeable Ryo could not interpret. Then the humans fell like lice from the sides and rear of the harvester, and were running remarkably mobile zigzag patterns through the field of shoulder-high weoneon and asfi.

It's doubtful that their numbers would have overawed the well-trained AAnn soldiery. On the other hand, the sight of several dozen alien creatures waving alien devices as they charged from supposedly empty jungle shrieking at the tops of their lungs and generally comporting themselves like dangerous mental defectives would be enough to unsettle the most self-possessed warrior of any race.

The AAnn guards fired wildly and often blindly while the humans picked their shots with surprising accuracy. Bonnie, Captain Sanchez, Dr. Bhadravati, and all those whom Ryo had come to think of as peaceful, gentle scholars were blasting away with an enthusiasm that made Ryo feel very sad for them. He was no longer frightened of the possibilities they presented. Fear had become pity.

They need us, these poor bipeds, he told himself. He watched as an energy bolt seared the wingtip of one shuttlecraft. They need us far more than we need them. They are the ones who should be crying for alliance.

The earth erupted and he ducked below the harvester's roof for protection. A shot had struck something more than volatile within the body of the farther AAnn ship. It disintegrated in a storm of flaming plastic and flying metal shards. The explosion knocked the other shuttle over on its side, crumpling landing gear and one of the four wings.

Several of the humans had been shot, but the damage had been done. The startled AAnn who had not perished grouped themselves into a surrender formation, threw down their weapons, and linked arms in a gesture of defiant submission. They glared through slit pupils at the peculiar beings surrounding them.

Ryo watched and wondered what the commander of the AAnn base ship orbiting somewhere above must be thinking. He did not know if the AAnn suffered from panic. Other AAnn were staggering from the intact shuttlecraft. Those returning hastily from the underground corridors of Paszex took note of the submission ceremony their fellows were performing and joined in.

It was not until evening that it dawned on the invaders how greatly they outnumbered their captors. By then it was too late to organize any resistance. Besides, they had performed the submission ceremony. Regardless of their anger, they had committed themselves. So they contented themselves with much internal grumbling, intense study of the alien victors, and disparaging comments about their officers, who'd mistaken strangeness for superiority.

By then the inhabitants of the stricken community had begun to emerge. The local Servitors were joined by ordinary citizens who'd armed themselves with utensils and manufacturing implements. The captured AAnn regarded them with unconcealed disdain, their tails twitching listlessly as they shuffled about under the watchful gaze of the humans. Meanwhile the hivefolk kept their distance, their curiosity focused more on their fearful saviors than on the belligerent AAnn.

Eventually someone noticed Ryo standing among and conversing with the bipeds. He reluctantly made his way to the strangely garbed Thranx, striving to get no nearer the monstrous aliens than was absolutely necessary.

"I am Kerarilzex," the Elder announced. His antennae were withered, but not his voice. "I am Six on the Hive Council of Eight. We would give our thanks to these peculiar visitors"—he'd been about to use the Thranx word for monster and at the last minute thought better of it—"but I would not know how to do so. It appears you can converse with them." Then he made a slow gesture of third-degree uncertainty coupled with one of rising amazement. "I believe—I believe I may know you, youngster. Can it be that you are of the Zex?"

"I am called Ryozenzuzex, Elder."

"The young agricultural expert who vanished so long ago. Truly do I remember you!" He paused, thinking furiously. "Word came to us all the way from Ciccikalk that you had become something of a dangerous renegade."

"Something of that, yes. I am a renegade from and danger to the blind, the callous, and the reactionary. No one else has anything to fear from me." Now that the AAnn had been neutralized, other problems—in their own fashion more serious—were beginning to resurface.

"Rest deep and warm, Elder. Neither I nor my friends," and he indicated the monsters, "are any threat to the hive. The contrary is true. All will be explained." I hope, he add silently. "All that matters is what I have accomplished in my absence."

Bonnie had walked over to stand next to him. She was gazing with interest at the Elder, who found the attention very upsetting.

"Who are these . . . creatures, and how have you come to be among them?" he asked.

"It's a long story," Bonnie said via the appropriate whistles and clicks.

The Elder was flabbergasted. Reflexively, he threw back a stream of questions.

"I don't understand," she told him patiently. "You'll have to speak more slowly. I'm not very fluent yet."

Ryo translated the rough places for both of them. The Elder's active mind was homing in on another unsettling thought.

"We thank you for our hive's salvation. I think we will be safe from AAnn depredations from now on. Would you by any chance know what happened to six children who were taken from the Nursery several months ago? Their Nurse vanished with them. A heinous crime."

"And a necessary one, I'm afraid." Ryo was past caring what local Elders thought. Having broken so many important laws in a comparatively brief span he had no compunction at mentioning yet another perfidy.

"The Nurse Falmiensazex had nothing to do with the disappearance." He had to hesitate before he could go on. "She lies in a comasleep. That was my fault. It was also necessary."

The Elder was watching him shrewdly. "You call it necessary, yet you show signs of remorse."

"She is—was—my premate."

"Ah." The council member was trying to sort events in his mind. "And the larvae?"

"All are well, healthy, and maturing." In areas you can't begin to imagine, he added silently.

"There will have to be an adjudication, of course," murmured the Elder.

"Of course."

"What are they talking about?" Bonnie asked him.

"My most recent crimes. I will have to surrender myself soon to confinement."

Bonnie hefted her rifle. "Not if you don't want to, you won't. You're too valuable, too important to the Project to languish in some cell while we try and muddle through first contact without you, Ryo."

"I assure you everything will turn out all right." He put first a truhand and then a foothand on her arm. "A society functions because its citizens choose to abide by its laws."

"That sounds funny coming from you."

"So I am selective." There was no accompanying gesture of humor. Bonnie wondered if that was for the benefit of the watchful Elder.

"The matter must be discussed, Bonnie. It will take time."

As it turned out, it did not.

An echo of the thunder they'd hidden from earlier now rose out of the south. It grew to deafening proportions as half a dozen sleek shuttlecraft passed low overhead. They commenced a wide turn that would bring them circling back toward Paszex.

Bonnie and the other humans had a bad moment until they noticed the loud and clearly celebratory reaction of the hivefolk. "Our ships," Ryo told her in response to the unasked question.

"Late again," muttered the Elder Kerarilzex, "but at least in force this time. I hope others caught the command ship before it could flee orbit. Words will be composed," he added darkly. "This is the fifth time in the last seventy years. Other hives endure worse. I do not believe the people will stand for it much longer."

"And well you shouldn't," Bonnie agreed in passable Low Thranx.

The Thranx commanding officer, of the fifteenth rank, had stared through his compensating viewer as his modest armada passed low over the site of Paszex. He made mental note of the two ruined AAnn warshuttles, the cluster of AAnn prisoners, the armed hivefolk, and the astonishing aliens in their midst.

There was no immediate way of ascertaining which side the horrific bipeds were on. He could not fire on them since they were mixed in with the hivefolk. It was very frustrating.

The military of both species were livid. The bureaucrats were most upset. The politicians were confused and angry. The scientists were disturbed.

Each group had dreamed of holding center stage when an intelligent, space-traversing race was contacted. Instead, the moment of glory had been usurped by some secretive researchers, a mutinous human crew, and an outcast alien agriculturalist.

There were pains and problems. The parents of the boys and girls who'd traveled to Willow-wane as part of the Project did their best to muster a feeling of betrayal. True, they had agreed to commit their children to Project control in return for a year of free room, board, and education, but to some of them the whole business still seemed like kidnaping. None had thought to inquire as to the precise location of the Project school or its distance from their homes.

The idea of lifting a group of impressionable youngsters and then plunking them down among a bunch of pale wormlike monsters grated against the public conscience. No one, of course, gave a thought to the effect the children might have had on the impressionable Thranx larvae.

The Thranx populace had an advantage because it had already been exposed to two semi-intelligent species and the AAnn. It was their highly developed sense of propriety that suffered most. Events had not unfolded according to carefully prepared procedures. When procedure was violated—well, the Thranx were very strong on organization and rather less so at improvisation, and you simply did not improvise first contact with an alien race.

There was also the matter of larval abduction. Unlike the humans, Ryo did not have the permission of parents to enroll their offspring in the Project school. His action was kidnaping, whatever the motives.

Ryo didn't care. He agreed with everything the adjudicators said. All that mattered was the Project. Its apparent success was vindication enough for him. None of the larvae had been harmed, physically or mentally, by their experience. The Nursery supervisors who attended them could attest to that.

It's very hard to rouse public opinion against someone who politely agrees with everything his prosecutors say while patiently awaiting martyrdom.

His strongest condemnation came not from government or public but from Fal. Under proper care she recovered rapidly from her comasleep, whereupon she laid into him far more devastatingly than any hivemother. Against her list of outrages he could offer only one thought in his defense: the fact that he had succeeded.

As to the avowed success of the Project, even the most jingoistic member of either species could not deny the evidence. Not only did the Thranx larvae and human children tolerate each other, they had grown nearly inseparable. Monster played happily alongside monster.

Recordings showing human children gamboling with their Thranx counterparts rapidly dispelled the initial outcry that had arisen on Earth and her colonies. How can something be considered a monster when a seven-year-old girl with pigtails can ride it bareback, or a couple of boys can tussle with it in a sandpile and all three are obviously having a wonderful time?

Reaction among the Thranx was, in accord with their nature, somewhat slower in forming. Grudging acceptance began to appear when chips revealed that the horribly flexible alien adolescents had no intention of butchering and barbecuing their larval companions.

A major ticklish problem was partially resolved when the Radical Agnostic theologians of Earth discovered their exact counterparts among the Aesthetic Philosopher sect of

Hivehom. They answered the nervous and awkward question raised by many as to which side the Deity might be on by proclaiming that he was most likely sitting back and watching the whole business with considerable amusement.

Twenty years would pass before the first treaties were drawn and more than that before the boldest among both species brought up the specter of Amalgamation. For the time being, preliminary agreements were sufficient. They were attested to and duly recorded by wary officials on both sides whose hands had been forced, not by strength of arms or superior intellectual power, but by children cavorting in a playroom.

Ryo was formally relieved of his long-neglected agricultural duties and assigned to the permanent contact group. This was placed outside Paszex, which now assumed an importance beyond the export of vegetable products and handicrafts. Many of the latter, incidentally, were traded to the humans of the Project. Once again the pioneers had stolen a march on the official planners. Trade had begun.

The airfield was hastily enlarged so it could handle shuttlecraft. First official visitors were exchanged, and as a few handicrafts and mechanisms traversed the gulf between the stars, it was discovered that the profit motive was another characteristic human and Thranx shared.

So it was that contact was not forged so much as hastily cobbled together. But it was a beginning, the most important part of understanding.

Even Fal eventually reconciled with her now famous premate, though he was still regarded as a traitor among some of his own kind and an enemy spy in certain unrelentingly paranoid human circles. Wuuzelansem was brought from Ciccikalk, still suspicious of humankind but more flexible than most Thranx. His conversion came rapidly when some of the humans became fluent enough to admire his poetry.

"I don't know how we did without them for so long," he once muttered to Ryo after a recital. "Their appreciation of true art seems as boundless as their enthusiasm. The government may acquire an ally, but I have acquired something far more valuable."

"Which is?"

"A new audience!" and Wuu returned to the display chamber to acknowledge the humans' peculiar form of applause.

Ten years passed. A day arrived when several of the original Project members had to return to their homes. Two would travel to Centaurus, one to New Riviera, and several to Earth.

Jahan Bhadravati was one of them. Bonnie was another. They stood next to the Paszex shuttleport's human-service area, still clad in Willow-wane duty uniform, which was to say practically nothing, and waited for departure call. It was a lovely midseason day. The temperature was 35° C and the humidity hovered near 92 percent.

No officials saw them off with speeches. In the intervening decade the coming and going of humans at Paszex had ceased to be worthy of special notice. There was a farewell party, however. Ryozenzuzex was there, accompanied by a young Thranx adult named Qul and a tall, skinny human named Wilson Asambi. They were working together to help develop gentler strains of a hybrid fruit.

Bonnie took a last look around the surface of Willow-wane. The distant lines of orchard and jungle, the little thickets of air-intake stacks, the shuttleway, all were old friends to be left behind but retained in memory. She looked much the same as she had when she'd first set foot on Willow-wane ten years before. The world was a fine place for keeping fit. There was gray in her hair now, and contentment in her expression.

"I suppose you'll continue at your post," she said to Ryo.

He shrugged, a human gesture that was becoming quite popular among Thranx, and uttered a confirmatory whistle of agreement. He reflected on the gesture and its meaning. We give so much to each other, he thought. Gesture as well as science, habit as well as art. Especially poetry. He smiled inwardly. Two years ago, old Wuuzelansem had fled to wherever it was old poets retreated to, fighting and kicking and disparaging the state of the universe all the way, but not before he'd seen his poetry wildly praised by the very monsters he'd once sought to avoid contact with.

Ryo missed Wuu. Even if they hadn't seen ommatidia to ommatidia all the time.

A high-pitched whistle sounded from behind. Fal was waiting near the entryway to Paszex. She still would not have close contact with humans. Her trauma was understandable, since they'd been responsible for luring her premate away and forcing him to strike her. She would barely tolerate them.

Toleration first, he told himself. Friendship later. If anything, progress on the latter was ahead of schedule.

To his surprise, he noticed that Bonnie was making eye moisture. Ryo waited to find out whether it was significant of happiness or distress. Water of delight, water of depression, Wuu had called it in one of his poems.

"I'm crying out of both," she told him. "I'm glad that things have turned out so well and I'm sad that after all these years it's finally time to leave. I just can't turn down a university position on Earth. Loo—Loo would have liked the way things have turned out."

"There's still a lot of work to be done," Ryo said. "I'll retain my position as long as I'm able to help."

Bhadravati shuffled his feet and said nothing. Conversation had never been the scientist's strong point, Ryo knew. He felt a great sadness within himself at the coming departure of two of his oldest human friends.

"There is no reason to cry, my friend," Ryo told Bonnie. "We have nothing but reason for happiness. We shall meet again someday."

Bonnie was too much of a realist to believe that. Circumstance and distance, the ancient enemies of acquaintance, would conspire to prevent it.

Nevertheless she replied with a smiling, "I hope so, Ryo," as she reached out both hands to touch the tips of his proffered antennae. The interspecies gesture was now as automatic as a handshake. Ryo repeated the gesture with Bhadravati.

"These youngsters here," he said, indicating Asambi and Qul, "will be taking on the truly important work now. Nothing can prevent the deepening of our friendship." She was still crying and he made a gesture of gentle third-degree admonishment.

"Please, friend, let there be no more tears at this parting. Not water tears from you nor crystal tears from me, would that I were able to manufacture them. It's a gesture I envy you. A small but intriguing physical difference."

"The only significant differences between us anymore *are* physical," said Bhadravati.

"Only physical," Ryo agreed, "and that means less each day. Shape and composition mean nothing when understanding is present."

"I thought old Wuu was the poet and not you," Bonnie said.

"A little of everything you admire eventually rubs off on you. I'm sure you'll be happy to live for a while now with less weighty matters on your mind."

"Well, I will have my classes," she admitted, "and Jahan his research and his books to compose." From the way they gazed at one another Ryo thought Bonnie might mate after all. The soft beeping sounded from around them. Other passengers began to move toward the waiting shuttle. Not all of them were human.

"We should board." Bhadravati put a hand on her shoulder. She nodded, didn't speak, looked back down at Ryo. Then she reached out and hugged him. Blue-green chiton slid against soft flesh. It was another gesture Ryo had learned but which he'd always observed performed by two humans. It was much too rough to be civilized, but he politely said nothing.

As they moved toward the shuttle he made the human gesture of farewell, waving two hands at them. He followed with the far more complex and subtle four-handed gesture of Thranx good-bye. At the base of the ramp Bonnie imitated it as best she could with only two hands. Then they disappeared into the ship.

He started toward the burrow entryway that led down into the busy terminal. The impatient Fal had withdrawn into the comforting confines below.

Bonnie and Dr. Bhadravati appeared content, and that thought made him happy. Everyone deserved contentment. They'd worked hard and long and deserved their share of mental peace.

The fruit he'd struggled so hard to plant had taken root. It had done more than survive. In ten years it prospered enormously and now showed signs of flowering into something far more than he'd ever dreamed of, more than mere friendship. The relationship between human and Thranx was becoming more than deep. There were signs, signs and portents, that someday in the far future it could become truly symbiotic.

And there was another benefit, one Ryo had not considered. One he hadn't thought much about during the last busy, exciting ten years. The realization came as a shock.

He found something useful to do with his life after all.

About the Author

Born in New York City in 1946, Alan Dean Foster was raised in Los Angeles, California. After receiving a bachelor's degree in political science and a Master of Fine Arts in motion pictures from UCLA in 1968–1969, he worked for two years as a public relations copywriter in a small Studio City, California, firm.

His writing career began in 1968 when August Derleth bought a long letter of Foster's and published it as a short story in his biannual *Arkham Collector Magazine*. Sales of short fiction to other magazines followed. His first try at a novel, *The Tar-Aiym Krang*, was published by Ballantine Books in 1972.

Foster has toured extensively through Asia and the isles of the Pacific. Besides traveling he enjoys classical and rock music, old films, basketball, body surfing, and karate. He has taught screenwriting, literature, and film history at UCLA and Los Angeles City College.

Currently he resides in Arizona with his wife JoAnn (who is reputed to have the only extant recipe for Barbarian Cream Pie).